INTO
AFRICA

KERRY McDONALD

WITH BOB COLES

This book is printed on acid-free paper.

Published by:
Level 4 Press, Inc.
13518 Jamul Drive
Jamul, CA 91935
www.level4press.com

Library of Congress Control Number: 2019943922

ISBN: 978-1-933769-94-3

Printed in the USA

Other books by
KERRY McDONALD

THE LOST TREASURE OF LIMA

THE NAZI GOLD TRAIN

JIM LORD

THE GREEN CATHEDRAL

THE AMBER ROOM

1

—

Raining. Heavy downpour. Not unusual. It was expected in the village of Ujiji in January, when the air stayed wet with constant showers, and drizzle poured over the Ukaranga ridges that fed the streams running into its Liuche Valley; Ujiji, in the heart of East Africa on the shores of Lake Tanganyika, the oldest, deepest, and largest freshwater lake in Africa, famed for its huge variety of fish—over three hundred species—and its stunning sunsets; Ujiji, a foremost Arab slave station along the trading route that stretched from the island of Zanzibar to Bagamoyo on the Indian Ocean and from there to Tabora two hundred miles west; Ujiji, a place of huge importance during the time of caravans that crisscrossed Tanganyika daily, carrying guns, ivory, and human cargo to be sold in Africa and the distant lands of Arabia, Europe, and the Americas.

Dr. David Livingstone, a middle-aged white man, turned and tossed on his sleeping platform in the middle of the night. Beads of perspiration had gathered on his gaunt face and long, gray beard. At times, raindrops dripped down from the leaking thatched roof of his hut and mingled with his sweat. He was dressed in a long, white nightgown, and he wore brown canvas pants day and night. The leaking rain aside, Livingstone was determined to get up. He turned on his back and pushed himself up, but he cried out in pain as he fell back down.

He had been in Ujiji since August 1871, after he witnessed the massacre of nearly four hundred men, women, and children by slave traders in the village of Nyangwe on the western side of the lake. Before that, these same traders had saved his life, when he was lost and starving, his own caravan members having deserted him and stolen his medicine chest. The Arabs knew he hated slavery, but, it seemed, he had turned a blind eye to their activities in order to complete his endless quest to find the true source of the Nile River.

"How long will you be gone?" Janet had asked as she walked beside him through the gardens at Newstead Abbey, the former home of Lord Byron. David had been staying there during his last visit home in 1864, the guest of a big game hunter he had met in Bechuanaland.

"Two years, Janet, no more."

"Your children won't like it. Have you told them yet?"

"No, I've got time."

"And what if you stay more than that? What if you get lost again?"

"I know the land. I know the people. I know where I'm going." He put his arm around his younger sister's shoulder. His breathing was heavy. His steps were long and laborious. "Two years. That's all I need."

"And where are you going?"

"Africa in its interior is full of fast-moving rivers and huge lakes. If I can find a connection between them, I will have solved what the great men of antiquity failed to do. From Homer to Herodotus, all of them."

He had first come to Africa in 1841 as a missionary but found greater success as an explorer and had undertaken three other major trips to the region. He was the first British man to cross Africa on foot from the east coast to the west and back again, and he had discovered the waterfall known as the "Smoke That Thunders," and renamed it Victoria Falls.

"Look, Susi," he'd said that day, "the whole mass of the Zambezi waters rush into a fissure, right across the entire riverbed."

"Yes, bwana. Good to look at. Very beautiful." Susi, Livingstone's assistant, pointed to the churning white froth at the bottom of the waterfall.

"You're right. It is beautiful to look at, but not as beautiful as the Zambezi itself. We must continue downriver and reach Tete before I have another fever attack. I want to bypass the Batoka tribe. I don't want to get sick in their territory. Come, let's take some measurements and get back to camp and get ready to go."

He had mapped and charted the only part of the world's major landmass that was still unknown by Europeans and had contributed to the white man's knowledge of Africa, especially its vast lakes and rivers.

Upon his brief return to Great Britain in 1856, he was often mobbed in the streets of London by fans; he had gained fame from a best-selling book that detailed his travels. He had done this all in the name of God, but somewhere along his path, he became obsessed with Africa itself, with exploring its vast interior. He had other motives, to be sure, but all of these paled in comparison to his absolute desire to rid the continent of slave trading in the wake of the massacre at Nyangwe.

Now, he was unable to walk and mentally chained to his room after years of wandering and exploring in complete freedom. Even before the Nyangwe massacre, he had suffered from dysentery, ulcers, and malnutrition, causing some of his teeth to loosen and fall out. In Great Britain it was reported and widely believed that he was dead. No white man had seen him since 1866. In truth, he was dying, and he knew it. The pain in his abdomen and intestines was sometimes so bad that he fell unconscious. It was only a matter of time before he'd never wake up again.

In this depth of misery and despair, he was surrounded by a group of African children he had adopted as well as his mixed-race daughter, Baraka, who was always with him and attended to his daily needs, such as providing him medicine, feeding him, and giving him massages between his bouts of physical stress; a ten-year-old boy, Kalulu, ran his errands, brought his food, and relayed his messages to local officials and nearby villages. There was also Susi, a man of about forty, Livingstone's most trusted servant, who had been with him through his many travels. Susi saw to it that he was bathed and cleansed every day. He also cooked Livingstone's meals and emptied his bedpan. Lately, as Livingstone's health grew steadily worse, other Ujiji villagers, Africans and Arabs, had joined these others in a kind of vigil, paying their last respects to a great man who soon would be no more.

Livingstone leaned forward and struggled to get back up. He pushed the mosquito net that surrounded him away and looked across the room. Nearby stood his table on which he kept his journal, pen, and paper.

"Help me please, Baraka."

"What you want?"

"I need to get to the table. I have something important to do."

Assisted by Baraka, who held on to his waist, he put his right arm around her neck and shoulders and dragged himself to a chair next to the table and fell into it.

"I feel so tired."

With his hands shaking from the constant, surging waves of physical torment, he took from the table an envelope and wrote out the name and address of his sister Janet, in Scotland. Then, he handed the pen to Baraka and took from his neck a crucifix on a silver chain and put it into the envelope, sealed it, and placed it into a waterproof leather pouch.

"Kalulu. Where's Kalulu?" He looked at the group of African children behind him staring at his every move. A youth stepped forward, thin and wiry.

Kalulu took the pouch and tied it to a leather belt around his waist. Livingstone nodded.

"Chuka gura. Take it, go." The boy took off and disappeared into the forest.

2

—

"Let us not forget, we are the elect, the chosen few."

Mr. James Ewing stood upright in his pulpit, as he had done every Sunday since he had taken over as preacher of the Hamilton Congregational Church of Scotland. He was a tall man, slightly balding. Like many men of his era, he wore a beard, although it was graying, neatly trimmed, and without a mustache. From a distance, he looked like the old-time Protestant preachers of the past, filled with fire and brimstone, lashing out with the full force of his righteousness, at sin and Satan. In truth, Reverend Ewing had a sense of humor and knew how to add the personal touch when speaking to his congregation, who sat before him, twenty-five loyal souls, families from the surrounding villages and towns, rapt in their attention as his sermon reached its peak. He stepped from behind the pulpit and approached his flock. As he came closer, he threw out the palms of his hands, as if he were trying to embrace them.

"We have been selected by the Almighty Himself."

His crescendo rose even further, rising but not yet to its full volume, not yet to the final climax that would cause individual spirits to explode and see the light. And then, he paused and looked each and every one of his congregation members in the eyes.

In the second row of the pews, sitting by the window near the bare white walls, Janet Livingstone watched and listened with everyone else. She was slightly younger than Reverend Ewing, in her mid-forties, her reddish-brown hair tied into a tight bun, her arms and legs covered by a long woolen dress. She had walked that morning from the town of Blantyre, Scotland, nearly two miles away, as she had done every Sunday for the past forty years. When she was a girl, she traveled that distance with her family: her mother, Mary Hunter, her father, Neil the younger, and her brothers and sister—David, Charles, and Agnes.

"Now, lads, make religion the everyday business of your life," Neil Livingstone said one such day after the family had been walking together for about a mile, he and Mary in the lead, followed by David, Charles, Agnes, and Janet. They were dressed in their Sunday finest.

Neil continued. "For if you don't, temptation will get the best of you."

"Aye, and make the best of unpleasant situations," Mary added.

Janet, a girl of eleven, didn't understand why they had to walk to their congregation every Sunday. "Is that why we walk to Hamilton? To make the best of it?"

Neil, who set a sturdy pace for everyone, making it difficult for Janet to keep up, turned to her as he moved. "We walk because we don't own a carriage."

"But why do we refuse rides when offered?" asked Janet.

"Because their carriages are small and can only hold one or two of us. We stay together," Mary chimed.

"You must build your strength of body and character, self-reliance and perseverance, so you will be ready to receive the Holy Spirit when it comes," said Neil.

"Remember the time we walked to the outdoor service at the parish in Shotts?" Charles, who had been quiet so far, sought to provide an illustration of his father's point. "And it started to snow."

Janet laughed. She also remembered. "The snow came up to our ankles."

Suddenly, David, who was always reticent and never talked, blurted out, "Is that what you mean by perseverance?"

"Yes, David. That's exactly what I mean. The snow came up to my ankles but I didn't feel any cold that day. The good Lord gave me all the warmth I needed," said Neil.

"But, Father," David continued, "why didn't I feel the warmth? I live by His example and for He who died on the cross, and yet I do not feel His warmth in my heart. I do not feel His spirit."

The family walked on in silence until Mary spoke again. "You're young, David. You haven't lived long enough."

"Someday the spirit will claim you," Neil rejoined, "and when it does, it will strike you like thunder and shake your soul. Meanwhile you must prepare yourself."

The Livingstones were famous for their independence and self-reliance. They never asked for help from anyone and made it a point to act in accordance with their beliefs and nothing else. The Livingstones were so independent that they brought their lunch with them to the chapel as well as coffee, tea, and sugar so that the only thing they asked for from the congregation was hot water.

Janet continued to make the trek every Sunday after her father and mother had long since passed away, and after her brother Charles had moved to the United States.

"Let us not forget our duty to uplift the downtrodden, heathens, and slaves, and the dispossessed. We were put on earth to help those who cannot help themselves. Even though they have been cast out, we must save them. So let us not forget the example of Dr. David Livingstone"—the minister stopped to look at Janet directly—"who has devoted his entire life to saving the savages of Africa."

When his crescendo had been reached, Janet wanted to stand up and applaud but dared not to, since any outward display of emotion would be frowned upon by her fellow members. Once Reverend Ewing saw that he had the full attention of his worshippers, once he knew

that their spiritual emotions had been truly moved, it was time for him
to finish.

"Let us pray."

After the sermon, Janet wanted to talk with Reverend Ewing, so
she made her way over to him. She wanted to thank him for his refer-
ence to her brother, even though in most of his sermons for the past
two years he had made similar references, usually near the end of his
sermons. Indeed the presence of Dr. David Livingstone remained viv-
id to everyone. His name was often invoked, or he was talked about.
Yet Janet never grew tired of this habitual adulation and respect, never
grew tired of hearing his achievements cited. As she walked toward the
minister, she stopped and said hello to various people she knew.

"Hello, Mrs. Scott. It's good to see you."

"And you, too, Miss Livingstone. You're looking well."

"Hello, Janet," another woman called to her.

"Martha Giles. How is the good Lord treating you?"

"The same. His light is always shining. By the way, I'll be going
back to Blantyre after the service. Would you want a ride?"

"That's kind of you to offer, but no thank you. It's a nice day.
I'll walk."

"I knew you would. Just thought I'd ask. I don't see how you do it.
Two miles each way. You must be strong as an ox."

"The Lord gives me my strength, Mrs. Giles."

These conversations were brief in relation to her insistence to talk
to Reverend Ewing. Soon she reached him.

"Reverend Ewing. Reverend Ewing. I need to talk to you."

He was talking to someone else, so she waited. Other women, and
a few men, also wanted to talk to him, and as they approached him,
they bypassed Janet until a small crowd had gathered around him,
shutting her out. A sudden flash of anxiety crossed her face, a sudden
realization of her own helplessness. She really wanted to talk, needed
to talk, but realized she couldn't, so she turned around and walked out.

The following morning, still fired up, her spirits lifted by Reverend

Ewing's sermon the day before, she walked along Main Street in downtown Blantyre. Her gait was steady and straightforward, almost like marching, as if she knew exactly where she wanted to go. The early morning sun had just come up in full view, casting its rays on two-storied buildings made of brick or stone, well-made structures to keep out the winter wind and snow. Most of the buildings had tall chimneys that rose toward the sky, and in the distance, the pinnacle of a Presbyterian church steeple stood proud over the town. On the street, horse-drawn carriages rambled by. A few children ran and played.

When Janet slowed to cross the intersection at Main and Victoria Street, just before she looked both ways to see if she could pass, a stray dog sidled up to her. All it wanted was some attention or affection and it bowed its head as if it were used to being petted by strangers, but Janet gave it a wide berth and sidestepped it, muttering inside her mind that the dog looked disgusting, a feeling she often felt when she came around animals, particularly dogs. She crossed the intersection and kept going forward, the sound of her heels pounding the concrete path. She pushed herself ahead until she reached a store with a large sign above: BOSWELL'S BOOKS BOUGHT AND SOLD.

As she entered the shop, she was greeted with hundreds of books that lined the shelves. All kinds of books, from famous novels by Thackeray, Austen, Fielding, and Defoe to poetry volumes by Shakespeare, Byron, and Shelley. There were scientific studies on geology, botany, and the new science of chemistry, and almanacs, both used and new. Boswell's was also well supplied in travelogues and boasted of its collection of texts by British-African explorers: Richard Burton's *Lake Regions of Central Equatorial Africa* and John Hanning Speke's *The Journal of the Discovery of the Source of the Nile*, and it had Mungo Park's famous *Travels in the Interior of Africa*. Park was the forerunner of them all, the first Westerner to have traveled the Niger River in central Africa and a major influence on David's career. In former years, Janet had read all these books along with her brother.

Now, however, she kept moving forward, beyond the shelves until she found Mr. Boswell himself in the back, with his assistant, taking books out of a box and shelving them. Boswell looked like a bookseller: round face, slight build, squeaky voice.

"Good morning, Mr. Boswell." She spoke softly. Mr. Boswell looked at his clerk, puckered his lips, and raised his eyebrows. He wasn't glad to see her.

"I was just passing by, and I thought I'd . . ." This time he turned away. He wanted to get back to his unpacking.

"How are you?" Janet tried again, only louder.

"Fine, thank you."

"I was just passing by . . . why have you taken Dr. Livingstone's poster down?" She looked at the poster now, resting against the wall in a corner of the store.

DR. DAVID LIVINGSTONE'S INTERNATIONAL SENSATION: MISSIONARY TRAVELS IN SOUTH AFRICA. NOW ON SALE. INQUIRE WITHIN.

"Don't need it. Everyone knows who he is. His book is ten years old and still selling well."

"But don't you think people need to be reminded of his extraordinary significance, his uniqueness, especially young people?"

"I do, Miss Livingstone. I do. But we must sell other books as well. Perhaps if he returns."

"When he returns."

"When he returns from Tanganyika, he can publish another book."

Janet's patience was running out. "Please put the poster back up, as a favor to me."

He reluctantly nodded his head yes.

"Praise the Lord," she said as she turned and walked out. Boswell watched her go. When he was confident she could not hear him, he muttered to his assistant, "Fanatic."

That evening, when she got home, after eating her dinner, she sat in her favorite chair and began to read the Bible, a nightly ritual. As a certified schoolteacher of reading and writing, she often brought papers home to grade, but no matter how busy she got, she always devoted at least an hour to her reading of the scriptures. She had to do it for her own peace of mind. It helped her get through another night and day. After a while, she would take a pen and piece of paper and walk to the dining room table and write letters, usually to her brother David, which she knew would go unanswered. Dozens of these letters she had written, wasting her money to buy postage for an envelope that would never get through. Yet, she wouldn't stop. She had to write these letters. She had to believe they would eventually get answered. So she sat at the table and began again:

"Dear David: I am writing in hopes that this letter will one day reach you. I have written dozens of times and will keep on writing."

As Janet composed, her brother was thousands of miles away sitting on his stool inside his hut in Ujiji. Before him stood a group of ten African girls, including Baraka, listening to him give a sermon. Outside, more Africans had assembled, but they watched out of pity rather than interest.

"Remember, my children, God is love. God welcomes all of you. All you have to do is open your heart and let him in." His words broke off as he felt another surge of pain. He frowned.

"You want medicine?" Baraka stood up.

"Sit down, Baraka. What did I just say?"

"Love God."

"What is God?" one of the other children asked.

"He is like your ancestors. You know your ancestors, don't you?'

"My family. They with ancestors now." Another girl spoke about her dead parents killed in a slave raid.

"God is like your ancestors, but instead of many there is only one, only one ancestor." The girls stared at him as if he were not making sense. When he tried to speak again, he felt another flash of pain in his abdomen, and he doubled up. Baraka ran to get him a dose of calomel.

Midway through her next sentence, Janet crumpled up the paper and threw it away. Although she wanted to write to David, and did so from personal need, at times she felt waves of despair descend upon her, waves of utter hopelessness that she had to shake. She was now so afflicted. *What's the use?* she thought. She folded her arms on top of the table and bent her forehead down, closing her eyes to rest or sleep.

3

—

The following day was Tuesday, and Janet waited patiently in line to get served at a butcher's shop, counting her change while she sucked in small breaths of air. Her tightly fitting bodice made it impossible to breathe, so she began to sweat underneath her undergarments, the moisture rolling along the cracks of her skin. Blood drained from her face, which looked as white as a sheet of paper.

Next to her stood her sister, Agnes, in her late thirties, more loosely dressed, her blouse and skirt made from cotton. Her face looked flush, as though she had just made love to someone. Her black hair curled and bounced a little beneath her pink bonnet and colorful shawl that hung from her shoulders.

Behind them, a small line of women and girls had formed, also waiting to order. The going was slow with only one butcher to serve them all at the evening rush hour when everyone hurried to get home for dinner. Despite the long line, the butcher would not be pushed. Indeed, it seemed now he moved even slower than before. At last, the woman ahead of Janet paid for her meat and left. With her eyes cast down, Janet stepped forward.

When Janet looked up, she met the eyes of a short man with a square mustache hovering over his lips. He looked directly at her, trying to stare her down, trying to intimidate her. This created an awkward silence until Agnes jammed her elbow into Janet's side, jolting her to speak.

"One pound of the braising steak, please."

The butcher began to cut the meat. When Janet saw he had sliced mostly fat, he stymied her attempt to protest or object with his gaze of gratuitous scorn, but Agnes would have none of it.

"Could you cut another piece without the fat?"

He gritted his teeth. He threw the bad piece away and cut another portion without the fat, wrapped it, and gave it to Janet, who paid him and walked out.

Outside, the sisters walked along Main Street. Already, leaves were starting to fall. It was early October, when nights grew cool but days remained hot enough to keep summer alive. They passed beneath a couple of towering elm trees with solid trunks that blended well with the two-storied brick and stone buildings below. Ahead of them, a white stone fence enclosed a graveyard. To the north and east, the Clyde River ran, unseen, unheard. To the northwest, most roads led to Glasgow eight miles away. A rustic smell drifted through the air to remind them that they lived close to the Scottish countryside, with farms, hedgerows, and fields just moments away.

Once Agnes saw that they were alone, she stopped. "Why do you put up with it? He was cheating you."

Janet turned to her. "I know." With even more emphasis, she repeated, "I know!"

"Then why didn't you say something, Janet? You can't let people trample you."

"I guess I didn't want to start—I mean I didn't want to make trouble."

They walked together in silence. People passed them by, many of them factory workers leaving their shifts at the Blantyre Cotton Mill where Janet had once worked twelve-hour shifts on a spinning jenny. She sold her labor as did her older brother, David, who worked as a piercer tying broken ends of threads. She remembered the feeling of quitting time. She could rush home and get something to eat, a happy moment when, at last, her time was her own, though living at close quarters with hundreds of other mill families gave her little room for privacy. Her parents, brothers, and sister all lived in a barracks-like tenement owned by the company, where six people crowded into a single, square room with two alcoves.

On Main Street, carriage traffic had picked up, mostly consisting of farmers and families of the middle class. The pubs were open, and more and more people came and went into the shops and stores. As they walked farther, Janet and Agnes passed a billboard.

DO YOU HAVE A FEVER? TRY DR. LIVINGSTONE'S
ROUSER PILLS. TESTED IN THE AFRICAN JUNGLES.
GUARANTEED OR YOUR MONEY BACK!

Next to these words, the image of a younger Dr. Livingstone, with a monocle over one eye, held up a bottle, his forefinger from his other hand pointing at it. Janet and Agnes stopped to look at him.

"Have you heard anything?" asked Agnes.

"No, nothing, only rumor." They both studied the image as they had often done, but each time, it seemed they were looking at it for the first time. They turned and continued walking.

"What's the latest?"

"Rumor?"

"Yes."

"Which one?" The tone in Janet's voice conveyed frustration. "Well, I hear *The Times* has a witness who swears he saw him two months ago."

"Two months ago? Where?"

They approached Janet's two-storied brick house on a quiet, clean street. She had lived there as a tenant for about ten years, ever since David's return trip to the Zambezi. Many of the clerks and shop owners of Blantyre lived nearby. The workers at the mill had to stay in the company-owned apartments, two miles away, where her family had lived when she was growing up. But now she could afford to rent her

own house, having secured her school teaching job and monthly royalty checks from David's popular-selling book. Standing next to a small
iron fence that lined the front of the house, a boy in baggy trousers and
a gray cloth cap waited.

"Miss Janet Livingstone?"

"Yes."

"An envelope for you." Janet frowned as she took the brown package from him and scrutinized her name scrawled in faded ink with tiny
print. For a moment, she shuddered; she recalled she had seen that
handwriting somewhere before but couldn't remember where. She hated to get mail, especially when it brought bad news, and with personal
letters, you never knew until you opened them. As she turned to walk
through the front gate, she noticed the boy still standing there.

Why is he still here? she thought.

"That'll be four pence for the postage." She took out the money
from her purse and paid him.

Janet and Agnes walked into the living room, sparse but clean.
Perhaps two hundred books filled the bookcases within, mostly collected by David Livingstone and her father, Neil, over the years: a
Latin grammar book; an English and Greek dictionary; books on human anatomy, biology, and botany; numerous travelogues and philo-
sophical texts; and of course, the King James Bible in various editions,
as well as several books by classical Greek and Latin poets—Virgil and
Homer—and *The Book of Psalms.*

On the walls, Janet had framed paintings and sketches, which
looked more like mass-produced posters of religious scenes, such as
The Nativity, The Resurrection, and *Daniel in the Lion's Den.* There were
portraits of her mother, father, brother Charles and sister. Finally, there
was a larger than life portrait of Dr. David Livingstone himself, as a
young man in his twenties with the glowing eyes of an idealist, confident and untested. Above his brown, curly hair, a large plaque read:

BY THEIR FRUITS YE SHALL KNOW THEM.

She laid the package of meat on the dining room table and opened the envelope. She used her thumb and forefinger to pull out a letter, but nothing was there. Instead, she could see some kind of object on a silver chain. She pulled it out, a necklace with a crucifix attached, nothing else. Then she turned the envelope upside down and shook it to see if she had missed anything. She hadn't. She examined the envelope again, the handwriting.

Yes, I have seen it before. I am certain of it now.

As her mind raced to identify where, she could feel her heart beating. She could feel some great force rising inside of her, as if she were going to explode. And then it hit her, like an eruption jolting her back. She staggered across the floor. A swell of dread and ecstasy swept over her.

Yes, I have seen this handwriting before, and now I know. Everything came together to make sense.

"What is it, Janet?"

"David is alive." She grasped Agnes's arm. "He's alive."

Two hours later, upstairs in her bedroom, she sat at her desk, weeping from both sadness and joy—joy from what appeared to be a breakthrough after years and years of unrequited searching, her constant struggle to never give up; sadness because Agnes didn't believe the necklace proved anything. Agnes argued with her, especially after Janet said she had made up her mind and would go to Africa to find him.

"It's impossible. It's out of the question."

"But I must go."

"It could be a hoax, like before."

"Yes, but they were all obvious frauds. I know this necklace. I gave it to him for his birthday."

"It looks similar but—"

"And the handwriting on the envelope. That's David's writing, small and crimped."

"How can you be sure?"

Janet stood up and wiped her eyes. "I've made up my mind."

Agnes went to Janet and placed her hands around her arms. "How can you go to Africa when you've never left Blantyre your entire life? And where will you go? You have no idea where he is. Even if he was still alive when he sent this, he could be dead by now. No one knows. The whole world has been looking for him without success."

"He's alive, and I'm going to find him."

Agnes released her hold and began to pace. "You're not strong enough to go to Africa."

"The meek shall inherit the earth," Janet replied.

At this point, Agnes lost it. She turned back to her sister and spoke with vehemence. "Oh, please! Don't start quoting scripture to me now."

Agnes resented when Janet quoted Bible passages no matter how trite or mundane. At such times, she thought her sister was trying to lecture her or assert her moral superiority. This reinforced Agnes's guilt. She knew she was not as devout as Janet, and that bothered her. It made her feel less worthy.

"I can't help it. I'm a Christian."

"And so am I," Agnes pushed back, "but you, Janet, and David, too, both of you . . ."

"I'm not a saint," Janet blurted, knowing full well what Agnes was thinking.

"But you act like it. Your devotion has completely overtaken you."

"I'm going to Africa. David needs me. I'm going to find him."

4

—

Janet alighted from her carriage on Fleet Street in front of the London Bureau of *The New York Herald*. It was a cold December morning. The building before her was a typical brick structure, three stories high, unlike the main office in New York City's Herald Square with its ornate columns and statues, its distinctly French or Italian architecture. She was dressed in a black fleece coat with a fur collar, black leather gloves, and earmuffs. In her right hand, she carried a small leather briefcase. After she paid her cab fare, she went through the front door amid the comings and goings of office workers and visitors whom she passed.

She had a ten o'clock appointment with Donald Pomeroy, the junior editor. This was not the first time they had met. Twice before in 1869 and 1870, after rumors had been spreading about the whereabouts of her brother, she met Pomeroy to gain support for a *Herald*–funded expedition to find him. She knew newspaper reports had been circulating, and she knew about the newspaper wars when rival publications tried to outdo each other to be the first in publishing worthy news. *The Herald* was the best at this kind of journalism, willing to stop at nothing to get a story. So far, the strategy had paid off. *The*

Herald had the highest circulation in the world, all due to its aggressive and ambitious search for news.

When she first talked to Pomeroy, she initially sought to talk to the editor in chief, the flamboyant and colorful Gordon Bennett Jr. who was responsible for the newspaper's ascension. He was the one who had successfully pushed the paper toward its current mode of operation: human interest stories, interviews, sensational exposés, and, spurred on by the Atlantic underwater cable completed in 1866, international news from Russia, Asia, and Europe. Bennett had also championed the first major newsworthy articles about David's whereabouts, which she had read.

She learned that Bennett was in London to promote his newspaper and sought a meeting, but she was told that he would not be in, that he had to return prematurely to the USA. She tried again in 1870. This time Bennett was in, but he refused to talk and sent her back to Mr. Pomeroy. On both occasions Pomeroy functioned as Bennett's hatchet man, always telling her no, offering excuses why *The Herald* could not help.

So now she was back again, though this time she had no illusions. She would prevail. Bennett, who she knew was in his office, still refused to see her, a clear sign that her meeting with Pomeroy would be in vain. This time, however, she had new evidence to bolster her claim, and soon she found herself sitting in front of Pomeroy's desk once again. She had already laid the crucifix on top of it and explained the necklace's origins and significance. She was waiting for his reply.

The noon hour approached. Through Pomeroy's wide-open door, she could hear the sounds of employees working, lots of shouting and running to make deadlines. Outside Pomeroy's window, she had a fine view of the building across the street, another indistinct office building with small windows.

Pomeroy, now in his mid-twenties, continued his silence. From time to time, he scratched his thick black sideburns or straightened his dull, brown tie, as if to show he was considering her proposition seriously, but she knew better. He bent down to look at the necklace again, studying it in detail. He shook his head.

"I don't know. I'm still skeptical."

She knew this, so she took the envelope out of her briefcase and placed it before him. "Here's the envelope it came in. That's David's handwriting." Pomeroy continued to shake his head.

"Only he and I and my sister know I gave this to him. Who else would send it to me?" She tried to hammer her points across, hoping to get Pomeroy to stop shaking his head.

"Maybe he told someone about it. And they sent it."

"Why would anyone do that? There are only a few Europeans in that part of Africa."

"We've already been through this. We need a corroborating letter or something in writing, or we need a valid European witness."

"You've already got his letter."

"But it's two years old. And no white man has physically seen him in five years. The Royal Geographic Society sent two expeditions to look for him and came up short. A total waste of money."

At this point, surprisingly enough, Gordon Bennett slipped into the room.

He looks immaculate, Janet thought, with his handlebar mustache, which he kept stroking, and his pinstriped suit, not to mention the smell of his expensive cologne.

He looked older than his age, late twenties. Maybe it was because he carried himself like a boss. One look at him, and you knew he owned *The Herald*. Pomeroy also glanced at Bennett, causing him to pause in his reply to Janet. As Bennett walked farther in, he took a position leaning against the wall silently as if to say, *Please go on. Don't mind me*. Pomeroy continued.

"Every week someone says they saw him. Crackpots from all over the globe. One person says he's in Cape Town. Another says he was in Bombay. And now you bring in this necklace that could have come from anywhere. Why don't you accept the truth?"

"All I'm asking is—"

"No. I'm sorry, Miss Livingstone. We cannot fund another expedition. I wish I could help you, but I can't." Pomeroy ended with a tone
of finality, confident his words would impress his boss.

Janet looked at both Pomeroy and Bennett, stalling for time to see
if either of them might provide her with any sense of hope. Instead,
they both remained silent. She reached across Pomeroy's desk, picked
up the necklace, and put it back into the envelope. Then she placed
the envelope in the briefcase, taking her time. She closed the case and
turned around. Despite her attempt to maintain her dignity by refus-
ing to say goodbye or to thank Pomeroy for meeting with her, she was
internally devastated, and it showed in her movements. As she passed
through the door, she ignored Bennett and continued on.

Once out in the hallway, her head bent down, Bennett came up to
her from behind.

"Miss Livingstone?" She heard him call, but she did not respond.
She really didn't want to hear him re-emphasize what Pomeroy had
already said. She kept walking.

"Miss Livingstone?" Bennett caught up to her. "I'm Gordon
Bennett, the editor in chief."

"I know who you are."

"Do you have a moment?"

A few minutes later, she stood in Bennett's office, looking around.
Maps of numerous countries hung on the walls, along with trophies of
animals he had shot and killed, and photographs of famous American
personalities—Grant, Sherman, Custer. Bennett's office was designed
to impress anyone fortunate enough to get inside. His desk was made
of mahogany and stood out like a volcanic island in the center of the
room. Next to it was a smaller table on top of which a pot of tea
steamed. Two chairs were placed under the table.

"Tea?"

"Yes, thank you."

While Bennett was preparing the tea, Janet walked to the

photographs, looking at each one until she stopped at the portrait of a man with flowing blond hair and a buckskin jacket. After pouring hot water into two cups, Bennett went to Janet and gave her one. They sipped as she continued to stare at the picture.

"That's Wild Bill Hickok, the lawman." She moved closer to his photograph. "*The Herald* did a feature on him a couple years back. They say he killed a hundred men."

Janet frowned and turned away. "Then why isn't he in jail?"

"He never killed anyone who didn't deserve it," Bennett replied.

"No one deserves it. We are all God's children."

Bennett felt he needed to say something in Hickok's defense but decided not to. Instead, they strolled back to the tea table, and Janet sat, sipping her tea in silence. Janet knew he had something up his sleeve but couldn't quite figure out what. She knew he was a crafty fellow so she had to be careful and not make mistakes.

He was just about to sit down but stopped, as if he suddenly remembered something. He put his teacup on the table and walked to his office door, which was open. Not only did he close the door, but he also locked it, a move that did not go unnoticed. He seemed to tiptoe back to the table before he sat down and began to speak in a low voice, almost a whisper.

"I just received a cable this morning from the American consul in Zanzibar." She put her teacup down and sat up.

"An Arab slave trader says in his travels he came across an aging white man with a gray beard about six months ago." Upon hearing this news, Janet sighed. She was used to hearing such rumors.

Bennett stood up and walked to a map of Tanganyika on his wall. He pointed. "At a place called Ujiji. There's heavy fighting in the region, slave raiding mostly."

Upon hearing the name Ujiji, she became attentive. "Ujiji? That's near where David was last seen by another slave trader two years ago. A hundred and fifty miles from Nyangwe."

"Yes."

"Then he is alive. I knew it."

Bennett sat down. "That's not all. The trader says he's very sick."

When Janet heard this, she leaped up, overturning her teacup. "That's why he sent this." She reached into her briefcase and pulled out the necklace. Bennett looked puzzled. "Don't you see? He needs my help. He's too sick to write a letter." In her excitement, she moved even closer to Bennett, bending down into his face. "We've got to find him. Will you fund a rescue mission?"

Bennett promptly replied, "If he's sick, it'll take months to find him. He might be dead before we do."

"He's not dead yet."

"Not yet, but—"

"He's a doctor."

Bennett pulled back and twisted his brow. He hadn't considered David Livingstone a doctor, but if any European could remain alive in Africa, it would be him. Nevertheless, Bennett had to be convinced. "Not to mention the expense. These kinds of trips are very—"

"He's alive! I know it!"

Something in Janet's determination pushed him over the edge. He decided to gamble. "I'll fund it on one condition. I choose the leader."

On that same evening, the Cannon Street Pub in East London was filled with men, except for the parlor girls who wandered around bumming drinks and two women gamblers playing poker at one of the tables. Most of these men were day laborers, merchant seamen dressed in canvas trousers and slouch hats or caps, and a few clerks and businessmen with homburgs and derbies.

They sat at the bar drinking beer or Scotch, waiting for the dancing girl to emerge on a stage that rose in a semicircle behind the bartenders. The liquor bottles were lined up in a row up front. Surrounding them, the pub was dark, with a few oil lamps lit to provide just enough light to see inside the large room, filled with cigar smoke and the brash sounds of drunken voices. Near the entrance door, two portraits of local boxers with raised fists crookedly hung.

Henry Morton Stanley sat at the bar on one of the few stools available. He had been sitting there for a while, drinking warm beer in a big mug, big enough to last all night. Once it was finished, he would not order more. He detested getting drunk. He detested anything that would cause a man to lose his self-control. He accepted beer because the alcohol content was low enough to give him a slight buzz, just enough to help him relax. He was currently reaching his limit as he sat, his face slightly flushed, his black hair ruffled and hatless. He was in his late thirties, pudgy, with a mustache. He looked like many of the other men who surrounded him and who had come to this pub for the same reason—to drink (or get drunk), relax, and watch the dancing girls.

Soon, she came out, a blonde in a Cassandra dress with a fully boned corset and a red walking skirt that fell to the floor but was cut high in the front to show off her legs, adorned in fishnet stockings and a garter belt. She wore black lace elbow gloves and black leather ankle boots that made her look tall and naughty. This was her third performance that night, and Henry had seen them all. He felt like he was beginning to connect. Once, earlier, she had looked at him and winked, so he was hoping, after her number, he might buy her a drink, find a corner table, and pour out his soul.

She began her routine, strutting left and right. She bent down to show her breasts and twirled around, lifting her leg high for all to see. To the tune of a piano, she then began to sing in a raucous voice, the voice of a hard woman, which Henry liked, experienced and mature, knocked around by life, someone who understood men like him, or so he thought.

I woke up this mornin'
What did I see?

Henry gawked at her, his eyes glued to her legs. She seemed to be dancing only for him, especially when she winked at him for a third time, which got him all excited and aroused.

Just then, Gordon Bennett walked in. By the way he was dressed in a black frock coat and John Bull hat, he clearly looked out of place, but by the way he carried himself, you would think he owned the joint. After he entered, he looked at the bar and saw Henry. Without hesitation or uncertainty, he went over.

"Hello, Henry."

Henry turned, a little shocked. Not only did he not expect him, but he had also arrived at the wrong time. "Mr. Bennett. Don't tell me you're slumming," he blurted out, half in anger, half in delight. At some level, he was happy to be joined by a companion, any companion, despite the bad timing.

"I have to talk to you."

In the background, the dancing girl continued to sing, even louder now, when she saw her potential mark being distracted, and she looked directly at Henry, trying to redirect his attention to the stage.

I don't like café
I hate cabaret
But in the saloon
My cares fade away

Henry was pulled back to her. Now he wished Gordon would leave so he could get it on.

"What's it about?" he queried. He wanted to ask Gordon if it could wait.

"You know what it's about." Henry perked up. He knew it could only be about his last assignment a year ago in which he was secretly dispatched to find David Livingstone.

They walked to the rear of the pub, the farthest table from the bar, and sat down. Gordon began recounting the events of that morning, his conversation with Janet Livingstone and his decision to fund the expedition. Henry listened attentively, but, as Gordon went on, he remembered they had had many of these same discussions in the past.

"Last time I went, I spent four lousy months in Aden, waiting for nothing. No word came about Livingstone."

"But I had nothing then. All I had was a hunch that didn't play out. It happens sometimes."

"But there's no concrete evidence now, either. What you've got is thin."

"Then bring back the evidence. Anything. Dead or alive, Livingstone is still big news." The dancing girl had now finished her routine. She looked around and spotted Henry.

"It's going to cost you, a lot more."

"You can draw a thousand dollars."

"Now you're talking."

"And when that's gone, draw another thousand, and when that's done, draw another and another. I don't care how much it costs. Find Livingstone!"

As soon as Gordon finished, he saw the dancing girl weaving her way to their table, and just before she approached, he added, "And one more thing. Keep your mouth shut. Don't tell anyone why you're going. And when you find him, get him back here quickly. Get in and get out. Do not delay!"

The following morning, Janet returned to Bennett's office. She was introduced to Henry Stanley, Bennett's choice to lead the journey, but as they began to talk, she kept using the pronouns *we* and *us*, as if she would be directly involved, as if she, heaven forbid, would be coming along. When they sat down to talk further, Henry sat as far away from Janet as possible. So did Bennett. The tenor of her enthusiasm unsettled them. Their discomfort was soon corroborated when Janet announced, "I'm going, too."

"Oh, no, you're not," Bennett quickly responded.

"Yes, I am."

"No, goddammit!" Henry reemphasized.

"Mr. Stanley, please do not use the Lord's name in vain."

"I'm a professional. I've been to Africa. I covered the Abyssinian campaign. What have you done?" Henry rolled his eyes and ran his hands through his hair. There was no way she would be coming, absolutely not.

"David is my brother. I insist."

"If you insist, then I will call it off. Africa is no place for a lady," Bennett said.

Janet got up amid a long moment of silence. She walked to the window to look out. Bennett and Henry thought this was the end of the matter, taking her silence as a sign of defeat, so they got up to leave the room. Just as they were about to go through the office door, she turned and spoke loudly. "I hear *The Times* is planning a rescue expedition."

Both men froze. She had gotten their attention. She turned from the window toward them. "You do know *The London Times,* don't you?" The tone of her voice disturbed them. If she was bluffing, she was doing it well.

"Is that why all the secrecy, Mr. Bennett? You're afraid they'll get the story before you do?" She had them on the run. Yes, *The London Times* had also funded two previous trips to locate Livingstone. In England, *The Times* was *The Herald*'s biggest competitor.

Bennett tried to put his best spin on it. "Our mission is humanitarian, to find your brother and help him."

"Then why did you choose a reporter to lead it?"

"I run a newspaper, not a mission." Already, he could feel his argument slipping.

"Perhaps *The Times* will be receptive if I ask them to fund me. Of course, they don't have the resources you do, and they don't know where David is."

Henry turned and kicked one of Bennett's tea table chairs, breaking it. He stormed out of the room.

5

—

Henry stood amid a group of Africans in an open courtyard of a white, flat-topped house. The courtyard was enclosed within two white walls. The rear wall, which faced the Indian Ocean, was missing. Behind it, a narrow dirt road ran along the beach, proceeding north and south toward other white-washed buildings that lined narrow alleys filled with sounds and smells of Africans and Arabs crouched on stoops or in dark corners, laughing and talking, or bargaining for food and goods—ivory tusks, spices, gum copal, and hides. With the full sun bearing down, the smell of sweating, semi-naked bodies mixed with the smell of urine and feces, tar and garbage, cooking fish and roasting goat meat, and, occasionally, sweet fragrances of flowers, fresh fruit, and plants.

Along the sea, dozens of boats plied in and out, including two British men-of-war, dhows, canoes, and an assortment of skiffs and other vessels. There was also the daily ferry that carried passengers to and from Zanzibar.

He was in the town of Bagamoyo, the main coastal settlement between the interior of Tanganyika and the island of Zanzibar, twenty-five miles away. Zanzibar was the capital of the Omar Republic, an Islamic state that claimed eastern Africa as part of its empire. In

Zanzibar, any goods, such as ivory or slaves, the most lucrative commodities in the African trade, had to pass customs inspections before they could embark by ship to other countries. Any goods coming into this region of Africa had to pass through Zanzibar.

Bagamoyo was also a starting point of all traded goods. To get to Zanzibar, you had to pass through Bagamoyo. Likewise, all caravans that sought to travel into the interior to obtain items for trade, or to sell guns, clothing, or cloth to eastern African tribes, had to originate in Bagamoyo. Even missionaries, who sought to spread the word of God, or traveling Europeans in search of missing white men, had to pass through Bagamoyo.

Henry wore khaki pants, a white cotton shirt, and Wellington boots. He also wore a holster with a gun, a clear symbol of his authority. Before him, a group of African men had formed a line. Some of these men were porters, looking for work as carriers by foot of bales and boxes of supplies. Others were traders who sought to sell anything of value, such as grain or rice, anything Henry might need for his long journey.

For the porters, if he signed them up, he usually paid by bales (one bale, or doti, equaled approximately four square yards) of calico, cotton, silk, or other highly prized cloth that the Africans used as currency in exchange for other goods, such as food, or used to make clothing for important tribal rituals and ceremonies. Henry also traded in glass beads and wire but reserved most of these items for the interior to sell to women as body ornaments. Once he paid any good or service, he always drew up a written contract or returned a receipt, which he used as evidence of sale.

It was late afternoon. Henry was tired. He had been bargaining and trading since early morning. Nevertheless, he pushed himself to keep going, aware that time was short. He had to get to Livingstone before he died or before other newspapers could find him first.

Surrounding Henry in the courtyard, dozens of African families had already begun to prepare for dinner. Women, wearing wraparound cloths of different colors, were bent over pots of fish stew or roasting pigs turning on spits, giving the courtyard a sweet smell. Men were naked except for white loincloths around their waists, or they wore loose, baggy clothes that covered their legs. Families had gathered to talk with their children. A few of the husbands smoked clay pipes. Amid the drifting smoke and conversations, the sound of a forlorn wooden flute could be heard.

Janet sat on a large chest, part of the supplies Henry had brought earlier from Zanzibar, reading the Bible, trying her best to keep out of Henry's way. She had the page turned to the Book of Psalms, which she often read for inspiration. Yet, somehow, she couldn't concentrate on her reading. She seemed ill at ease. Everything around her was unusual and strange.

She was dressed in white riding breeches and a long-sleeved blouse, her reddish-brown hair bouncing down her neck and shoulders. She looked even odder next to the Africans close to her; *too close*, she thought, to those who had *probably never seen a white woman before*. Despite her discomfort, she continued to read or at least pretend to read. The Bible was like her shield. As time passed, a small crowd of beggars assembled—Africans who had nothing to buy or sell, some deformed or crippled. To them, she looked like she had money and wealth. To her, she couldn't tell the difference between an African who was a beggar and an African who was not.

Soon, an elderly beggar leaning on a crutch approached her and held out his hand. His fingers and knuckles were twisted into knots. Janet backed away. He approached a second time but now more aggressively.

All I want is for you to go away. Please go away, she thought, but he kept thrusting his gnarled and twisted fingers in her face, and then he began to talk in words that sounded guttural and harsh. Only when he touched her did she pull out her purse and give him a copper coin, the only way to get rid of him.

Within seconds, dozens of other beggars descended on her: sweaty faces, arms, and hands.

A hideous display of humanity, she thought. She got up and walked away, but they followed her and began to tug at her skin, blouse, and hair, which caused her to panic in horror and revulsion.

As the crowd swelled around her, Henry took notice and ran over to her just after she fell to the ground, shouting and screaming, "Leave me alone!" Henry picked up a stick and began to thrash the beggars.

"Get back," he thundered. "Get back!" He kept thrashing away until only a few beggars were left. Then, he pulled out his pistol and shot in the air, clearing out all those who remained.

"What happened?" he asked as he lifted her from the ground.

"I don't know. I was just standing there and—"

"Did you give them any money?"

"Well, yes, one man."

He looked at her in anger but seemed to be addressing himself. "I told you not to come. I knew this would happen."

"Knew what would happen? I don't understand."

"There's a ferry boat going back to Zanzibar in the morning. Make sure you're on it."

He started to walk away; she reached out and grabbed his arm. "It wasn't my fault."

He turned around. "If you start falling apart with helpless beggars, what's going to happen to you in the bush? Out there!" He pointed toward a line of hills that rose along the horizon. "In the jungle, it's every man for himself, and you wouldn't last ten minutes. Take the boat while you can."

As he continued to walk away, she stopped a moment to collect herself, her mind spinning and churning. Sea waves behind her crashed along the beach. Henry had gone near a wooden crate filled with loose pieces of cloth. When he reached down to grab a few pieces, she caught up with him.

"I understand how you feel," she said. "I must look terribly dumb."

For the first time, he softened to her. He even looked at her with some compassion. "You're not dumb. You're just—this is all new to you. Once it was new to me."

She cast her eyes down. Then she looked back at the ships on the ocean and spoke. "Maybe you're right. My sister, too."

He bent down and took another piece of cloth from the crate. Someone called him, "Bwana, bwana." Despite wanting to get back to his business, he felt he owed her a few more moments of his time. It would be worth it if she decided to go back to Zanzibar.

"Your sister?" he asked.

"She said the same thing you did before I left. She said I wasn't strong enough."

"Then take her advice. No one will think any less of you." Someone shouted again, "Bwana, bwana!" He needed her to hurry up and decide. He stared at her with impatience.

Blue waves continued to crash onto the shore. She turned away from him to face the sea, and then she spoke softly to herself. "No, no. I can't run away." She had made up her mind. She turned back to him. "I can't."

"Can't what?"

"I'm not going back," she said with greater force.

Henry threw the pieces of cloth on the ground. "GODDAMMIT!"

She looked at him, her eyes widening with even more determination. "I came here to find my brother and find him I must."

He stepped forward and waved his forefinger in her face. "Then stay out of my way! If you slow me down or cause trouble, I will beat you like a nigger." He stomped off but quickly came back. He reached for the Colt pistol in his holster and threw it at her feet.

"Here, take this. You're gonna need it!"

Janet picked up the gun from the ground. She had never touched a gun before and thought about giving it back. It was unchristian to keep it. It was unchristian for her to kill.

What did he mean when he said, "You're gonna need it?"

Doubts and fears arose in her mind. *Should I go back to Zanzibar? Is it too late to change my mind?* She looked again at the courtyard before her, trying to make sense of how she should act.

By this time, campfires were burning and the sun had gone down. Various groups of Africans were laughing and singing, eating and drinking, or telling stories. One group of men was gambling, pitching coins against the wall.

Mr. Stanley—she refused to call him Henry; he was not a friend—*is paying more men in cloth to join his caravan.*

"Twelve shillings a month," he said to one of the porters.

"Fifteen, bwana."

Henry hesitated. "Thirteen."

"Fourteen." Henry nodded in agreement and pulled out a written contract for the porter to sign. He gave the man several coins. "Seven now. Seven in Tabora."

A second porter stepped up. "No want coin."

"Three doti."

"Four doti. Cotton, silk, calico, sash."

"No silk, no calico. Just cotton."

They both walked to two large wooden crates filled with pieces of cloth tied in bundles. The porter looked inside and pointed. "Two cotton. Two sash."

"No sash. Just cotton."

As they continued to negotiate, suddenly there was fanfare, the sound of loud talking, laughter, the music of flutes, the beating of drums. A small entourage of twenty Africans, mostly men, entered the courtyard from the open space in the back. As they entered, they surrounded a tall black man in his late twenties, who was the center of their attention. Unlike the other Africans, his hair hung down in long dreadlocks. He wore clogs made of wood and cork, strapped to his ankles by a leather strip. His white loincloth hung loosely from his waist and covered his thighs and knees. A short blue cape trailed his lean body, and he walked in a dignified manner.

Goma Foutou strolled with his retinue to Henry and stopped. Everyone grew silent. Janet put Henry's gun at her waist and walked toward him, fascinated. As Henry and Goma continued to stare at each other, Janet thought that they had a long history between them but was unsure whether that history was good or bad. Somehow, they seemed incompatible, almost opposites, like two strong personalities who always competed, trying to outdo each other.

Goma began to speak in exaggerated obsequiousness. "Me want ten pounds masa and twenty shillings each for me family." His right arm swept toward his entourage who erupted in applause and approval.

"Cut the shit, Goma!"

"But masa." He broke out into a fake smile.

"You bastard. Talk to me straight or not at all."

Upon mention of the word "bastard," Goma stepped forward and pointed to himself. "Me? A bastard?"

Henry, who always carried himself imperiously, was disarmed. He backed off. Goma shrugged his shoulders, winked, and smiled. His laughter grew louder as he turned and walked away, his people following him.

Later that night, Goma continued to hold the center of attention and gave a performance in the middle of the courtyard. "Him bukkrah! Him spear up his ass." He strutted and waddled like a penguin, back and forth. He stuck out his buttocks then pulled them back as if they were struck. The crowd erupted with laughter and derision. "Him no kiti. No Meizi Mungu. Him disease. Mukunguru. Him ghost. Him walking dead." And then Goma began to dance, a slow, foot-stomping ritual amid background sounds of drums.

Janet's fascination soon turned to dread. She drifted closer to Henry, who sat in the background, looking away. "Tell me I'm not seeing this? Why don't you stop it?"

"Stop what?"

"He's mocking you—us! It's rude, disgusting."

"It's all an act, nothing more."

Goma continued to dance and shout. "Me a black man! African!" He thumped his chest with his fists. The men in the courtyard imitated him.

Henry stood up, unconcerned, more perturbed by Janet's sanctimoniousness and naïveté. "Miss Livingstone. I want to be alone for a while. Please."

She followed him and wanted to speak again, but he cut her off. "He's just trying to get me to pay his price. Don't be concerned."

"You mean he's coming with us?"

6

—

Daybreak. Drums beating. Two groups were lined up, ready to move out. At the head of one group stood Goma bearing a rifle. Behind him stood a drummer and forty Africans next to their packs and supplies that consisted of small, tightly packed bales of cloth, wooden and metal boxes or chests, long poles with brass wire wrapped around them, or canvas bags of dried meat and rice hanging down, not to mention folded canvas tents, cooking utensils, tools, and a host of other smaller things. Joining the line of porters, who also carried knives and swords fastened to their waists, were ten gun-bearing soldiers, or guards, and a cook.

Behind Goma's group, Henry rose at the head of a second unit that looked the same as Goma's, except he had a flag bearer with an American flag, to symbolize the trip's American sponsor. Henry also had an African guide, and he had several donkeys with saddles and packs. In addition, Henry's group remained sitting or lying on the ground next to their loads, smoking or talking and looking relaxed and unorganized. Some of Henry's men continued to sleep or doze, unaware of what was going on.

Henry nodded his head and raised his hands. "Okay, Goma.

March!" Goma's group picked up its equipment and slowly marched out of the courtyard.

When Janet saw Goma's group on the move, she felt her adrenaline running.

So this is it. We are on our way at last, into the great unknown.

She felt exhilarated, like running, like jumping, like shouting to the world that she was going. As Goma's group finally disappeared into the tall grass and trees, a few women and dogs straggling behind, she picked up her pack and strapped it on her back. She too began to march, that is, until she noticed Henry's group had remained immobile on the ground, not moving an inch.

"Come on! Let's go!" She shouted to Henry and waved her arms forward as if she were in command, but the men in Henry's group only snickered and laughed. This made her angry, so she turned and began to run after Goma's group to catch up until Henry grabbed her arm and pulled her back.

"Not you."

"Let go of me." The men laughed at her again. Her exhilaration crashed.

Henry continued to grip her arm. "We travel in separate sections. Goma's group goes first. We follow."

"But why split up? It doesn't make sense." She relaxed somewhat. Henry released his grip.

"If one group gets attacked, the other will continue the mission."

"Continue the mission? You mean if—"

"One group gets wiped out and killed."

Janet's mouth flew open. She was horrified at the prospect.

"Or if one group attacks and needs help," he added. "Have a seat, we'll be here for awhile."

Hours later, Henry's caravan bounced along a worn dirt path through fields and streams and low rolling hills. Antelopes scattered. Hartebeests roamed. Strange cries were heard from unseen places. Everyone was happy to be moving at last. From a distance, Henry appeared at the head of the procession, and directly behind him, his guide. Behind the guide, a drummer beat heavily as the Africans shouted, sang, and made as much noise as possible.

Behind the drummer, the flag bearer, then came the porters bearing their loads on their heads, and sometimes with three-legged stools tied to their backs, and then a few women and children, and in between, scattered throughout the line, armed guards with rifles, donkeys, and dogs. Henry set the pace: they marched faster and faster.

Through ravines, valleys, and small villages, past zebras, giraffes, and hippos, spirits stayed high. Through open forests of ebony and calabash, past planted fields of Indian corn and manioc, fruit trees loaded with bananas and mangos, fast-moving streams cascading down from low-lying hills. They moved without stops. As they reached the top of a hill, somewhere near the valley of the Ungerengeri, at the foot of the Uluguru Mountains, Henry halted to look at the staggering beauty of the land set before him—a lush, green paradise.

He spotted a grove near a small lake and looked up. The sun bore down. It was hot. "We'll rest here! Till the sun goes down!" he shouted to the group. Everybody stopped and lowered their packs. Some ran to the lake for water.

An hour later, Janet rested on a cot inside her tent. She dozed off but was awakened by the sound of voices. She got up and looked outside. She saw Henry shouting angrily at two porters who muttered back and shuffled away. When she saw he was alone, she approached him. Her mood was upbeat. She had hoped to draw from him some semblance of cheerfulness and goodwill.

"We're making good time, Mr. Stanley."

Instead of showing goodwill, he glared at her.

She took a deep breath. Invigorated by the fresh air, she spun around, her arms flailing. She tried again. "What a beautiful land God created here. It reminds me of the Scottish Highlands. The smell of life and the living."

"Don't get too comfortable," he replied in a sour tone, causing her to frown.

"Why are you so hostile?"

He didn't feel like talking. He stooped down and entered his tent, took out a razor, and poured water into a bowl. He set it on a chest, crouched down, and sat on a stool. Janet, who was left standing outside, her anger now beginning to rise, entered. He lathered his face, placed the razor to his skin, and began to shave.

"You're more savage than the savages," she said. When he accidentally dropped his razor into the bowl of water, she knew she had hit a nerve. "Your skin is white, yet inside you're black. Very black."

He picked up his razor and began again. "You don't know anything about me."

"That's the problem."

"I'm not here to make friends or chitchat. Go do that with the Africans." He continued to shave.

"They're just as unfriendly as you. In fact, everyone is. We all hate each other." She drew closer to him. "And that man. What was his name? How can you trust a man who mocks you to your face? And the way he looked at you when you called him a bas—"

Henry sharply turned to her and glowered, as if warning her not to repeat that word—*bastard*.

She paused to watch him shave and decided to change the conversation. "And you tell me not to be concerned."

He continued shaving. "I meant what I said."

"Then you tell me not to get too comfortable."

Henry finished shaving. He placed the razor down and wiped his face with a towel. He spread a blanket down on the ground.

"Miss Livingstone, would you mind?" He wanted her to leave. She left.

Outside, she saw the lake glistening and strolled toward it. On the shore, she took another deep breath and turned around. The Africans seemed far enough away, so, on a whim, she unbuttoned her blouse and rolled up her breeches. Meanwhile, Henry, who had just lain down, got back up and looked. He saw her taking off her boots and socks. He picked up his rifle and walked down. Janet waded into the water, not seeing Henry coming. As she began to swim, a crocodile from the bank slipped into the water.

"You should join me," she shouted when she finally saw him. She waved her arms and continued to swim.

Henry saw the crocodile moving like a nondescript log toward her. He lifted his rifle and began to shoot, causing the crocodile to jump and thrash. He shot again and again until it was dead. Janet screamed, rushed to the shore, and ran out of the water. She screamed again when she saw a leech had attached to her shoulder. She yanked it off and fell to the ground and wept.

"Just like the Scottish countryside," Henry muttered.

The next day, the caravan snaked on through dense forests and dales, past sweet-smelling flowers, wild sage, shrubs, and indigo plants, past rich, moist soil and tamarind trees, acacias, and flowering mimosas, boulders and clefts, and dark green woods, mists, and vapors winding up mountainsides. Henry barked orders, imploring everyone to move faster. He barked orders again the next day and the day after that and the day after that. Days became weeks. The sun stared down. Janet stumbled.

They continued to make progress until one morning it began to rain.

They had now reached the Makata Valley where the lush countryside changed from forests and fields to gulches and savannahs with tall grass and bamboo trees, the ground below softening to slush and mire. As the rain thickened into a steady downpour, they entered gullies with marshes and fast-moving rivulets. The mire became a swamp and the caravan marched knee-deep in water. Donkeys brayed. Dogs barked. Some of the supplies fell into the slush. Janet pulled out her raincoat and put it on, but it didn't do much good. She would have been better off if she were nearly naked like the porters.

The rain hammered. The swamp grew deeper. Henry found an

island of dry land where they headed to make camp. Henry and Janet put up their tents, and a few porters put up the equipment tent to keep key supplies dry, but everyone else stayed out in the rain, wrapped only in blankets. Some found cover among fallen trees. At night, Janet shivered in her tent. When she tried to sleep, clouds of mosquitoes and flies attacked. She wrapped her blanket around her skin, hoping this would stop her from being bitten. It did not. And then she began to pray. She wound her brother's necklace tightly around her hand.

"Happy birthday, David. I have a gift for you." Janet's mind was back in her parents' tenement apartment in Blantyre. It was early morning just before sunrise, just before she and David were about to leave for work at the cotton mill.

"What is it?" inquired David.

"Open it." She took the small, wooden box and pressed it into his hand.

He pulled the top off and lifted out a silver necklace with a crucifix attached and dangled it from his fingers. "It's beautiful."

"Put it on."

"You mean around my neck?"

"Yes, silly."

With clumsy hands, he pushed his head through the silver chain.

"To remind you of your special mission on earth," she said.

"You know I don't like any kind of religious ornamentation, Janet."

"It's not an ornamentation. Like I said, it's a reminder. A reminder of Him."

"God should exist within us, not in external objects."

"Then think of it as a reminder of me, an extension of me."

7

—

The next day, the caravan kept moving. The rain had stopped. Swamps gave way to dripping woods, swaths of tiger grass, and decaying trees. A miasma of vapor from rotten mounds of filth and vermin left by former travelers made it hard to breathe. Horseflies, midges, mosquitoes, and wasps swarmed around Janet's head.

They came to a huge patch of black mud that blocked their path. Henry ordered the porters to keep going. Two porters stepped forward and inched along, their legs covered in the thick slime. The others refused to go. Then the first porter tried to walk farther, but his legs got stuck. The second porter, too, could not move. They both struggled to get out, the mud sucking them down like quicksand.

Henry grabbed a rope and threw it out to the first porter, who held on as the other porters and caravan members pulled him out. Henry tossed the same line of rope to the second porter, who shouted and screamed as he held on for his life, but he was too far down. He pulled and thrashed as he sank until he disappeared, swallowed up by the earth.

Immediately everyone ran, including Janet, to the toolboxes, took out axes, and began swinging and chopping small trees with straight limbs. Once they were felled, they were stripped of their limbs and branches and gathered to lay across the mud. Janet worked with the other men, lifting the logs and placing them next to each other while stopping to swat away insects that landed on her neck. When the tree trunks were in place, tightly packed together, they cut down weeds and papyrus leaves and assembled blankets and donkey saddles, placing them on top to form a bridge. Henry walked over it to make sure it steadied. The caravan crossed over the mud.

That night, after the donkeys were fed and cared for and the camp-fires were started for dinner, everyone crashed on blankets or cots from exhaustion. Three porters, however, woke up in the middle of the night. While everyone slept, they took two rifles with ammunition and some of the bales of cloth and bags of beads. One of them entered Janet's tent, walking noiselessly while she slept, and grabbed some of her clothes and personal items, put them into a sack, and slipped away with the others into the forest.

When Janet awoke at daybreak, she heard the cook putting water into pots for breakfast and some of the men collecting wood for the fires. She got dressed and looked for her comb and brush. They were gone. Also missing were a few bars of soap, pills she took to prevent fever, a porcelain cup, a belt, and a pair of slippers.

At first, she surmised that she must have lost her things in the confusion of the previous day with the black mud, but then she re-membered she had worn her belt the day before, and she had combed and brushed her hair before she slept. As she rummaged further just to make sure, tossing everything in her tent around her, she heard Henry's voice arguing nearby.

"More. Must carry more!" he shouted.

"Why gunman, ni beba!" shouted back the porter.

"Gunman, ni beba. No carry weight," Henry replied.

Just then, Janet came out of her tent and strode up to Henry. "Mr. Stanley!" she shouted. "Mr. Stanley!"

Henry's eyes remained on the porter in front of him. "Not now!" he growled back at her.

"Mr. Stanley!" she repeated again.

Henry turned his head. "I said not—"

"Someone stole my things!"

He turned away from the African and confronted her. "Miss Livingstone, last night three of my porters deserted and now the others don't want to go on. I said not now!"

"If not now, when?"

"Get used to it, Miss Livingstone. I don't have time to listen to your whining about some lost garments and underwear!" He turned back to the African. He took out his revolver and pointed. "Pick up the pack or I shoot you, dead."

"No." The porter shook his head, but Henry came closer and cocked the trigger.

"I said pick it up!" He put the pistol barrel on the man's forehead.

The caravan kept moving west. After crossing the Ungerengeri River, they were in sight of the Usagara Mountains. The peaks, rising above two thousand feet, were the largest mountains they had seen so far. Before them, they could see the land rising steadily like ocean waves. They could see slopes and ridges with grass and fields, forests and jungles, leading up to isolated crests whose jagged peaks rose above the clouds. Add to this exploding landscape antelopes, buffaloes, zebras, and giraffes.

It was now mid-May, but the spring season had long since passed away. Days were hot, unbearably so, with the glare of the white sun. Night temperatures plunged to cool. The caravan's state of mind, which by now had been tested, had deteriorated from the initial euphoria two months ago. At this moment, it picked up again, now that they had left the swamps and rain. Henry continued to push his team faster. This caused the primary source of tension in the group besides the heavier loads each man had to carry due to the dead and deserted porters. Henry drove his group relentlessly, and everyone hated it.

The porters objected that the guards carried nothing but their guns and a small backpack. Henry, however, protected the guards, who would also desert if they were forced to carry loads. To him, the guards were more important, especially when they would have to face hostile attack. It was not a matter of if, but when.

Janet had somewhat adjusted. She used a rope instead of the stolen belt with her riding trousers and traded one of her shirts with an African to obtain a new comb, bigger and better and made of ivory. She managed to get more fever pills from the medicine chest, though nothing could stave off the itching caused by insect bites.

By keeping her mind concentrated on marching ahead, she could ignore any sense of physical discomfort, at least until she went to bed, for at night, pain and swelling often kept her awake. At such times, she would light a candle and read passages from the Bible. She would always go back to the Book of Psalms or the Book of Job, to words that helped her cope with suffering. And then she would pray to her Lord, confessing to Him her thoughts and feelings as if He were sitting next to her. This always helped her get to sleep and carry on through the next day.

One night, just before she dozed off, she heard herself repeating a couple lines from psalm 121.

"The Lord is thy keeper. The Lord is thy shade upon thy right hand."

David added the next line. "The Lord shall preserve thy going out and thy coming in." He was sitting opposite her at the living room table in Blantyre.

"And even forever more." Their father, Neil, had the last word, just before the Livingstones joined hands to pray. They were eating their last breakfast together before David and Neil were to walk to Glasgow, where David would catch the Liverpool steamer bound for South Africa.

"Well, David." Neil spoke as he passed a plate of hot biscuits to his son. "How does it feel to be a missionary at last?"

David took a biscuit and passed the plate on to his mother. "I am optimistic and confident, Father. I look forward to Africa. The hand of providence will be my guide."

"There was a time when you weren't so sure."

"Yes. I waited to receive His blessing, which never came. But I was looking for Him in the wrong places."

"Where did you find Him?" Janet asked. She already knew his answer but wanted to hear it again.

"Inside myself, through love. It was not divine blessing I should have been seeking, but divine love. I feel His love more than anything, even now inside of me, deep within my soul. Right now, I can hear the angels singing, all around me. Can't you hear them, Janet? Such a glorious gospel." His hands began to shake, as if possessed by a spirit.

Try as she might, all Janet could hear was the sound of his voice and everyone around her chewing food and sipping coffee. How desperately she wanted to feel what he did.

Yet, now, she felt very much alone. Mr. Stanley made it clear he would not be friends and continued to resent her presence. At first, she thought he resented her because she threatened his authority.

Yes, that's part of it but not all. He seems to resent anyone who challenges him, as if he has something to prove to the entire world, as if he has to always win.

Anything short of that, any failure, he couldn't tolerate, even though she knew no human being was perfect.

And she knew Mr. Stanley would die rather than fail to find her brother, but that was the way he was, no matter what the objective. He lived the extremes. Everything to him was a matter life and death, with nothing in between. Anything ordinary, common, or average simply did not exist.

Yes, I am beginning to figure him out, but there's something else, something I don't quite yet know. As for the Africans, I still don't know them at all. I am embarrassed because they all look the same. Try as I might, I can't tell one from the other.

She rarely talked to anyone in any deeper conversation. It was silently understood that there was a line. She knew and they knew how far to go, and when they reached it, she turned her back or they clammed up. In the villages they had passed, she was often stared at, touched, or followed by Africans who had never seen a white woman.

At such times, I despise them. They are nothing but repulsive savages. Why can't they just leave me alone?

She didn't want to think that way, but she couldn't help it.

If she needed anything or had complaints, she always went to Mr. Stanley, though he made her uncomfortable, especially when he used his donkey whip or gun if any African opposed him.

But the Africans seem so different to me, their habits, their culture, the languages they speak, and they have an ability to relate to animals that frightens me. All this was strange and difficult for her. *Perhaps*, she thought, *this is what God intended.* And then she remembered, *I am a Christian and it is my job to spread the gospel, even among savages, just like my brother David.* It bothered her that she couldn't surmount the gulf between her and the Africans.

The caravan began to ascend the Usagara Mountains, low at first, the foothills. Bubbling springs with fresh, sweet water gurgled from dark recesses and cracks, rushing down from boulders of granite and in between sandstone and quartz. All around them, mimosa trees and acacias, thorn bushes and bamboo. They kept trekking higher, ridge upon ridge, plodding up the steep slopes. The group walked slower now, worn out by the ordeal in the Makata swamps, especially the porters who were carrying heavier loads.

Although the guards still carried nothing but their rifles and a backpack, the guide, drummer, flag bearer, and cook were ordered to carry twenty-five new pounds on top of their weight, which made them angry. Why should the guards be exempt? Morale as a whole waned more and more. Henry remained sullen, and Janet began to lag behind. Then, abruptly, one of the donkeys fell down dead, its pack scattered all over the ground. Janet crossed over to look.

"What is it?" she asked Henry.

"Tsetse fly, from the swamps."

It shouldn't have come as any surprise that the donkey dropped.

Henry was warned before he left Zanzibar not to take the donkeys. He was told by the British consul, John Kirk, "You journalists know nothing about Africa."

"That's not true. I have been to Africa before. This is not my first time," replied Henry.

"Then why are you taking donkeys and horses on the caravan?" John Kirk said with a sneer on his face, as if he were talking to an ignorant child.

"Why not? I need them to help carry the packs. More porters will slow me down. My mission requires speed."

John Kirk burst out laughing. "The tsetse fly will kill the horses first, once you get to the swamps. Then your donkeys will die."

Henry reflected for a moment. "Okay, I'll leave the horses behind, but you're wrong about the donkeys."

The fly, also known by the Africans as chufwa, attacked horses, cattle, and donkeys in the woods, jungles, and swamps, and people were vulnerable, too. Every year, the tsetse fly caused thousands of human deaths in East Africa by subjecting them to fever, also known as sleeping sickness, causing chills, sweats, and delirium. To be sure, sleeping sickness was not the same thing as malaria, a fever caused by the mosquito, but it produced nearly the same effects.

Yet, Henry was stubborn and skeptical about such claims, and he was victim to his own foolish denials that the disease would affect his caravan. Even after the donkey fell, he continued to minimize the threat of flies and insects. The porters cleared the carcass from the path. Its pack and saddle were now carried by others, which further demoralized the expedition.

After a brief rest, they carried on until someone shouted, "Bwana, look!" Everyone turned their heads to the front. Goma Foutou was coming down the trail, accompanied by two armed guards.

"Goma." Henry was not happy to see him. Goma kept coming forward until he stopped.

"What are you doing here?" asked Henry. Goma just shook his head. He looked worried.

"You should be at least two days ahead." Henry knew something was wrong. Goma continued to shake his head. "What is it?" Henry pressed him.

"My men are sick. Fever."

8

—

oma led the caravan to a grove on a small plateau farther up
the trail at an abandoned village, a group of three thatch-
roofed huts surrounded by trees. Goma had made this a
temporary camp. Stretched out in front of the huts, Goma's men who
were not sick sat around in small groups, resting and talking. Some
were drinking water or eating peanuts or fruit. Some just seemed to
stare ahead, their faces worn. Some were tired and lay prone on the
ground with their eyes wide open. As with Henry's group, they lacked
enthusiasm.

Henry walked inside the first thatched hut that contained the
sick men, shaking violently in blankets, their teeth chattering. Henry
moved among them as they babbled and shouted out loud or screamed
from hallucinations. He gave each man a dose of quinine poured into
cups, and rouser pills, Dr. Livingstone's invention to stave off African
fever sickness, which they chewed and swallowed. He also gave them a
shot of brandy. He moved systematically from man to man, perform-
ing his task perfunctorily.

In the second thatched hut was another, larger group of sick men.
Goma and Janet worked inside, dispensing medicine. Goma, who
knew all his men on a personal basis, gave them quinine and pills, but

at the same time, he would bend down and talk, whispering words of encouragement in their ears or smiling and grabbing their hands. He touched them and pulled their blankets closer to their shaking bodies.

"Here, brother, take some of this."

"Thank you, my brother."

Janet watched and listened as they spoke in Swahili. She couldn't understand exactly what they were saying, but from their tone and body language, she could infer their intent.

"How you feel, big fellow?" Goma moved to another porter with tattoos on his arms and tribal scars on his cheeks.

"Not good. I feel weak."

"Here, drink some of this. Soon you be strong and back with your friends."

"I'd rather be with my wife."

"So would I. So would all of us, my friend."

If the sick men jabbered and prattled nonsensically, he talked to them as if their gibberish made sense, as if they were having a normal conversation. Janet, too, tried to help these men, but she still feared them, and her hands shook as she gave them their medicine. She was also distracted by Goma, watching him do his work with effortless ease.

She hadn't thought about him since his caravan began the march over two months ago, except that she was relieved he had gone ahead. From his first appearance in Bagamoyo, his arrogance and insolence upset her, and she thought him callous and self-centered, not to mention ignorant. Most importantly, she felt she couldn't trust him.

There was something in his behavior that revealed a hatred for white Europeans, the kind of man who would smile in your face but stab you in your back. Now, watching him show compassion for these sick Africans gave her a slight ray of doubt. *How can a man who works among the sick, not unlike Christ, be all those terrible things?* Soon, she found herself staring at him again until he noticed and stared back, causing her to drop her eyes.

Later, after the caravan members had eaten dinner, when the men sat around campfires looking sullen and gloomy, Goma and Henry walked away to be by themselves. They went about fifty yards near a grove of trees that separated them from the rest of the caravan. Janet thought it odd that they would go off like that, as if they wanted to make sure no one could hear their conversation. This intrigued her. She wanted to know why Henry and Goma, who seemed so different from each other, would have anything to say that required privacy. She followed them, making sure the night shadows and the sounds of crickets and bullfrogs would be enough to cover her.

As she came nearer, she could see them huddled around a fire, trying to get it to burn brighter. They threw more twigs on it until yellow and red flames burst into view, giving her just enough light to see them clearer and get closer. As she tiptoed farther, she saw a huge sycamore tree far enough away for her to safely hide behind, so she went to it. After standing a few minutes behind the tree, she couldn't make out what they were saying but knew from the tone of their voices they were engaged in a heated conversation. She saw another tree, closer to them. She tiptoed over and hid behind its trunk.

"I don't care. You should've kept going. This increases the chance of attack. You know that, Goma."

"Like I said, my men are sick!"

"But you have medicine."

"We needed to rest, and I didn't know you were moving so fast. I won't push my men like you do."

Henry stood and walked to the tree behind which Janet hid listening. As he came closer, she pulled herself around to the other side in hopes he wouldn't see her. He came closer and closer, almost directly in front, opposite her.

"No, Goma. I know you. You're not telling me everything. Tabora is a few days away. Even with the sick, you could have made it." A long silence followed.

Janet held her breath. Maybe he knew she was there but didn't say anything. Maybe he was waiting for her to make a sound. Should she come out? As his silence continued, she was about to step forward and reveal herself when he stirred, turned around, and walked back to the fire.

"Give it to me straight, Goma."

"I need money. Gold."

"Gold? For what?"

"For tribute. The Manyema tribe. We have to pass through them to get to Tabora."

"You have beads and cloth. Give it to them."

Goma shook his head as Janet strained to hear him speak. "They don't want cloth or beads anymore. They want money, gold or sterling, so they can buy muskets or rifles."

"Then go north. Go around them."

"Can't. Masai."

"Masai? This far south?"

"Henry, I need money. I can't go any farther without it."

"If you're holding back on me—"

"When have I ever held back?"

"You could take the gold and go home."

"Nyamwezi? No." Goma paused and sighed. "I am not welcomed there. Because of what happened."

"But that was years ago."

"My people don't forget. Neither do yours." He paused again.

Janet didn't need to stay for the resolution; she got the gist. Goma was as single-mindedly focused on money as he'd appeared to be the first day. Janet steadily backed away and tiptoed toward her tent.

In the morning, Henry's expedition awoke early. Those who weren't sick rolled up their blankets and relieved themselves in the bush. The cook began to make breakfast, a kind of porridge that he boiled in a pot. In another pot, he boiled water for coffee, which they had in abundance. When Janet came out of her tent, fully dressed and ready to move out, she saw Goma sitting alone by the fire, drinking from a cup, contemplating. Hazy smoke floated through the air. Shouts in the background echoed from Henry giving orders.

Although she normally would not approach any African unless she needed something, she was intrigued by Goma. Last night's conversation with Henry only made her more curious. For one thing, she was shocked that he could speak English properly. *And why would an educated African, which I have never seen in my life, pretend to be something he was not? And what did he mean when he said he couldn't go home and his people did not forget?* She watched from afar, sitting and drinking. When he caught her staring at him again, she felt compelled to go over. She poured herself a cup of coffee and sat down next to him.

To her complete surprise, he got up and walked away. *Rude and vulgar,* she immediately thought and reverted to her former impression. She was livid but even more so embarrassed that she could let this man, this savage, this beast, get the best of her. She was doing him a favor by allowing herself to talk to him. Instead, he insulted her. Indeed, from the very first day she saw him, he made it a point to mock her or Henry, to treat them both with disrespect. *He was compassionate with Africans because they were black like him. Perhaps, he was trying to undermine Henry's authority so he could take over. I will not let myself be caught off guard again!*

Usually, Henry's team, now combined with Goma's, tried to move out from camp by 7:00 a.m. Henry insisted they made more time in the morning before the sun rose. By noon, it became so hot that they couldn't go on, at which point they made camp or rested until the next day, or they rested in the morning and afternoon and marched again at night.

In reality, they seldom left camp in the morning when Henry wanted. For various reasons, they had delays: arguments about who would carry what, bickering between guards and porters over the guards' higher status. Now, he faced missing porters who had deserted or left overnight to be with their wives or local women who followed them. A few days ago, one of the porters fell down dead for no apparent reason or cause.

That morning, the procession left even later. The usual conflicts were compounded by the large group of men afflicted with African fever. It was a common occurrence in any caravan trip; it didn't mean they couldn't travel. Although physically weak and wracked with pain, some of the men could walk, although slowly with the aid of wooden staffs or hastily made crutches. Others had to be carried on litters and stretchers. And one man had to ride on one of the two remaining donkeys, shifting the donkeys' packs to the backs of the porters, making their loads even heavier. Morale was low. Most of the men, regardless of their job, didn't want to go on, and Henry knew it. It was only a matter of time before something would happen.

An incident came quickly enough. As the caravan began to move, less compact than before, with numerous stragglers lagging behind and scattered over a distance of a mile, another donkey carrying a saddle and two thirty-pound bales collapsed—dead. When Henry ordered the bales to be assumed by two other porters, one of them, a young man with bulging muscles, refused. Henry ordered him a second time, and still he wouldn't budge.

"Mimi beba fifty pound. No eighty pound. Hapan mkataba."

"I pay for extra pound in Tabora."

"Ni taka now!"

"Not now. In Tabora."

When the porter continued to resist, growing even more adamant, some of the other men began to get restless. The porter could see they agreed with him. All this could lead to an open revolt. Henry had to act. He took out his revolver and pointed it to the porter's chest. "Pick up pack!" The porter shook his head no. He didn't move, even though he knew Henry never bluffed.

Goma, who had remained passive so far, eased himself over to the resisting porter, taking his time, as if he had all day. He looked at the porter, and, after a pause, he said, "Twenty shillings, I pay in Tabora."

Henry scowled. This was an unusually high sum, and he knew Goma
didn't have it.

Goma repeated, "I pay twenty shillings in Tabora." He placed his
forefinger on the porter's chest. Then he pointed it to himself. "I pay.
Fedha." Goma was telling him he would pay in money.

"Twenty shillings?" the porter asked of Goma. Already, his resolve
started to crumble.

"Yes, in Tabora. Everything good." Goma balled his hand into a fist.
The porter likewise balled his hand. The two fists met. They agreed.
Janet studied Goma with even greater fascination. Henry said noth-
ing further.

The caravan ground on, sluggish and unsteady, past giraffes eating
leaves and buffalo herds running, past small hills with large granite
boulders that protruded out like magnificent rock sculptures. Henry
stayed up front, trying to speed up the pace. Janet, too, walked near
the front, trying to keep up. Yet, somehow, in spite of herself, in spite
of her doubts and counter-arguments, she kept looking at Goma, who
walked in the middle of the procession, carrying one end of a stretcher
with a sick man on top, and every time she looked, he turned his head
away from her. The harder she looked, the more he turned away. This
made her even more insistent on finding out more about him.

What do I have to fear? After all, I am white. She lagged back until
he caught up. When he walked past, she lockstepped with him as the
caravan kept moving.

"Where did you learn to speak English? I thought you were illiterate."

He only sneered.

Her exasperation returned. "Did I say something wrong?" She decided she would have it out with him if necessary.

"Think about what you said."

"I merely asked where you learned to speak English. What's
wrong with—"

"All Africans are illiterate to you." For the first time, he acknowledged her.

"I'm just trying to talk to you, Goma. Is that so bad?" Her anger was returning, her frustrations building. *Oh, what's the use,* she decided and walked away, back toward the front of the line. Then she heard his voice call her.

"I once studied at Oxford."

She turned around and came back. "You mean Oxford University in England?"

He nodded his head yes.

"That's amazing! You must be very proud." Instead of the positive reaction she expected from him, he sighed and seemed to sink into depression. After moments of silence, she picked up her pace and went ahead, but suddenly, she stopped. She was dying to ask one more question. She came back again. "Are you a Christian?"

"I was," he replied.

"Then why do you work for a man like Mr. Stanley?"

"Why don't you ask him?"

From the Usagara Hills, they traveled through the Marenga Mkali wilderness, crossing remote spurs that stood between higher ridges that surrounded them. These spurs, isolated from the steeper slopes, allowed the caravan to pass through the higher elevations.

They marched across ten miles of relentless jungle with monkeys and rhinoceros in abundance, and numerous streams and rivulets. Rock formations gave way to more jungles with thorn bushes and great towering sycamore trees. The water tasted bitter, like salty urine, so no one took a drink unless they had to. And then came the winds, huge gusts that came down from the higher hills ahead, causing bales to teeter atop the porters' heads and some of the cloth and bags to fall, which got caught in the dense shrubs and plants.

As they continued to climb toward elevated ground, Henry saw something ahead and ordered a halt. Another caravan approached from the opposite direction. Since the footpath was narrow, he decided to let the other caravan pass them before they would resume.

It was a column driven by seven black Arabs—black Africans who had converted to Islam—in long white robes and turbans, heavily armed with rifles, swords, and whips, guarding a group of thirty naked African slaves, mostly women. The strongest-looking men and two women walked up front, their necks fastened to "slave sticks," straight pieces of wood with forks at each end that were fastened around their necks. In addition to these sticks, their hands were bound behind their backs, making the task of walking in bare feet extremely difficult.

Behind them, another group of about twenty women and two older men trailed, bound in chains. They were mostly left to themselves, with only two guards to watch them, and seemed to be freer in their movements, though their emaciated condition made it difficult for them to keep up. A slave driver brought up the rear with a whip that he brought down on anyone who lagged behind. The caravan passed, slowly weaving along the narrow lane in silence. No one spoke from either group. No sounds were heard at all except moans and cries from those who were suffering.

Once the slave caravan had passed, Henry's group resumed its journey with the buffeting winds blowing down on them, making their passage slow. They had not walked but a hundred yards when a small group of three women appeared, female stragglers from the slave caravan, no longer bound or in chains.

They were even more emaciated than those ahead of them, their ribs sticking out of their flesh. They seemed to be wandering aimlessly, their eyes hollow, not able to recognize anything before them, as if they were unconscious of their surroundings. It was clear that these slaves had given up and looked like black ghosts, the walking dead.

Henry pushed his group farther on, now slashing through the jungle that had grown denser. Using their machetes, they had to hack through thick vegetation and sometimes a fallen tree in their path. Usually, they could climb over these obstacles, but with the donkey they had to unload and go around. Henry walked ahead with his rifle ready, until, once again, he ordered a halt.

Ahead of him was a small glade with a tall tree, but as he came closer, he saw a group of ten naked bodies that looked like the women they had just passed, only these were dead, and someone had tied their necks to the tree, which had made it impossible for them to escape. Already, ants and other insects had covered them, and their odor had filled the space around them, so the caravan slowed down but kept on moving.

Janet was rattled but also buoyed when it seemed such destruction and death would be behind them.

"Do you think that's the end of it?" she asked Goma.

"End of what?" he replied in an irritated tone.

"Those slaves." She pointed behind her.

"What are you asking? What do you mean?"

"Will we see any more slave caravans like that?"

"There's never an end to it. There are dozens, hundreds of slave caravans. Thousands. Don't be surprised if you see them again."

"Where are they going?"

"To Bagamoyo. Most will die before they get there."

Janet kept marching along with everyone else, the thick jungle now thinning, with only the wind to reckon with. An hour passed. They picked up their pace. No more signs of slaves or slavery. Just as her positive outlook came back, Henry stopped the group once more.

Now what? she thought.

She hated to stop, for usually it meant something was wrong. She heard sounds of snarling and growling, a pack of wild animals tearing at something. They sounded like hyenas, which she sometimes heard howling at night or saw tracking their caravan during the day. Henry lifted his rifle and fired, causing the hyenas to run away.

And then she saw them, a larger group of slave bodies at the base of a tree, their heads and limbs eaten away with blood and flesh, bone and body parts scattered along the ground out front with a horrible smell, so thick and foul that it stopped the wind. As Janet staggered past, her stomach boiled and churned. Try as she might to stop it, she vomited again and again until her legs collapsed, and she fell to her knees.

9

—

Janet pulled herself up. She had to keep going, one foot in front of the other, almost in a trance. So long as everyone else marched, so would she, like they were one huge connected body. She had to keep walking no matter what. If she fell or got left behind, she couldn't help but think she would face the same fate as those fallen slaves behind them, and why not?

The hyenas were following them, too, lurking behind trees for the next victim, anything that lingered and fell behind. She looked around. Henry thrashed ahead. With his hatchet, he cut down limbs and branches. The guide behind him, who was called Asmani, followed in silence. *What guide?* she thought. Henry had talked to him, but he never really consulted him. Rather, he used the guide as a crutch to back him up and uphold decisions he had already made. At a small clearing inside the thick woods, Henry stopped again. Janet's body shook with dread when he raised his rifle.

From the surrounding trees and bushes, a group of thirty African warriors leaped out with spears and shields raised, screaming in a language Janet did not understand. Their arms were cocked and ready to throw, ready to kill them on the spot. Henry froze and pointed his rifle, and so did the armed guards. Everyone else remained in their place. The warriors seemed to be taunting them, moving back and forth, their weapons braced to strike. Just as it seemed that they might assault them, their voices rising to a blood-curdling crescendo, Goma dropped the stretcher he was carrying and ran up the side of the path.

"No fight! No fight!" he shouted. The warriors continued to taunt and test them. Facing Henry and the guards, they beat their spears on their shields. "Hapana pambano! Hapana pambano!" Goma shouted again and ran to the guards to shove their gun barrels down. Then he turned back to the warriors. "No fight! No fight!"

Henry lowered his gun. "Jambo! Jambo!" He smiled at them and nodded his head. "Jambo!" Then, the warriors lowered their spears and silenced their strident voices. Henry stepped forward and began to talk to them in broken English.

When everyone on both sides had lowered their weapons, Janet proceeded to Goma. "What's going on? Who are they, Goma?"

"The Manyema tribe. We'll have to go with them."

"Why?"

"To pay muhongo. A tax to pass through their land."

The caravan followed the Manyema soldiers along the same path they had been walking until they came to a large settlement with dozens of sun-dried mud huts. They followed the path into the center of the village, passing hundreds of Africans lined up on the sides. Men, women, and children stared at them, or fought with each other to get a better view. Some of the men wore wrap-around loincloths. Some wore goat skins suspended by a knot tied around their necks like a toga. The younger women were heavily decorated, adorned in necklaces with carved pieces of ivory, hippo teeth, and small boar tusks or cowrie shells.

Older women and mothers carried sleeping babies in sacks tied to their backs. Those without children tied down their breasts with cords that wrapped around them. Boys were naked or wore short white pants that looked like underwear. Girls wore little grass skirts.

Janet was oblivious to everyone; everything became a blur. As she passed the Manyema Africans, she became a target again. Women pulled her hair or rubbed her skin to see if her white flesh was real. Their fingers poked her ribs, arms, or shoulders. She feared she might get stabbed. She shrank back in horror and revulsion. She prayed that she wouldn't fall down and kept her legs moving forward just behind Goma.

They came to an area with a dead African man, his body bloated and propped up below a sluice of running water that appeared to be cleaning and softening him. Just as Janet was passing him, a Manyema man took out his knife and cut a small piece of the bloated man's flesh and ate it. He chewed it and shook his head with disapproval, as if the taste was not quite right. He bent down, grabbed a handful of salt from a box and sifted it out.

Then he cut the salted meat and put it in his mouth, shaking his head with approval. When Janet saw him devour the morsel, she screamed. Her fear had finally overtaken her. Immediately, Henry ran back and clamped his sweaty hand over her mouth, stifling her ability to breathe. She almost passed out.

"Do not panic. Stay calm!" she heard him say as he dragged her along until they reached a central square.

In front of them, Queen Mother sat on an elaborate stool. Tall, black, and self-assured, she exuded feminine grace and strength. She wore a blue and red wrap-around cloth that covered her breasts, loins, and legs. Her hair was plaited with copper coins that draped her upper forehead. A bluish ochre covered her lips and eyelids. Two huge elephant tusks surrounded her, in a kind of shroud, with four men from the council of elders flanking both sides of the tusks. They were older men in red robes, bearing staffs. Behind them, four boys stood fanning them with ostrich feathers.

Henry stopped. Queen Mother stood up from her stool and walked forward. She looked at Henry and then Janet, who was now standing by herself, her body shaking as she struggled to look composed.

Queen Mother began to speak in Swahili. Goma stepped forward to translate her words. "I know what you're thinking. Do not be afraid. We only eat those we killed in battle."

"It's wrong!" Janet blurted. She didn't want to say it, but something inside of her pushed the words out. She couldn't help it.

Queen Mother frowned but quickly recovered her poise. "Do you know about the Zimba tribe?" She addressed Janet directly. Goma continued to translate.

"No."

"They originated near the Zambezi. You know the Zambezi?"

"I do," said Henry nervously, "the great river in the south."

"Many years ago, when the Portuguese controlled the coast. You know these Portuguese?"

"Yes," said Henry again. "They—" He wanted to say something else, but she cut him off.

"Whites like you kidnapped our people and made them slaves." Queen Mother stared at Janet as she spoke. "And took away our gold."

"They were our enemies, too, Queen Mother," Henry added, citing the Portuguese rivalry with the British navy. He was trying to smooth over the damage Janet had done.

"The Zimba tribe lived on human flesh. They ate people. One day, they rose up and marched from the Zambezi. They killed and ate all the Portuguese on the coast and all those Africans who helped them. Thousands were eaten." Queen Mother continued to stare at Janet.

Henry knew he had to change the subject. "Where is your chief, Queen Mother?"

Queen Mother kept her eyes on Janet. "Our chief has been killed. I am in charge." She shifted her attention back to Henry.

Henry turned to Goma. "Tell her we have what she wants." As soon as Goma told her what Henry had said, she smiled warmly and spread out her arms in a welcoming gesture.

That night, the situation calmed down. Fireflies came out, and dozens of torches flickered at the end of poles. The Manyema villagers went back to their huts or gathered in the village center to sing and

dance. Henry sat on a stool near Queen Mother and her elders talking
and gesturing, trying to communicate with them as they ate dinner.
Next to Queen Mother, a small tin box of gold coins lay open for
her to see.

The rest of the caravan members sat on mats near them, eating
and drinking pombe, a popular alcoholic drink that tasted like beer.
Everyone was in an upbeat mood. Even the sick ones were coming around.

Janet sat next to Goma, trying to eat the grand array of food set before them: rice, millet, corn, sweet potatoes, peanuts, dates, tomatoes,
roasted chicken, and goat meat. It was the best meal they had eaten
since they left Bagamoyo. Janet only picked at her food; she wasn't very
hungry. She was still shaken by the earlier displays of Africans being
eaten by animals and by man.

*Eating a dead man is the same thing as hyenas who devoured fallen
slaves, a despicable and savage practice.*

Whenever she put anything into her mouth, she thought of the
bloated man. Goma, however, wolfed down his food and drank large
amounts of pombe until he was drunk. This further incensed her.

"How can you gorge yourself when human beings are being eaten?"

"Because I'm hungry. We all must eat, including you."

"Where is your compassion? How can you get drunk when they are
being killed and devoured in the most hideous ways?"

"It's no more barbaric than when the English drew and quartered
political prisoners." In the background, Manyema men and women
started to dance an elaborate dance. Drums were beating. Goat horns
were blowing like bugles.

"It's not the same thing." Janet had to raise her voice against the
steady pounding of the drums.

"Your people chopped off heads with an ax and hanged people with
ropes. What's the difference?"

"But we didn't eat each other. Not even our enemies."

"You burned witches at the stake, thousands of them!"

"Two wrongs don't make it right!"

"You sent innocent men to the gallows!" At this point, Goma shouted at her, and his eyes turned a watery red. Sensing that she had hit a nerve, Janet stopped talking. Nevertheless, she was shocked by his reaction, as if he had taken their discussion personally. She looked at him, puzzled by his tears.

10

—

The caravan stayed on an extra day, which gave them all a chance to rest. For those who were sick, it was a time to heal, and they received a visit from the Manyema medicine man. He gathered a group of them and told them to sit in a circle around a stool. Janet, who had an interest in medicine just like her missing brother, joined the group to observe. The medicine man pulled one of Henry's sick porters up.

"Sit here," he told him in Swahili. "Relax."

With the sick man's head already bent down, the medicine man draped a towel over it. Then he took a steaming bowl of liquid and placed it under the sick man's nostrils with the towel acting to keep the vapors concentrated.

"Breathe in," he instructed. "Breathe long."

The sick man inhaled the murky cloud deep inside him. When the medicine man removed the towel, the sick man breathed out and smiled. He felt better already.

The medicine man looked around to see who would be next. This allowed Janet to move closer and see the vapors were caused by a root suspended in a pot of steaming water. Thinking that she was also afflicted, he gestured for her to step up.

"No sick. No sick." She waved her hands back and forth. "No sick." Another ailing porter got up instead, sat on the stool, and the process began again.

As the day continued, caravan members were free to wander around and interact with the Manyema villagers. Janet kept to herself, yet found her eyes once again drifting toward Goma, closely observing him. As in Bagamoyo and in the abandoned village they had left just days ago, she noticed a pattern in his behavior.

He always seemed to attract Africans by going out of his way to communicate with them, to smile and talk, and not only that. She saw that he seemed to cultivate attention to himself by individual acts of kindness, such as helping a child carry a bucket of water or fetching a walking staff for an elderly man. And when he was among any large group of Africans, he would always perform, sing, tell jokes, or dance. She wondered whether all this came naturally to him or whether he had some ulterior motive.

Janet wandered farther around the village. It was a small village by African standards, no more than a thousand residents. All the huts looked pretty much the same from the outside. Inside, she saw how Africans lived on tamped-down mud floors with blankets and mats. Chickens and goats came and went, and most huts were inundated with insects, especially ants that scurried on the floors and huge spiders in corners. She also saw rats and mice. In one hut, she confronted a young Manyema woman.

"This filth is appalling. You need to clean this hut."

But the woman didn't understand her. "Nini?"

"You should clean this dirt. It's unhealthy. You need to learn proper hygiene."

"Nini?"

"How can you live this way? Do you have a broom? To sweep?" Janet used her arms to suggest the sweeping motion of a broom.

But the woman just smiled and said, "Asante tafadhali. Asante."

And then a goat wandered in and began to nibble at a leather bag.

Janet seized the goat by the head to push it out and turned back to the woman. "No animals. No good. Keep goat outside hut." She pointed. "Outside."

The woman, who had by now lost her smile, still kept repeating, "Nini?"

Janet also noted that during the day, men and women were segregated and performed their daily tasks separately. She saw women cooking and washing or pounding corn in wooden mortars with sticks. Some were making baskets from strips of bamboo. Some were dyeing cloth by soaking it in red- and blue-stained water.

Many of the young men were absent, either hunting for meat in the countryside, searching for ivory, or passing caravans to pay tribute. In the village, men worked on projects, such as carving wood into stakes, poles, stools, masks, and mallets they used for pounding. She was intrigued by these carved objects, by their detailed complexity and beauty. Another group of men worked with ivory, stacking it to sell to passing caravans or cutting it into smaller pieces for necklaces and jewelry.

Men were also involved in iron making, where they took heated ore from charcoal burners underneath the ground and shaped it in various ways. Instead of a blacksmith's hammer, they used two heavy, smooth stones, one that held the molten metal, the other used to shape it by pounding down with their hands encased in gloves. To Janet, it was a primitive process, but the finished products—mainly knives, hatchets, spearheads, and hoes—looked quite effective and accomplished.

She also observed the children. Young girls stayed with their mothers, helping them with their tasks, or they looked after the younger children. A few of them sat on stools while another girl twisted their hair into short cords that shot out in all directions from their heads. Boys, like the men, were not around, except the very young. She saw some boys with spears going into the bush. She saw others leaving to go out to the pasture to oversee goatherds.

At the end of the day, Queen Mother summoned Henry to talk.

Janet saw them assembled with Goma, so she also went over. Queen Mother looked elegant with her mass of kinky hair combed straight back from her forehead, her full lips smiling. Around her, torches blazed. Shadow and light flickered. Her council of four elders flanked her near the elephant tusks.

In the background, Janet could hear sounds from horns and drums. She also heard a large group of women chanting a lyric. One voice would yell out a line, followed by a chorus who repeated it. This chanting went on and on without stop or variation. After a while, it seemed monotonous and repetitive. Soon, Henry and Goma sat down on a mat. Janet followed suit as Queen Mother began to speak in Swahili, Goma translating.

"You are welcomed, Mzungu, to stay for as long as you like. You are my guests."

Henry smiled and nodded. "I thank you, Queen Mother, for your generous hospitality, for your food and drink, and helping our sick recover."

As Henry spoke, Queen Mother leaned over to one of her elders, who whispered in her ear. She sat back up and gazed upon them somberly. "I have some news. There's going to be war. Mirambo has assembled a large army."

As soon as she mentioned the name Mirambo, Henry's face dropped, and, for a moment, a flicker of anxiety crossed his face. "Mirambo?"

"You know him?"

Everyone who knew Mirambo considered him a military genius. For years, he had waged war successfully against the Arab caravans whom he blamed for taking power away from his father, the chief of his tribe, the Uyowa. When his father died, Mirambo assumed the throne. He accused the Arabs of encroaching on their lands and monopolizing the ivory trade upon which the Uyowa relied. The Arabs endeared themselves to other African tribes that competed with the Uyowa, and the Uyowa were slowly cut off from the trade. Additionally, he hated the Arabs for the slave trade, turning Africans against each other in order to sell slaves. The Uyowa, were forced into slave trading when they were cut off from ivory. Mirambo hated the disunity the Arabs had caused among the Africans and decided to unite his people and fight back. With growing numbers of fugitive slaves flocking to him, many of them teenagers, he had threatened the Arab strongholds and vowed to stop the caravan traffic altogether.

Goma, too, perked up when he heard Mirambo's name. "They call him the black Napoleon." Goma knew Mirambo had assumed his reputation from the number of victories he had garnered against all of his enemies.

Queen Mother turned to her elders and laughed. Then she became serious. "Soon he will attack Tabora. When he does, he'll block the road to Ujiji."

"Ujiji?" Janet uttered. "That's where my brother is."

Henry also shook when he heard the news. If Mirambo attacked Tabora, the caravan could not get to Ujiji and Dr. Livingstone. "When, Queen Mother, will he attack Tabora?"

She leaned once again to her elders and turned back. "Wood already touched by fire is not hard to burn."

After their meeting with Queen Mother, Goma, Henry, and Janet assembled in a nearby hut to talk, hastened on by the new information. The three of them looked dark among the shadows now without torches or light. Insects swirled all around—fleas, flies, mosquitoes, gnats. The night was hot, their foreheads dripped sweat. Tensions began to rise.

Henry paced back and forth. "We'll have to leave tonight and pray we can get to Ujiji before Mirambo launches."

"Together," Goma said.

"No. You keep your people here," replied Henry.

"No, we leave together."

"I agree," Janet chimed.

Henry would have none of it. "Bad idea. We'll be sitting ducks."

"In Tabora, there's money. The porters want their pay," Goma said.

"If Mirambo attacks, no one gets paid." Henry spoke with finality.

"If we stay here, they'll run away." Goma knew that without his porters, the entire caravan would be in jeopardy.

After a long pause, Henry made his decision. "All right, but when we get to Tabora, we split up again. I go ahead with my group to Ujiji. You follow."

That night, the caravan moved out of the Manyema village, everyone now rested, those who were sick now recovered, the porters carrying their packs. Unlike Bagamoyo, this time there was no fanfare, no beating drums, no carrying of the American flag, no singing or shouting, no racket, no noise. As they left, with Henry at the helm once more, Queen Mother bade them farewell and good luck. Many of the Manyema villagers came out and lined the pathway that led to the surrounding dark hills. Some waved and smiled and shook hands, some continued to stare, some frowned before they turned and went back to their huts.

By morning, the caravan had made good time, Henry driving them at a very fast pace. At noon, they stopped to rest. The sun was blazing once again. They ate some food and made camp. Henry suggested they all try to sleep because they would soon resume the march, once the sun went down. Just before bed, Janet noticed Henry talking to a young African who then slipped away into the bush, but she dismissed it; she was too tired. Since the ground was dry, she did not put up her tent. For once, she slept in the open, just like the Africans. Soon everyone was wrapped in blankets and slept. All was quiet.

What she didn't know was that they had camped in an area infested with snakes crawling through the low grass, one of which slithered toward her. She tossed to one side within her blanket away from the snake, now slinking closer to her. When she opened her eyes, she saw it on her chest, looking into her eyes, its tongue shooting out. She jumped up and screamed. She took out her pistol and fired it for the first time, killing the snake instantly. Henry rushed over. He looked at her. She looked at the smoking gun in her hand.

"Makes you feel powerful, doesn't it?"

"What?"

"To shoot. It makes you feel—"

"No," she cut him off. "It makes me feel empty."

The next day, after they had been marching during the night, they reached the top of a knoll. Henry ordered everyone to stop. He took out his spyglass and climbed a tree. Through the lens, he could see an open plain surrounded by low hills in the middle of a vast irrigated field with gardens of corn, peas, cassava, tomatoes, cucumbers, and orchards of planted trees—mango, banana and pomegranate. He saw pastures with roaming herds of goats, cattle, and pigs, and a dirt road leading to a large populated town of dried-mud huts and houses with thick plastered walls, all of which was surrounded by a vast stockade of stout posts and stakes, an oasis in the middle of the wilderness. They had reached Tabora, the principal Arab settlement in central Africa.

11

—

The procession entered the town. Unlike in the dozens of villages they had passed and the Manyema tribe, with its hundreds of Africans who lined the route leading to the center of the village, Henry's caravan aroused little attention from the people inside, so used were they to arriving and departing convoys. Instead of curious villagers who had never seen a white person, Tabora streets were filled with Africans from different tribes who had come to trade or buy supplies.

Tabora had a large Arab population, since it was their primary trading station in the region, of both Muslims from Oman and black Arabs, indigenous Africans who had converted. It also had a large group of half-castes, mostly mixed-race children who ran openly through the mud-packed streets along with African children, goats, and dogs. And there were slaves, hundreds of them, recently kidnapped, brought to the market to be sold.

Tabora was alive with buying and selling, rich with the sounds of vendors and merchants hawking their wares: teapots, Persian rugs, baskets, ropes, earthenware cups, even Chinese porcelain. Asians from India owned the banks. Gun-toting Africans kept the peace. Henry's

group found an open space near the stockade wall and made camp. His
next task was to find Sheik Sayd Bin Salim, who was expecting him.

"I have to find the governor. Goma, will you come with me?"

"Is he expecting us?"

"I disposed a messenger—Saburi—to announce our coming. We
need to talk to the sheik immediately."

"About Mirambo?"

"Yes."

Janet, who had been listening, spoke, too. "Can I go?"

"No," Henry replied emphatically.

She decided to go with them anyway. They walked briskly. Goma
asked a passerby in Swahili where the governor lived, and they found
his house easily enough. It was surrounded by lavish gardens, the front
door made of carved teakwood with brass knockers that Goma lifted
and pounded. Soon a huge African slave, dressed in an embroidered
jacket and turban, opened the door and let them in, blocking Janet.
When Janet insisted that she enter, the doorman blocked her again and
turned to Henry.

"No women," he said.

She tried again. "But—"

"No women! No! It's against their religion." Henry spoke as he
turned and walked inside. The doorman shut the door in her face.

Outside, Janet looked around. Now what? She didn't want to go
back to camp and sit around, reading her Bible. It was not the time
for that. She decided to take a tour of Tabora itself. That seemed to her
worthy enough. She left the sumptuous gardens in front of Sheik Sayd
Bin Salim's house and proceeded down the street toward the central
market area.

As she walked, she noticed the preponderance of Arab men who
looked different from the Africans. Some of them were dark-skinned
or black with Negroid facial features, some of them were lighter with
thinner lips and narrow noses. Yet, what distinguished them was not
their skin color or how they looked, but their dress, quite different

from the semi-naked Africans. Most of the Arabs wore long white robes and a belt within which was tucked an elaborate knife or scimitar. Some wore long shirts like nightgowns that hung to their knees.

Around their heads, they wore a white turban that covered their hair, unlike Africans who never wore hats or caps and whose hair was always on full display. Also, these Arab men carried themselves differently, assuming an air of importance, like Goma or Queen Mother, as if they were kings. These Arabs reminded her of the slave drivers she saw on the caravan trail, men who were used to being in control. Men who took whatever they wanted.

Once she got to the market, she saw numerous vendors selling their wares in small makeshift stalls, separated from each other by wooden partitions or blankets suspended from wooden poles. As she walked to the various shops, men shouted at her in different languages, urging her to come and buy whatever they were selling.

"Bonjour. Hola. Hello. English? Portuguese?"

"Scottish."

"Scottish. English. Same thing."

"No, it's not the same thing."

"Yes. Same people. White people. Smooth hair."

"We have different cultures. Different history."

"Same language."

"No, different languages. Different accents."

"Okay, Irish.

"No. I'm Scottish, not Irish."

"Okay. Scottish. You buy my chocolate from Belgium. I give you good price."

Many of these goods were now what she considered luxuries— things like sardines in cans or caviar, a vast array of European wines and bottles of brandy, embroidered jackets trimmed in a gold sash, leather boots, and Persian rugs.

When she looked closer at who was purchasing these items, once again she saw they were mostly Arabs or a few Asians from India. Asians, who were less in evidence, dressed in baggy trousers that came down to their knees, long-sleeved jackets, and fezzes or skullcaps on their heads. Asians were also distinct from the blacks, with copper-colored skin and straighter hair. Like the Arabs, they appeared to be members of the master class.

She entered another open area nearby. Here she saw more Africans dressed in loincloths or cheap, white wrap-around cloths that covered their chests or legs, just like the porters in Henry's caravan. Although many of the Africans came from different tribes with different styles of dress and physical attachments to distinguish them, Janet was not able to notice these differences.

All she could see was an ocean of black Africans buying from vendors with cheaper goods and basic needs: baskets, rope, hoes, knives, spoons, spices such as salt and pepper, rice and beans, and packages of coffee. A few women were buying medicine. A few men were buying tobacco and cigars. As Janet walked farther, the crowd got thicker until it grew into an assembly in front of a one-story house. They had gathered to watch a large group of slaves being sold, about a hundred of them, mostly young women, some holding the hands of their children standing next to them.

It was a horrible scene. The slave women looked sad and afraid while the men, Arab slave traders who looked like those she had seen earlier, walked up and down, examining them. One of these men squeezed the buttocks of a beautiful slave woman.

"Yes. Yes. Such a tight, firm ass," he said in Swahili. "What is your name, my beautiful?"

"Towfika," she whispered.

He smacked her buttocks hard, which sounded like a whip cracking. "I can't hear you!"

"Towfika," she spoke again louder.

"You be my slave, Towfika? You want that?"

"Yes, master."

Then he ran his fingers along her breasts and pinched her cheeks. As he did so, she cried, the tears falling silently down her cheeks. Standing next to her was her boy, squeezing her hand, his head bent down in dejection. Other traders walked up and down, fingering and touching the women and children, their hands roving all over their bodies.

To conclude the sale, the trader went to another man, an Arab, to make payment, which consisted of a whispered agreement in the Arab's ear. Then, he took the woman by the arm to escort her away.

"Please, master. You take my boy, too. Please, I beg you. He's my only child."

"No. I want you. I don't want him. Come. We go now."

"Please, master. Let me take my child with me. Please!"

"No!"

"Please. I'll do anything you want. Just take him." She continued to clutch the child's hand, squeezing it even harder.

"I said no. Don't ask me again."

"I must have my boy. Please, master. Please!"

And then he beat her. With his fists, he punched her in the stomach and face until she doubled over. He dragged her away, leaving the child screaming and running after his mother as they were separated. In the crowd of Africans surrounding them, people were protesting, their voices howling against what they were seeing. Perhaps they were relatives or friends who knew the woman now being sent into slavery.

Yet any signs of overt challenges or attempts to stop these proceedings would be met with Africans who were also slaves, guards who kept their fingers on the triggers of their outdated muskets. Everyone was helpless to do anything against this brutality, and for the first time during her visit, Janet became enraged, truly infuriated that this practice could go on. She now understood why her brother was in Africa. She understood why he hated slavery. As Janet stood there, looking helplessly at the horrible scene unfolding before her, an Arab man smiled at her.

"Hello, pretty white girl. Such lovely red hair." He spoke in Swahili, but Janet could understand what he wanted.

He drew closer to her. "Come with me, yes? I take good care of you."
*How can this man be smiling when lives are being ruined? How can
he not feel outraged?* In disgust, she turned and bolted away.

In the meantime, while Janet rushed from the slave mart, colliding
with Africans in the surrounding crowd, Henry and Goma sat in luxu-
rious surroundings inside Sheik Sayd Bin Salim's spacious living room
with huge, finely carved rafters. They sat and crossed their legs on a
comfortable Persian rug. They leaned their elbows on satin pillows. The
sheik's slaves, all of them young black women, were bringing out silver
dishes loaded with delicacies and laying them out on a huge, round
tray upon which rice and curried goat meat were already steaming.

Across from Henry and Goma sat the sheik. He was an older Arab
from Oman, the commander in chief of Tabora. As such, he ran the
town as any mayor did, collecting taxes and overseeing security. He
had been on the job for almost two years, having been appointed by
Sultan Barghash Bin Said, the Omani ruler of Tanganyika in Zanzibar,
but the sheik's rule was limited. Although he ran armed security police,
he lacked any real military strength and was vulnerable to any incursion from a well-organized African tribe.

But now the sheik looked relaxed and unconcerned as he sat in
traditional clothes: white gown, turban, black slippers, and a carved
dagger hanging from his belt. On top of this, he wore a blue calico
robe that looked like a shawl elegantly draped around his shoulders. In
the midst of a heated discussion about Mirambo, he dipped a piece of
bread into the shredded goat meat and began to eat.

"Who knows when he will attack. When he comes, we will be ready.
We have Winchester rifles. Like yourself."

"Do not underestimate Mirambo. He's got many tribes on his side,"
replied Goma.

The sheik slammed his fist down on the carpet. "So do we!"

"You exaggerate, Sheik Sayd. I assure you." Goma knew that Arab
rule in the region was more in name than actual fact. In truth, the

Arabs had very little political or military influence except along the
ocean coast.

"Most Africans want us here," the sheik continued. "They like trade.
We sell them what they want."

"But they hate slavery." Henry couldn't help but say what he
thought should have been obvious.

"If we didn't trade slaves, the Africans would. They would sell their
mothers for gold."

Goma's eyes flashed with anger. "We are all greedy, Sheik Sayd.
The Arabs, too. That's why the tribes are killing each other."

Oblivious to this exchange of words inside the sheik's opulent living room, Janet continued to hurry away from the slave mart, as far as
her legs would take her, yet everywhere she turned, she encountered
slaves, some in chains from an arriving caravan, some walking in or
out of the numerous harems where they worked as concubines; some
were held as prisoners in large tembes, enclosed square huts with an
open court, guarded by armed sentries.

Janet slowed down when she reached a dirt-packed street that
looked like a residential neighborhood with small huts and families.
She saw a woman grinding corn in a mortar. She saw an elderly African
man sitting on a stool, mending a garment. She did not see any slaves.
She stopped and looked around.

Farther down the street, she saw a group of African girls playing a
game that looked like hopscotch. One of the girls tossed a small square
object onto the packed-dirt arena and proceeded to jump toward it
on one leg, turn around, hop back, pick up the object, and return to
where she began. As Janet drew closer, she recognized the game as what
she had played in Scotland when she was a girl. The only difference was
these girls had scrawled their rectangular patterns on the dirt, whereas
she had used chalk on concrete pavement. Otherwise, the same rules
of the game applied. This intrigued her, and she wondered how this
game had become a part of the African culture. She walked closer to
the girls in order to get a better view.

She remembered she had bought a couple of large pieces of chocolate from one of the vendors earlier, so she decided to offer each girl a piece. As she walked closer to the girls, who were still skipping and jumping, Janet took a piece and broke it up into smaller pieces. She stood next to them, silently watching. One of the girls, the skinniest and smallest of them, her hair shaped into dozens of tiny knobs that stuck out of her head, came up to her and smiled.

"Do you want some candy?" Janet gave the chocolate to her.

"Asante." The young girl smiled and took a small bite.

Janet was about to give the other girls a piece, but before she could, they surrounded the little girl and yanked the chocolate out of her hand. The little girl ran after them, screaming and protesting to give back her candy. When Janet saw her fighting to get back what was stolen from her, she, too, joined in and fought the girls to take the candy. Janet battled until she had her hand around the other girls' hands, which were clutching the chocolate, and they stood there, in the middle of the street, pulling and pushing each other.

"Give it back," Janet screamed. "Give it back!"

Then the other girls broke away and ran, taking the candy with them and leaving Janet and the little girl behind. Janet, however, remembered she had more chocolate in her pocket, so she turned back to the little girl, whose face had sunken into dejection, and gave her all of the remaining pieces. The little girl took them and smiled as she had done before, a gorgeous smile with big white teeth that looked like polished ivory. Janet lingered, put her arms around the child's shoulder, and drew her closer.

12

—

In the living room of Sheik Sayd Bin Salim's house, Goma, Henry, and the sheik were still talking. They had finished eating the main course of food, and the slave women now brought hot coffee in porcelain cups as well as sherbet. They continued to discuss the Mirambo threat, with the sheik pressing Goma and Henry.

"Mirambo, like most chiefs, wants power for himself. He doesn't care about the slaves."

"That might be true, but he has their support, and if he attacks, then we can't get to Ujiji." Henry really didn't care about Mirambo. He wanted to continue on his journey.

"Then stay here in Tabora and help us fight. The more soldiers we have, the better our chances."

"No, Sheik. I have business in Ujiji."

"I know what your business is. You want to find Livingstone." The sheik paused and smirked, as if he knew something that Henry didn't. "The word is out that your boss, Gordon Bennett, is paying you thousands of dollars, and if you find him, you will be rich and famous."

Henry merely looked at him. *Let him think what he wants,* he thought.

The sheik continued. "I wish you well, my friends, but take heed.

The London Times is right behind you. They, too, are getting ready to launch their own caravan right behind yours back in Zanzibar."

"I'm not afraid of *The London Times*. If Livingstone is alive, and I think he is, then I shall get to him first."

"Take my word for it. He's dead. Despite what they say."

"Have you seen the body?"

"No, but he has money and supplies in the storehouse. He never picked them up."

It came as a shock to Henry that Livingstone had left anything behind, and at first, he didn't believe the sheik. Henry told the sheik that he was flat-out wrong and even thought this information was a ploy to get his group to join with the sheik's army in fighting Mirambo. So he asked the sheik to take them to the storehouse and prove it.

"Sure, I can prove it. I can show you. All of his things are right down the street."

"Then take us there."

"Sure. Sure. We go soon. Relax. Drink your coffee. Do you want more? Perhaps more sherbet. Sherbet is good in this hot weather." Henry's anxiety was building, and the sheik knew it. He liked watching Henry squirm.

After they finished eating, the sheik led them out of his house to a storehouse nearby. The storehouse was well fortified, made from stone with a heavy, intricately carved wooden front door to discourage any potential thieves from trying to enter. Also, two armed guards stood outside. Everyone knew that the storehouse contained valuables, so it seemed more fortified than a bank.

The sheik took out his key and opened the door. Inside, it was dark. The sheik soon lit a candle hanging from the inside wall that gave them enough light to walk down a hallway filled with boxes, packages, bales of cloth, clothing, and equipment from an assorted group of owners. He led Goma and Henry farther down until they reached a dark corner and the sheik lit another candle. Before them stood another set of caravan packages—bales, bags, boxes of tools and other equipment, long poles loaded with brass rings, two canvas tents. There were even a few rifles and ancient muskets with barrels of ammunition and gunpowder.

The sheik waved his hand and pointed. "These are all Livingstone's things, all of what you see here."

Henry and Goma stepped forward to get a closer look.

"This is a lot of stuff," Henry exclaimed while picking up one of the guns. "Why did you say Livingstone left all these things here?" Henry realized there were enough valuables here to supply any large caravan for months.

"I didn't say."

"Then how did you get them? How did Livingstone deliver . . ." Goma, too, couldn't fathom the idea that Livingstone would leave these supplies unless he intended to quickly return for them.

"An expedition left them here. They were supposed to get them to Ujiji but couldn't get through. I was told by an Arab from Ujiji that Livingstone knew they were here. That was a year ago. I haven't heard anything since. That's why I think he's dead."

"How did Livingstone look to him? The Arab from Ujiji?" asked Goma.

"He said he didn't look good. Thin. Gray hair. He said his teeth were falling out. In some ways, he looked dead already."

"Have you tried to contact him since?" said Henry.

"Of course. That is until this Mirambo business. Right now, I am focused on preparing for an assault."

Henry shook his head. "Mirambo might have already cut off the road to Ujiji. That's why you haven't heard anything."

"Maybe. Maybe not. All I know is that he hasn't yet launched a full attack. Not yet." He paused and led them farther down the corridor. "There's one more thing I haven't shown you." He directed them to a tin box in the corner and, with another key, opened it. Inside, they saw a large collection of gold coins. "See what I mean? No man in his right mind would leave this amount of gold here unless he were dead."

Henry and Goma went to the box and then looked at the sheik.

He anticipated their question and, before they could speak, told them they were welcome to take the gold and whatever supplies they wanted given that they were trying to find the owner of these possessions who, in the sheik's mind, was already dead. He knew they would not use the funds for their own purposes.

"Now we can hire more porters," Goma said.

"And buy more guns," said Henry.

Later, back at the camp, a few of the caravan members were resting after they had eaten dinner. They were in a good mood, especially after Goma brought back enough money to pay off his men as he'd promised. Janet, who had since returned from her afternoon adventures, had earlier suggested they go out and buy the men extra meat so that they might have a feast, a sort of last supper, since they all knew they would be leaving in the morning.

Goma, however, nixed the idea. He knew the men would not be there. With extra money in their pockets, and knowing full well they faced an uncertain future in the face of Mirambo, they would all be looking for female companions in one of the brothels in town, or they would be with their girlfriends or wives. Some wouldn't return to camp until the hour of their departure, early in the morning. The camp was now deserted except for Henry, who retired to his tent, Janet, Goma, and a few porters who sat around a small fire to sing plaintive songs.

"I had no idea." Janet was strolling at the edge of camp, walking along a street near the stockade wall that fortified the town, Goma at her side.

"What? That the trip—"

"Would be strewn with slaves. Everywhere I turned today, I saw slaves. I saw young children being separated from their mothers."

They continued to walk in silence. The soft sounds of the porters' song drifted to them in the background.

"It's only going to get worse."

"And the women in town, the women in the harems. They're slaves, too?"

"Yes."

"And the African guards?"

"Yes, them, too. Most of the African soldiers and security forces. They are all slaves."

"How did it ever get this way? Whose fault is it?"

"It's the fault of the Arabs . . . and the British and Europeans. They tempt us with fine clothes, goods, and guns, so we must kidnap each other to pay for these things. If the tribes gave up selling each other, it would all end. But some allow their people to kill and plunder, so the others must defend themselves."

Daybreak. The caravan once again awoke. Although they looked groggy and had not gotten much sleep, those caravan members who had returned were in fine spirits and ready to go. Some porters had not returned, but Henry had anticipated this and paid some Arab masters to allow a few slaves to come and work for him, to help carry some of the equipment and supplies. He didn't see this as a problem since some of his initial porters were runaway slaves.

Slavery was so fluid that the line between free and slave was constantly shifting, depending on frequently changing circumstances. Masters hired out their slaves all the time if they were paid enough money. And if they were good masters, those slaves would always return to them rather than face the harsh reality of trying to find food and shelter on their own. The caravan now had about sixty members, smaller than when they started from Bagamoyo, but all caravans had an attrition rate as they progressed on their journey. Everybody knew that.

After campfires had been doused and everyone had eaten breakfast, porridge and biscuits made by the cook, and they had drunk their morning coffee, Janet and Henry stumbled into an argument. Once again, Henry had irritated her by saying she had to remain behind in

Tabora because the danger of Mirambo attacking them would be too
great. Indeed, Henry anticipated an offensive action and had prepared
for it. With the gold coins he had received from Dr. Livingstone's supplies in the storehouse, he bought new rifles and pistols for his guards,
including more ammunition. There would be a fight, and he didn't
want Janet involved. When she refused to be left behind, he ordered
her to stay.

"You can't stop me," Janet responded.

"Yes, I can."

"Why?"

Henry sat down on a stool. He bowed his head. He tried to speak
with honesty and sincerity, hoping to convince her without a struggle.
"Because I feel responsible for you. If anything should happen to you—"

"You want to control me. That's not responsibility."

Henry stood back up. Her tone irked him. He would have to be
more forceful. "Control you for your own good. To protect you."

"Because I'm a white woman?"

"When we leave here we will be hit. Do you know what that's like?
Have you ever killed a man? I'm trying to save you from that." His
voice rose almost to a shout. He thought to himself, *She just doesn't get
it, does she?*

"I don't want any favors. I want to find my brother!"

"And I say no!" He had raised his voice. "You stay here. If we find
your brother, we will bring him back!" He stomped away, but she ran
after him. She gripped his arm in a tight vise and pulled herself close
to his face.

"I'm going with you to Ujiji."

13

—

The expedition got underway again, Henry at the helm, behind him his guide, a flag bearer without the flag, a cook, a drummer, porters, armed guards, a few new donkeys. They moved quickly and with little sound. Janet walked up front, near Henry, her hand now resting on her pistol, lost in her private thoughts. Behind her were the palisades of Tabora and a rising blood-red sun.

Also left behind were Goma and his group of twenty-five. He had agreed on the last night of their stay in the Manyema village that once they got to Tabora, he would separate from Henry en route to Ujiji. Now it seemed to Janet that splitting up made even less sense. Henry's group, which numbered about thirty-five men with ten armed guards, didn't look formidable. She imagined Mirambo having hundreds, perhaps thousands of warriors. What could they do against them? How could Goma's group help if they came too late? It seemed to her they could be overrun quite easily.

That night, they made camp and posted guards for the watch. Henry chose a spot that was removed from trees, an open field. Why Henry chose this area, Janet didn't know. Once again, she thought if Mirambo and his people wanted to assault them here, they could be easily taken. Nevertheless, campfires burned. The donkeys brayed nervously. From time to time, she heard the sound of wild dogs in the distance, but she knew they were not wild dogs. These sounds she had never heard before. They could be the sounds of Mirambo warriors who were watching them. Everyone, including Henry, was on edge. When they went to bed at night to sleep, the sounds continued to keep everyone awake. She saw Henry sitting on a stool, his rifle cocked and ready.

"Splitting up the group makes no sense."

"What do you know about it?"

"How can Goma help us if he comes too late? It seems we could be easily overrun."

"Miss Livingstone, I don't feel like talking about it. You know nothing about tactics."

"I have common sense. That counts for something."

"You're a fool."

The next day, the caravan moved even faster. From Tabora, they had marched along an open dirt road across a ridge, mainly open grassland with few trees, and, although they had marched ten to fifteen miles, they could still see Tabora, now far away. Then, the terrain changed. After they crossed a second, higher ridge, they entered a dark forest, not quite jungle, but dense enough to cover Mirambo's soldiers, hidden from sight of the caravan.

The forest grew darker above the dirt road on which they traveled another five miles, the road breaking at two points to cross over rocks and fast-moving streams. Then the road became a footpath that slowed them down, but Henry kept them marching relentlessly, sometimes walking to the rear as they moved to determine if anyone was following them.

Soon they came to an open space within which a large square structure stood. It looked like a stockade, well-fortified outside with poles or sticks. A few conical huts surrounded it; the area looked like it had been cleared to build a larger settlement. It was dotted with tree stumps. Otherwise, there was no sign of human life anywhere. Before they approached the stockade, Janet went to Henry.

"What's this?"

"Kwihara. It used to be part of Tabora." He signaled for the group to go inside. The guide opened the front door and walked in. The others began to follow. "We'll stop here. Mirambo's men have been tracking us since we left."

"How do you know?"

"They've scared the birds and animals away. It's too quiet."

The caravan entered a large enclosed space surrounded by four stockade walls of three-inch-thick tree stakes daubed with dried mud. Inside, just behind the stockade walls, a series of poles were planted at intervals to support a narrow thatched roof under which soldiers could stand along holes pierced for observation and firearms. It was a small stockade, but perfect for Henry's caravan, whose numbers were low.

The caravan kept moving into the fort, but the armed guards were edgy, their rifles cocked and ready. Most of the porters, donkeys, supplies, the cook, and the guide were all inside when an arrow came out of nowhere and hit one of the guards, who staggered backward, dead. As he fell, he shot his rifle in the air.

Arrows and spears rained down on the remaining caravan members still outside, including Janet and Henry, the drummer, five porters, and three armed guards still standing. Another guard took an arrow in the arm as he swung his rifle up and shot, knocking down a Mirambo warrior. With his left hand, he broke the stem of the arrow off and fired again. Henry rapidly fired his Winchester at twenty of Mirambo's warriors who were coming at them in full battle gear with eagle feathers stuck into their thick, kinky hair. Capes were tied around their necks, and they carried buffalo-hide shields.

They rushed at the caravan from all sides with knives, hatchets, and short spears used for stabbing. Two more guards and porters got stabbed or slashed, but both guards and one of the porters remained standing as they grappled with the warriors hurling themselves at them. The remaining three porters drew swords from their scabbards and fought back.

All the while, Henry kept firing his rifle until his ammunition ran out. Mirambo fighters were able to deflect some of the bullets with their shields. Nevertheless, two of them got hit and fell.

As he stopped to reload, he turned to Janet. "Keep firing. Cover me."

Once reloaded, he stood next to her and began firing again. "Aim carefully. Don't waste bullets."

The Mirambo soldiers pressed closer. One of them lifted his spear to throw at Janet, who had one bullet left, which she fired, stopping him, as his spear came down a few inches from her face. She didn't even think about it. She reloaded and kept on fighting, like everyone, for her life. Henry, with three remaining guards still outside, kept firing and hitting more assailants. Soon, their rifle power was strong enough to cover themselves as they rushed toward the stockade.

"Everyone. Get inside!" shouted Henry. "Get inside!"

Inside, the battle raged with arrows and spears hitting the stockade walls. A few Mirambo soldiers used outdated muskets to shoot into the open loopholes, wounding another guard. Henry found an open space, reloaded his rifle, and fired. Janet stood next to him, also shooting her pistol. Among caravan members, everyone who had a gun or rifle shot quickly toward the Mirambo attackers who had now surrounded them and made several attempts to breach their wooden stakes.

Mirambo's people knew that only seven or so guards had rifles to shoot, and, despite their swift fire, there were gaps, areas along the wall that were barely defended. At these weak points, the warriors hurled themselves, chopping at the wooden stakes with hatchets, attempting to break open the palisades. They almost succeeded, only to be driven back by well-aimed bullets fatally wounding two of them.

The skirmish went on until the Mirambo fighters pulled back to a group of trees near the outskirts of the clearing where they could take cover. Then they suddenly ceased their assault, and the firing stopped.

Silence now, except for the moans of wounded men inside and outside the battered enclosure.

"They've stopped," Janet blurted.

"No, they haven't." Henry inspected his rifle to make sure it wouldn't jam. "There's more to come. A lot more."

"When will they attack again?"

"Maybe five minutes. Maybe tonight. It's no use guessing."

Night approached. Small fires began to burn inside the open space within the small fort. Everyone was exhausted, lying in scattered groups on the ground, spitting out blood or trying to find the strength to breathe. Others struggled not to scream from their pains. Janet walked among the wounded, applying bandages and alcohol to open wounds, or she gave them whatever medicine she could for gashes and cuts. She pulled the arrowhead from the arm of a guard who was hit. She set a splint for a porter with a broken arm.

Henry looked out of one of the loopholes to see if any Mirambo soldiers were near. Outside, it was dark. No signs of life. He turned to a young porter, who looked like a boy or a teenager, and spoke to him in a low voice, pointing with his forefinger to a door in the back of the compound. They both walked to the door. Henry opened it, and the youth slipped through.

Janet continued to nurse the injured, but she had not missed Henry's short talk with the young African. Just as Henry had closed the rear door, she approached him.

"What's going on?"

Henry pretended he didn't hear her. He continued to walk to the center of the courtyard. Janet pursued him. "What's your plan?"

Henry took up a rag from one of the trunks and began to break down his rifle, taking care to wipe any dirt from the metal parts.

She hated when he didn't answer her, something he had done many times in the past. She felt it was his way of not recognizing her, of diminishing her importance.

As he continued to clean the barrel and bullet chamber, he turned to her and finally spoke. "You fought good today. I was shocked."

"You sent that runner for Goma. Didn't you?"

"Now do you see why I wanted the group to split up?"

"What if he doesn't get through? What if Goma doesn't come?"

"What do you think will happen?"

She was at a loss for words. "I—I—"

"Remember, Miss Livingstone, I warned you this would happen. I told you not to come, but you insisted."

Suddenly, words came back to her. "I don't have any regrets."

"It won't be long before they try to burn us out."

The African youth that Henry had sent looked at the trees on the other side of where Mirambo's fighters had retreated. In utter silence and under the cover of darkness, he crouched and glided toward an open space. Then, he slipped through and dashed into the woods. He had not gone a hundred yards when he stopped out of instinct and froze. Close to him were two Mirambo warriors on guard duty. The youth tiptoed around them and ran once again through the brush, taking care not to make any sound. After he had gone more than a half mile, he saw the way before him was clear. He picked up his pace and began to run, hard and fast.

He ran up hills and down sharp gullies. His feet splashed in holes filled with water. He leaped over rocks. He jumped over fallen trees. He dashed through thick forests and sunken valleys. Without tiring or slowing down, he ran. Under vines and limbs, around thorn brakes and open fields, shrubs and high grass. The eyes of hyenas, jackals, and wild dogs watched him as he leaped, but they knew he was fearless. They knew he would not let anything stop him or slow him down. On and on, the African youth ran for minutes, for hours. He kept up his pace until he was silhouetted against the dawn horizon.

The sun had just cracked across the sky, sending out red and yellow bands along the low mountain ridges near Tabora. Goma and his group of twenty-five men were up eating breakfast and getting ready to break the camp. They had left Tabora right behind Henry and were only a few hours away. Normally, Goma would have lingered, being careful not to push his men. Normally, he would not have broken camp until the sun was much higher in the sky. But he also knew Mirambo's people were in the area, and the threat of attack was imminent, especially for the advancing group. He knew Henry would be hit first.

On a whim, he climbed a tree and took out his spyglass to view the country that lay ahead. And then he saw something. At first, he thought it was an animal running toward him from far away, but as it drew closer, he realized it was a youth, an African running with a grim, determined face, one of Henry's porters. Goma jumped from the tree and swung into action. Within moments, Goma's caravan was running with their guns, following the young African who showed no signs of tiring.

Back in Kwihara, Mirambo insurgents launched a fresh assault. Fire-tipped arrows flew through the air like burning rockets. They came down and landed on the thatched roof that lined the inside of Kwihara's walls. Anything made of wood or grass began to burn. All of the members of Henry's caravan rushed to douse the building now ablaze. Since they didn't have much water, they used their blankets to try and smother the flames spreading across the roof. Incoming arrows and more musket fire from afar prevented them from completing their work.

Conditions grew worse because the Mirambo fighters were out of range from Henry's armed guards; they hid behind the cover of trees on the other side of the open field. Soon, some of the flaming arrows hit the bales of cloth. Henry and his porters ran to save them, but, as they did, more incoming arrows hit two of the porters, wounding them. Janet stood at a loophole and aimed her pistol toward the woods, hoping to prevent the insurgents from launching more missiles, but she was only wasting bullets. The situation looked grim. The fire spread along the thatched roof.

The entire structure was soon engulfed in a swelling inferno when a great din of gunfire was heard outside. First, shouts and screams were coming from the woods and the sound of rapid rifle fire. Then, the missiles stopped raining down. Janet was the first to hear and see this as everybody else was fighting to contain the flames. As she squinted through her loophole, it soon became clear. Someone else was fighting the Mirambo soldiers. More shouting, more rapid rifle fire, and then she knew. It was Goma! The runner had gotten through! She ran to Henry.

"Goma!" Henry shouted when he saw Janet's smiling face. Everyone inside began to cheer.

Outside, Goma and his group continued to fight. Spears flew. Bodies fell. But Goma and his men had superior rifles, forcing the Mirambo warriors to pull back. As they did, he ordered ten of his men, those who had rifles, to stay near the woods and continue to engage any remaining Mirambo soldiers. Then he broke from the woods and ran to the fortress's front gate. To the members of Henry's caravan, he looked magnificent in his baggy white trousers that came down to his knees, his flowing black cape, his unruly dreadlocks, and especially his flashing Winchester rifle.

The rest of them, porters armed only with knives and swords and the courageous African who had been running all night and day, entered the fort to help stop the spreading fire. First, they worked quickly to save the threatened cloth. Then they moved to prevent the fire from running along the roof, which was soon reduced to smoldering, and then contained.

By midday, the fighting had stopped. Heavy smoke drifted in and out, death and debris scattered everywhere. Goma and Henry and the men who fought with them drew together. They drank water and hugged each other, happy to be victorious and alive. Janet walked to the young African who had broken through to Goma. For the first time, she recognized one of the porters.

"What is your name?"

"I am Saburi."

"Where are you from?"

"From Bagamoyo."

She wanted to congratulate him further, but others had stepped in to embrace him, to praise his courage and bravery. Henry also applauded the youth. He grabbed Saburi's shoulders and hugged him, revealing that he too was capable of sincere affection. For a moment, the entire caravan came together in a show of unity and hope. For those who had been with the caravan from the beginning, they had faced their biggest challenge yet and survived. Now they felt they could do anything, face anything. In comparison with what they had just been through, whatever happened from now on would pale, or so they thought.

Little did they know greater challenges were to come.

14

—

When the euphoria had quieted down, Janet found herself once again attending to the wounded. She worked hard with little help, and her medical knowledge was weak. She had to rely on what she had learned from her brother. From time to time, Goma would interrupt his work and assist her, but in reality, she was on her own. He was now preparing for a possible counterattack. All told, casualties incurred from both caravan groups included four porters who had been killed and seven who had been wounded. Among the guards, two had been killed, three wounded. These wounds were not life threatening, mostly arrows to be pulled from shoulders or arms. A few had some of their skin burned. There were also a number of gashes and deep cuts from knives and spears. One muscular porter, who had fought with distinction, had been shot in the leg and would need a crutch to walk on.

After she removed the musket ball and started wrapping a bandage around his leg, she looked him in his face. Then she realized he was the same man who had challenged Henry when the second donkey had died after they passed through the Makata swamps. Henry had pulled his revolver on him. Yes, she remembered because he was big with bulging muscles. He now seemed contrite and thanked her for her help. By working with these injured men, without Goma's help, she was forced to recognize them, forced to interact. This was good in that they became more human to her. A few weeks ago, she saw this African as nothing but a terrorist and a troublemaker. Now, she didn't know. She thought about it further. *I really didn't know who he was.*

Outside of these injuries, the main problem among the men was exhaustion. For those who had been in Henry's group, they had been fighting for two days, nonstop, and they needed rest, so Henry decided to remain at Kwihara another day. It was a risk. Mirambo's people could attack again, but Henry couldn't go on. At least with Goma and his men, they might be able to successfully resist any new incursion.

By late afternoon, most of Henry's group were sound asleep. Goma's soldiers stayed awake and kept guard, their rifles sticking out of the stockade walls. Earlier, in between her duties attending to the wounded, Janet managed to catch a brief rest. When she awoke, she saw Henry and Goma talking, so she joined them.

"His main force has surrounded Tabora. Ahead of us, he's blocked the road." Goma spoke in a calm, even voice.

"We can't go forward. We can't go back. That's just great." Henry spat on the ground. They had achieved a victory only to be trapped with nowhere to go.

"There is another possibility," said Goma, "a trail to the southwest. We can backtrack to Lake Tanganyika and then turn and march north to Ujiji."

"A trail?" Henry didn't seem impressed.

"No one uses it. It's all wilderness down there with very few settlements."

At this point, Janet felt compelled to talk. She was always thinking about her mission to find her brother. "Can it take us to Ujiji?"

Henry broke off from the conversation and went to wake up the guide, Asmani. Henry wanted a second opinion.

"A detour, yes, but we get to Ujiji." Asmani yawned. He was still tired. He was a short African with broad shoulders. During the fighting in Kwihara, he had distinguished himself by saving the lives of two porters. Unlike the guards, he didn't look down on the porters, even though he carried a rifle.

"Can you lead us there?" asked Henry.

"Yes. I take you."

"Are you sure? Can I trust you?"

"Yes. I get you this far. Why you ask me that?" Asmani resented the questions. Hadn't he proved himself in the fighting at Kwihara?

"I'm not going anywhere unless it leads to my brother" Janet interjected.

"To Ujiji. Yes. We go," said Asmani.

"It's risky." Goma felt compelled to add this new piece of information.

Henry studied Goma's face. "What else, Goma?" Goma hesitated. Henry drew closer to him. "What else?"

"It's crawling with lions. Man-eaters."

"You mean lion lions?" Janet used her arms to imitate a lion's powerful gait. She wanted to make sure that he meant the real thing.

Goma shook his head up and down. "Man-eaters."

They paused. Should they go on taking this new route as proposed, or should they turn back? In truth, they really had no choice. They couldn't go back, at least not now, not unless they wanted to keep fighting. Even so, Henry had to make a decision as if he had a choice. The caravan was now at a crossroads. Janet, Goma, and Asmani looked at him.

"I have taken an oath, an oath to be kept while the least hope remains in me, not to break the resolve I have formed, to never give up the search until I find Livingstone, dead or alive."

Henry stopped. He looked at Janet and Goma. He looked at the entire caravan, most of whom were sound asleep. "No living man or group of men shall stop me. Only death can prevent me, but not even this. I shall not die. I will not die. I cannot die."

"What about the lions?" Henry's oath notwithstanding, Goma wanted to know how they would get through their territory.

"We can handle lions. We've got rifles."

Once the caravan had rested, it moved out again at sunset. This time Goma's group and Henry's group marched together, which made Janet happy. Through early evening haze, they began to backtrack a few miles and then headed southwest, away from Tabora.

Everyone looked refreshed, but the pace was slower because of those who were injured. The wounded men had to limp along. Some placed their arms around another comrade's shoulder, helping them to walk, stumbling over rocks and shrubs they couldn't see. Some carried walking sticks or canes. One wounded man had to ride a donkey. Henry led the procession, as usual, followed by Asmani, and the drummer who now walked in silence. Goma remained in the rear with two armed guards. An attack from behind was just as possible as one from the front or sides.

Janet fell back away from Henry and drifted farther down the line where she could elude her own private thoughts and draw nearer to the other caravan members. After yesterday's fighting, and after attending to those injured, she realized that her life depended upon these men whom she'd barely noticed. If she was to survive, she had to get closer to them. She had to see them and understand their differences. She began with Saburi. Since he said he came from Bagamoyo, she thought he might understand some English. As she spoke to him, she used physical gestures when words broke down.

"Were you born in Bagamoyo, Saburi?"

"No. They take me from my village to Bagamoyo, a slave. My master was an African Muslim."

"How were you treated?"

"By my master?"

"Yes."

"Better than most. I had a skill. I could run. My master use me to take messages. Sometimes I run for many, many, many miles."

"How did you meet Mr. Stanley?"

"In Bagamoyo. My master need money, gold. Mr. Stanley need

runner. He buy me and set me free. Now I not a slave. I work. He pay me, Mr. Stanley. Sometimes extra."

"You mean he gives you a bonus when you run for him?"

"Yes. He pay extra. In gold. I run to Tabora to tell the sheik you are coming. Mr. Stanley pay me."

"Let me get this straight. When we were marching to Tabora, you ran ahead to tell Sheik Sayd Bin Salim we were coming?"

"Yes, it was me."

Janet thought back. She didn't even notice he was missing then. She didn't know he existed. "And the others. Do they know you get paid extra?"

"No. You don't tell them, please."

Janet said she wouldn't but was glad she spoke to him. Things were going on around her that she was completely unaware of.

She also engaged the cook, Ferrari, an older African from a tribe near Nyasaland in the far south. She noticed that when they ate dinner, he often pilfered extra rations for himself. She asked him about that.

"Why do you steal food, Ferrari?"

"Me? I no steal the food."

"I saw you."

"What you see? Tell me. What I take?"

"You take extra pieces of cornbread and lick the honey. You take fruit."

"Fruit is a part of nature. God's earth."

Janet smiled when he used God's name. *What does he know about God?*

"So is honey," he added. Then, he paused and smiled at her. "It is true, memsahib. That is why I cook. To get more food." She liked his honesty and good humor and acknowledged, as everyone else did, he was an exceptional cook. He knew how to make very little go a long way, and he could rustle up a quick meal of biscuits and coffee in five to ten minutes. Whatever he took for himself, it always came after everyone else was fed. She realized that all the other caravan members knew he pilfered, but they turned a blind eye. Ferrari was just adding

an additional amount to his pay, a sort of reward for his exceptional ability.

Janet looked at the other men she didn't know, those who didn't
speak or had very little understanding of English. One of these porters was from the Wagogo tribe. At night, around campfires, he told
hunting stories. From his tone, she could tell he bragged about his
exploits, standing up before the others and acting out various scenes,
something that Goma was good at. This Wagogo man would mimic
how he bagged a rhino or brought down a buffalo with one spear. He
would pull back his right arm and show how he threw it, after which
the others would laugh at him in disbelief.

Two porters from the Wajiji tribe looked like brothers or even twins,
but Janet was told they were not related. These two were superstitious,
always participating in rituals of sacrifice by pouring libations to the
earth or praying to their gods for safe passage. They often avoided
walking in certain places because they thought they were sacred, and
they constantly looked for signs and omens that foretold trouble ahead.

As the procession walked, she remembered that the porters rarely
talked to the guards. Indeed, they were hostile to each other. Then it
hit her that some of Henry's earlier arguments with the porters, near
the beginning of their long march, touched upon this animosity between the two groups. Porters resented the guards because they didn't
have to carry weight and they got paid more, a rule that Henry rigidly
enforced. Guards, on the other hand, resented porters because guards
felt they were better than porters and looked down on them, despite
the fact they were all poor Africans. But Asmani denied it, denied that
the divide existed.

"No. Untrue. Everybody equal."

"But they're not equal. Guards think they are better."

"No. Everybody does skill. I guide. Nothing else. Maybe you carry
some pack. That's what you do."

To some degree, it reminded her of the factory system in Scotland,
where the workers were separated from the managers. In Africa, whenever they stopped to rest or eat a meal, the guards always sat and

talked among themselves apart from everyone else. Of course, as they marched, the two groups communicated, and when they were in danger, they worked together, yet these subtle differences prevailed.

Among the guards, she thought one stood out, Selim, from Palestine, a quiet young man in his early twenties who looked different from everyone else. For one thing, Selim was not an African. His skin was copper, like Asians or Arabs, and he wore a skullcap all the time. He even dressed differently, in a long nightshirt and thin trousers that looked like pajamas. He carried his rifle slung over his shoulder, clutching the barrel with his right hand. At night, he often sat alone, away from the other porters and guards.

The only other people he talked to were Saburi and Ferrari. Sometimes Selim talked to Henry alone, and when Henry went out hunting for meat, he took Selim with him. During the fighting in Kwihara, Selim always kept his cool and seemed to be completely unafraid. He always did what he was told and without complaint. To Janet, he was the perfect example of the silent hero. Yet, she was bothered he was so aloof, not just to her but to everyone.

There was one other thing that bothered her. She remembered that when the caravan began, a small group of black women followed Henry's group and, as the march continued, those women had dropped off, at places unknown, to be replaced by other women at various points along the way. This continued all the way to Tabora. For answers, she turned and walked back to Goma, where he was still protecting the column's rear.

"Who are these women? Where do they come from?"

He spoke, all the while looking to see if anyone was following. "They are the wives and girlfriends of some of the porters and guards. They come from their home villages or from villages we pass."

Sometimes, at night, she had seen them in the bushes or behind trees. *I don't have to ask him what they're doing there.*

"At night, during the march, they go off with their husbands into the woods," he said.

"But where do these women go when they disappear? They stay with us for a few days or a week and then they're gone."

Goma shrugged his shoulders. "They can leave at any time. They know the land. They know where they are. There are dozens of trails scattered everywhere. Women are walking all over Africa. Some of them have friends and family in other tribes, despite tribal warfare. You have to realize that you and Henry are trapped in this one caravan. Outside of it, you are lost. To us Africans, we are free to walk anywhere. This was true in the old days, but now with slavery, it is making travel more difficult. We have to be careful we don't run into kidnappers. The women followed us for protection. That is why you don't see any women now. Any wives of these men are still back in Tabora. You are the only woman who has come along."

After the caravan had backtracked, walking east a few miles, it turned from the main footpath and followed another. This led them to a ridge that climbed to a higher elevation. As they hiked, the dirt path became rocky, granite rocks and massive boulders interspersed with dwarf trees. Everyone grew silent as they kept their eyes focused on the steps ahead of them. It was now dark, the sky had turned bluish-black speckled with stars. The column tightened itself into a shorter unit winding upward to the top of the ridge, barely able to see farther up. Once they had ascended almost to the peak, a porter shouted:

"Look!"

They turned their heads. They saw a large yellow glow that lit up the sky far away to the north. After staring for moments without uttering a word, Henry broke the silence as he sadly shook his head. "Tabora."

"Oh, my God!" Janet blurted after realizing she and Goma had just talked about the wives that the porters and guards had left behind. She also thought about the slaves she saw in the market and the little girl she befriended playing hopscotch. She wondered what would happen to them all and whether they were still alive. The glow in the sky appeared immense. Tabora was burning.

15

—

They kept going, south by southwest, down from the ridge, over dark green fields merging with jungles and quick-moving streams, a land that looked like paradise once again. They sallied on past the slow-moving waters of the Gombe River and grassy knolls. It wasn't long before such breathtaking scenes were filled with herds of wild boar, buffalo, antelope, zebra, and giraffes. These were the biggest herds of wild animals they had seen so far. As they traveled, they stopped a few days in order to hunt the game. Henry and a few guards went out and killed enough meat to last a week.

They also passed a few small villages, mainly with families that had fled Mirambo's fighters. These villages were friendly and welcomed Henry's group without any attempts to exact muhongo. They only wanted to be left alone. The caravan also passed two burned-out villages, signs that tribal warfare and slave kidnapping still existed, even in this unknown region, and it was possible Henry's group could still be attacked.

The beauty of the land continued to reveal itself until they entered a region where water became scarcer. Instead of rivers and rivulets, they encountered dried riverbeds and lakes with large amounts of iron hematite. Now and then, they came to a small lake already occupied by a large buffalo herd. Fruit trees filled with sweet tamarind provided them with nourishing food and water. In the air above, eagles began to follow them along with honey birds that led them to the honeycombs of bees. Here, the caravan stopped as everyone devoured enormous amounts of golden honey.

Then the caravan pivoted west and entered a giant savannah that stretched into the distance. Through this land, they passed wooded groves where peach trees appeared, more fruit to fill rumbling stomachs. After a while, jungle growth began to increase. The grasses grew taller.

The guide, Asmani, proclaimed, "We near the big lake, perhaps one or two march away."

"You mean Lake Tanganyika, fifteen miles away." Henry turned to him.

"Yes. I think so."

"Do you think so, or do you know?" Henry asked.

"Yes, we near. I know for sure."

On this same plain, they soon stumbled over small strips of marshland. They encountered huge elephant tracks nearly one foot deep. The trees in and around this area were stripped of all vegetation, indicating these huge beasts were around. They also passed uprooted dead tree trunks that gave off a foul odor. Caravan members, including Janet, Henry, and Goma, avoided them, fearing their odor contained poison that if inhaled, caused fever, or malaria, as it later became known.

Little did they know that malaria came from mosquitoes and not foul vapor from dead trees. More uprooted trees and devastated branches stripped of their leaves eventually led to the elephants themselves, the first time the caravan had seen these lordly giants who stared at them with curiosity as they passed. Henry told the guards to be vigilant, as it was known that elephants would charge human beings if they felt threatened by them. To some degree, an elephant could be more deadly than a lion.

After the elephants, they entered a wilderness filled with hundreds of anthills, and after that, they passed a small stream close to a ravine.

This was the last low spot before they would have to cross a series of larger ridges ahead. It was still morning. The sun was just beginning to move higher in the sky.

Janet saw that Henry was walking funny. When they had passed the anthills, he seemed to be zigzagging. Asmani, who walked just behind him, had to stop him several times and point, showing Henry that he was going the wrong way. The caravan members also looked confused, constantly stopping and starting again. Goma, who was still marching in the rear, now came forward. He felt concerned. He approached Henry.

"What is it, Henry?" Goma asked. Henry stopped and threw up his hand, indicating for everyone to stop.

Goma looked around. It was a perfect campsite, but Henry never stopped marching until the sun grew unbearable. "But we can go farther. It's not that hot."

"We'll make camp here." Henry avoided Goma's eyes.

Goma got closer and looked at him. "You've got the fever."

Two hours later, Henry lay on his bed inside his tent, wrapped in a blanket. His teeth chattered, his body shook. There was no question now that he had the fever. He didn't know where he was. His eyes rolled upward into his skull.

"They're coming. Can't you see them? Look! Over there! Over there I tell ya!"

He screamed how ferocious monsters and wild animals were attacking him. He stood up and tried to grab his rifle. "Give me my rifle. Got to protect myself. I won't go down without a fight. I say, give me my rifle!" But Janet, who was attending him, grabbed his waist and pulled him down.

At times, Henry thought Janet was his mother. "Get out of my sight, you dirty whore."

Despite that she knew he was delirious, such words angered her.

And then he was moved to tears, pleading with her. "Please, please, don't ever leave me again. Promise me, Momma! Promise me!"

This went on for hours and into the night. When the caravan members had bedded down and were trying to sleep, he remained awake and cried out and carried on more imaginary conversations with people from his past.

By early morning, Henry finally calmed down. Janet stayed in his tent and slept on the ground. Caravan members also used this time to get further rest. Ferrari got up late and took his time making breakfast. After he made coffee, Janet left Henry's tent and poured herself a cup, relieved that Henry was finally sleeping. It suddenly struck her, after all these months, how little she knew about him.

She never forgot that first day in Bagamoyo when he threatened to beat her if she got in his way. She wanted to be friendly with him. She wanted to call him Henry rather than Mr. Stanley all the time, but she couldn't.

He won't let me get close. He won't let anyone get close.

With her coffee in hand, just as she was about to sit down, a loud roar disrupted her thoughts and shattered the morning silence. Janet jumped and yanked out her pistol. The guards and porters leaped to their feet, grabbing swords and rifles. Another roar came, and another. Goma, who was sleeping on a blanket nearby, also stood up. Janet went to him.

"Lions?"

Goma shook his head. "Just one. It sounds like more."

"It seems very close."

"It smells the food. It's hungry."

"Will it attack?"

"Probably not, but we'll have to post guards by the meat. Nothing will stop a lion if it's starving, and we've got a lot of food here." Soon, the roaring stopped. Everyone else stood down and went back to their blankets. Goma poured himself a cup of coffee and sat by the smoldering fire.

Janet sat down next to him. "I'm tired. I didn't get much sleep."

"What about Henry?"

"He'll need another day or two before the quinine takes effect. But he's sleeping now. That's a good sign. He'll be all right."

"You seem to know a lot about medicine. I watched you treat the injured men."

"I learned from my brother David. He taught me what he knew. When we were young, before he left for Africa, we studied together. We used to read while we worked in the cotton factory. And at night, after work, I sometimes went with him to school."

"Sometimes?"

"No one could keep up with him. I've never met anyone on this earth who was so insistent on learning."

"You never went to university?"

She shook her head no. "I taught myself, and, of course, I had my brother. He was a great teacher."

"I learned to read in a Christian missionary, The Nasik School, near Bombay." Goma spoke with the same excitement he once had for learning.

"That's where you learned English?"

"Yes. I also had good teachers . . ." And then Goma hesitated, the enthusiastic thrust of his emotions and energy deflated. Something had gone out of him. "Well. Most of them."

Janet was quick to feel the full meaning of his pause, the undercurrent of emotions that suddenly became obscured. "You hate the British, don't you? That's why you left Oxford." She finally let it out, something she had wanted to say.

He looked at her, startled, although he had half expected her to ask it, so he wasn't totally shocked. "No, I don't hate all British. Only some of them. "

A day later, Henry still looked sick. He had lost weight. His skin had turned yellow, and he could barely walk. Yet, he decided they should carry on since his fever had broken and his head was clearer. He ordered everyone to break camp, and they began moving again. Slowly and cautiously.

Henry still preceded them, now riding on a donkey, even though he had not yet fully recovered, and the whole group knew it. He was unsure of himself, teetering on the edge of a dark abyss. Selim, the Palestinian guard, carried Henry's weapon and led the donkey by the reins. Asmani followed behind Henry's donkey, sometimes scurrying ahead of it and then scurrying back. The porters and guards held their positions, moving forward like a machine without any problem or delay, just a slow, steady grind. Meanwhile, all eyes remained on Henry. They knew all about the fever—many of them had gotten it earlier from the tsetse fly. They knew his hold on consciousness was precarious at best. Yes, he looked better, but that didn't really mean anything, not yet, not until he could assume command and not merely ride ahead.

Janet and Goma walked together, drawn by the complete disappearance of their mutual distrust. Ever since the fighting at Kwihara, she knew she would need Goma. They would all need Goma. Now she knew she was in the real Africa, not an imaginary Africa born from books and hearsay from Blantyre, a view of Africa as seen only through European eyes and told from a European perspective. Her need for Goma was natural and logical.

Nature, too, she began to see in a new light. For months she had lived in the depths of open forest, close to a world far removed from man or his control. She was now forced to see her surroundings differently. The natural world of Africa had thrust itself on her whether she liked it or not, forced by the necessity of what this environment threw in your face, constantly and powerfully, pitted against death so near that death itself was no longer something to be feared.

She remembered that first day in Bagamoyo when she screamed because an African beggar had placed his mangled hand before her to see, compelling her to acknowledge his suffering. She looked back on her reaction as a mistake, her first big mistake in Africa.

Back then, I was forced, forced to act in that stupid way because that was all I knew, all that I was taught. And I was afraid, terrified to face these unusual and strange people. Now I seem to be losing my fear.

She thought about whether or not this new reality conflicted with her Christian beliefs, whether she had changed.

In the first few weeks, I turned to the Bible and the Psalms to give me strength, but now I am mostly turning inward, to my inner self. I must look deep inside myself and my beliefs. Perhaps now I am an even greater Christian than before. Perhaps, I am now closer to God.

She thought about the lions and how she would react.

Have I gained enough courage and nerve to face this new challenge?

Those first few roars in camp stunned and paralyzed her. But then she knew that roar was just the beginning. She had now come to always expect the worst.

She remembered when David was mauled by a lion during his early years in South Africa. When he returned to Scotland in 1856, he told her, "For the first time in my life I had no fear, no fear at all."

"I don't believe you. All of us have fear, even you."

"No, Janet, I tell you I wasn't afraid, even when he bit into me. Not when he tore at my arms and breast."

"But why is that? If not fear, you must have felt pain."

"No, not even pain. I didn't feel a thing. It's as if I were dreaming."

She pushed him further by suggesting he was lying to her, trying to make his attack look romantic. "You're just boasting or bragging to me because I am gullible—your gullible sister who doesn't know anything."

"No, Janet. You know me better than that. I don't brag or boast! We humans are more fearful before we are attacked, when we think about what is going to happen. When I was attacked, it was as if the lion knew how to kill me, knew what exact nerve it had to disable so I wouldn't feel fear or pain. When I was lying there, all I saw was the hand of fate. It does the same thing to animals. Their fear is when they're running and still alive, not in the moment that they are killed."

Now she knew what he meant, knew that he had no choice but to face the lion, and that took away the fear. Fear was a luxury in a land where luxury, comfort, and safety had rendered her helpless against the universe, the temple of stars that guided them day and night.

16

—

The caravan moved even slower now that they had entered another thick wood with much vegetation and growth that became denser and denser until their path ahead darkened with only sporadic sun, splashing through the thick leaves with speckled yellow spots of light. They marched behind Henry, still pushing him forward with little sense of control. The woods now got even thicker and darker. Then came a shroud of silence, darkness and silence, not even the sound of a monkey or bird.

An immense stillness settled in like the lost black night shimmering so far away, the path now descending into a valley, the procession winding down a narrow path. Ferns and bushes and low-lying branches smacked and bounced into the faces of the porters. Some pulled out their hatchets or swords and had to chop in order to move ahead.

At first, Janet thought she heard the sound of something breaking apart, a bag ripping and a high-pitched scream. But the caravan hadn't stopped, so she didn't think about it again until a rifle shot rang out, and this time a shout, a man's shout, and then another man shouted.

When the caravan stopped, she knew something was wrong. She turned to Goma only to see him bolting to the front to join Henry, who had his rifle jammed underneath his arm. Instinctively, Janet ran, too, following Henry with her pistol drawn. She ran past a broken pole where they stored meat wrapped in canvas bags, one of which was ripped open, another missing, and one of the guards was lying wounded on the ground. They had been attacked by a lioness, who jumped from the side of the path and ripped off a huge portion of meat, hanging inside a bag along a pole carried by two porters. The lioness broke the pole as she seized the meat between her teeth and vaulted into the bush unscathed. As she did so, she knocked down a guard who tried to get off a shot to stop her but fell backward, his head hitting a rock.

Janet ran through the thick jungle growth, hearing the sound of Henry straining to breathe as he dashed ahead. She could hear his heavy panting. He was heading for the lioness. He ran as if possessed, his eyes bulging like a demon, like he had this one last task to complete before his death, driven by sheer nerve and emotions.

They came to a clearing. Goma, who was ahead of everyone, now backtracked as Henry came forward.

"Henry, don't be stupid. Let it go. You can't get it back."

The lioness stood at the edge of the clearing, feeding the meat to her two cubs, oblivious of the human beings who were facing them. Henry pushed Goma aside and walked within a few feet of the lions and opened fire.

The cubs jumped into the air and fell back. The lioness was wounded, but broke away and ran. Henry reloaded and kept firing at the cubs until Goma grabbed his rifle barrel. Henry, fighting to get it back, punched Goma in the face. Goma punched him back, and they fought, tearing and clawing at each other like animals themselves. Janet had caught up and, seeing they would not stop, thrust herself between them to break them apart.

"Stop it!" she yelled as Henry's fist landed on her arm. "Stop it. Stop!"

They continued to fight until they were spent, and Henry fell exhausted to the ground.

A few moments later, some of the guards appeared on the scene to find all three of them—Janet, Henry, and Goma—sprawled on the ground. Then Goma lifted himself up and walked to the cubs, both of them mangled by a slew of bullets, their blood scattered on the green vegetation surrounding them. How helpless and innocent they looked in death. Janet and Henry joined Goma.

Goma turned to Henry. "You shouldn't have done that!"

"The only good lion is a dead lion."

Goma was shocked and now wasn't sure whether Henry had recovered from the fever. Janet, too, was alarmed by his brutal actions. Soon Goma calmed down but continued to stare at the fallen cubs.

"They're going to come after us." He looked into the surrounding bush as if he could see the lioness.

"What do you mean?" asked Janet.

"I mean they're going to come after us. Now that you killed the mother's cubs." He glared at Henry.

"Nonsense. They'd come after us anyway, cubs or no cubs. Out here, we must fight or die."

"But we must use our heads, Henry, before we fight."

"The trouble with you, Goma, is you're too cautious, too careful. Sometimes, you have to act without thought or calculation. Besides, I wounded the lioness. She might even be dead by now."

From that point on, Henry returned to his old self, as if the shooting of the lioness and her cubs sparked in him his exalted sense of command. When they resumed the march, he no longer rode atop the donkey but walked ahead with his usual confidence and swagger. Janet thought he was being cocky, being an exaggerated imitation of himself and his abilities. He talked louder than before, and the tone of his voice was harsher and crueler, announcing to the world, *Stay outta my way*. Goma, too, noted the change, a sign that the fever had not really left him, only that it had entered its final stage. Most malaria patients entered this phase after the sickness had left the body but not yet the mind.

Soon, they reached the outer edge of Lake Tanganyika. They could see its gleaming gray waves floating between high green mountains that rose two or three thousand feet above their heads, great peaks rising out of the lake folding around the open water so close there was no room for water to escape, mountains that blocked the caravan's entrance to it. But they were not going to the lake. They turned to the north and followed the mountains while keeping an eye on the lake hovering to their left.

As evening returned once again, the sun began to fall. Janet thought she heard something high above in the trees, high-pitched screeches, shouts, and hoots. She looked up. Chimpanzees sat on branches looking down. The caravan was surrounded by hundreds of them.

When Janet looked closer, she thought that the chimps were mocking them, scorning them for their physical limitations. Two of the chimps climbed down. From a distance, one looked at her with deep, inset eyes like a man, sizing her up and down, examining her with intense seriousness. His face looked human in that it didn't have any hair and had an upturned nose with pink flesh. Beyond the forehead, black hair and big ears. The other chimp was older and female with many wrinkles on her skin.

The caravan slowed. Goma spoke. "Don't be alarmed. This is chimpanzee country for the next ten miles. Leave them alone."

They pushed on in utter silence. Every once in a while one of the porters would suddenly break out into song, no longer able to bear the silence, and then he would be joined by the other porters, and a chorus of African music rang out in Swahili, as inscribed in their memory.

March, march, march,
through the long hard day.
March, march, march,
we go our weary way.
March, march, march,
over mountain, field, and stream.
March, march, march,
with nothing but our dreams.

High above the trees and in the sky overhead their sounds would echo and shake the hills, the chimpanzees scurrying with delight, a satisfied audience. This chorus would build, growing louder and louder. And then the chorus would stop, silence once again, and more hours of slow, steady steps, walking a tightrope in the center of the earth, straddling the line between safety and oblivion.

Periodically they passed an African villager standing by the path and staring. Some were friendly. Some were not. No matter what, the caravan members trudged and slogged. The blue-black mountain range now stretched to their back. They entered a strip of tall, matted grass and a few cultivated fields. Ahead of them lay one more summit. Henry, who was now sensing victory, pushed them forward to the top, and then they could see it not far away, Ujiji, lanterns and huts and the twinkling waters of the lake. They were just hours away.

"Now would be a good time to stop," Goma told Henry as though he needed to remind him.

"No. We keep going. I say when we stop." As soon as Henry replied, Janet and Goma looked at each other and, suddenly, they both knew his mind was still delusional. His sickness had not totally left.

Henry sensed he would be challenged. "Why should we halt when we're but a few hours away? Let us march a few more hours, and by night we'll be in Ujiji. We'll be eating fish from Lake Tanganyika."

There is no question about it. We have to stop. Has Henry forgotten about my brother? Was that all he cared about, eating fish? The men are tired. Night is already here. Everyone is hungry. Janet knew she had to speak up. "Goma's right, Mr. Stanley. We must stop and clean ourselves. Look at us. We are all in tatters, and you, your shirt is ripped and your boots muddy. Your pants are crawling with filth, and you need a shave. We can't go into Ujiji, one of the most important events in world history, looking like this. What will future historians say? That you met Dr. Livingstone and looked like a tramp, that you looked like you crawled out of a sewer?"

She whispered to him as though he were a child who had thrown a temper tantrum, and now she was trying to soothe him by appealing to his vanity.

17

—

The sun rose. A red line steadied across the horizon. Ujiji beckoned, hundreds of dried-mud huts and wooden houses, a few Arab residences with carved wooden doors and plastered walls. Ujiji stood nestled within a small cove along the lake with dozens of canoes tied along wharves. Inside the canoes were the nets of fishermen who went out each day. Amid the structures that lined the streets, tall palm trees swayed from the breeze that blew in from the water, their fronds flowing like green flags over a small Christian church and a market square.

Unlike Tabora, there was no stockade, no fortress with walls and guards posted. Goats, cattle, and chickens roamed the streets. The Africans from various tribes, the Waguha, the Warundi, the Wangwana, were dressed in white and blue cotton cloth wrapped around their loins and breasts, or baggy cotton trousers that fell to their knees. Their hair was nappy and cut into various shapes, and some of the women had bamboo rings in their mouths, making their upper lips thrust out. And, of course, there were Arabs and half-castes with their turbans and white cloaks and their hundreds of slaves and concubines.

In the early morning stillness, an African boy, Kalulu, came running into town.

"Somebody coming! Somebody coming!"

People had just woken up and were eating their breakfast of pancakes and mocha coffee. Some chewed on fried snails or crabs.

"Somebody coming!" Kalulu kept running.

At first, some of them panicked. They knew about Mirambo but had always thought he was too far away, though fear lurked in the air that he might come to Ujiji and burn them down. But Kalulu would have said so as he ran. This must be another Arab caravan, or French. There were rumors that a French caravan would be coming soon. A crowd began to gather along the main street, leading into the center of town.

"Somebody coming!"

The crowd swelled until almost the entire population seemed to come out.

Henry's group came down from the hills. Everyone was dressed in their finest. Henry had shaved and put on white flannels. He chalked his white helmet and oiled his boots. Goma, too, wore his blue cape and had put on a pair of knee-length pantaloons. He had washed his dreadlocks and twisted them tighter. Janet wore trousers and a clean cotton shirt. She, too, had oiled her boots and brushed her reddish-brown hair. The porters, the guards, the guide, and the cook, all of them were dressed in new cloth garments bought with the money that they earned from their trip.

The caravan marched down, Asmani blowing a horn and the flag bearer in front with the American flag fluttering, representing Henry's sponsor. The lake sparkled as the drummer began to roll, followed by a volley of pistol and rifle fire from the guards. And then the porters began to chant and sing a wild, uplifting song of triumph and celebration.

As they drew nearer, closer to the town, Janet's heart began to race. She had suffered and struggled to get here. She had fought against Henry's relentless attempts to stop her from coming. Before that, she had spent many years trying to get *The New York Herald*, as well as others, to fund this expedition and had on numerous occasions been told by Donald Pomeroy that she did not have the evidence to prove David was alive. She had written countless letters, night after night, that were never returned, and faced insinuations from the people in Blantyre that she was wasting her time.

In Africa, she had fought a pitched battle against armed fighters and almost got stabbed by a spear to get here. Although her health had not broken down, she had almost lost consciousness twice, once in the Manyema village when she saw a dead man being eaten and once when she saw the mangled bodies of dead slaves torn apart by hyenas.

As she looked at Henry marching ahead, his body bearing the stride of a conquering hero, she thought, *He looks like a clown, driven purely by narrow selfishness.* She knew he would get all the credit for this discovery, that he would be praised and venerated for his great accomplishment. They would say he overcame great obstacles, trials, and tribulations. Against all odds, he persevered and never gave up. They would say these things because he was a white man, one of two white men in all of eastern Africa. She knew part of his task was to boast of the greatness of Anglo-Saxon civilization against the backdrop of savagery.

She knew all this because she, too, believed in these ideals. She, too, shared this racial and national pride.

But that is not why I came. That is not why I, too, persevered against all odds to get this trip funded. I came for one reason alone: to find my long-lost brother, a true giant in a world of paltry and insignificant men. I will not rest until I find him. Even now, as they approached the very last stage of this long and difficult journey, she would not be satisfied until she saw him in person. For the first time in many weeks, she pulled out David's necklace and fingered the crucifix at the end of the silver chain.

And what will he look like when I do find him?

She remembered how she had used his sickness as an argument to Gordon Bennett. David had sent her the necklace because he was too sick to write, she had told Bennett. This was the proof she used to claim that he was still alive.

What will he look like? Is he sick, and, if so, how sick? What is the nature of his sickness? Will he be well enough to recognize me? Will he be well enough to travel with us back to the coast or to Zanzibar? If we can't bring him back, then what?

She remembered how David had looked the first time he returned from the continent, the heavy tread of his gait, his clear mind and mental discipline, his ability to speak many African languages. Back then, in 1856, he returned to Great Britain a hero after fifteen years of missionary work in South Africa, and he was about to publish his major book. He looked like a man who had seen both heaven and hell and wore the eyes of a god or superman. He had walked across southern Africa from coast to coast, the first European to do so. He had discovered Victoria Falls in the name of Britain as well as many other lakes and rivers. Everywhere he went he was mobbed by crowds. David's bearing and confidence made Mr. Stanley look like a two-year-old child in comparison. Even so, these accomplishments meant little to her and were far removed from what motivated her.

For her, David returned as a man who had fulfilled his promise as a Christian to improve the lives of a downtrodden people, the Africans.

He provided the only example I knew of what it meant to be a Christian. He showed me that his character and beliefs—integrity, honesty, compassion, self-reliance, independence, intellect, will—had triumphed in the darkest place on earth. For me, his return to Scotland was proof that these ideals could be achieved to the betterment of all humanity. For me, he returned as a leader, a man whose example I could uphold and even— yes—worship. No other man in England had stood up to this task. No other man in Europe could fill his shoes. This is the true mark of his greatness.

This was before he returned to Africa in 1858, a trip in which he sought to travel up the Zambezi River in order to open up a trading route for African goods to be sold—a series of trading stations.

"We can stop the selling of Africans," he would argue, "by developing trade among the natives so they can sell their rich minerals and agricultural products to the British and others and sustain legiti-mate incomes."

"How would that end slavery?" Janet asked. His ideas always in-trigued her, even though she sometimes thought they were too ide-alistic. But that's what she loved about him—his passionate belief in his hopes and dreams. At such moments, his eyes would glow and his arms would flail with intensity. Everyone around him would be drawn into his orbit.

"Once discovering the importance of trade, the Africans would no longer attack and sell each other to supply the slave caravans."

"But the Africans, they're not ready for trade." All of her life she had been told that Africans were still savages. They seemed unprepared for the task he was asking.

"We must help them get ready, but the elevation of Africa can only occur from within itself," he would tell her. "Her nations need to be raised to commercial centers from which civilization and commerce can radiate." Commerce and Christianity he espoused, and he sought to discover those African rivers that would support steamships to carry these traded goods.

"That's fine, David, but what about Christianity? How does trade encourage Christian values?"

"One thing I've learned, Janet, is we cannot progress as Christians in Africa until we deal with problems of income, of wealth inequality. We cannot build missions on faith alone."

But that expedition ended in disaster. The Zambezi proved unnavigable, shallow, and filled with rapids and rocks. He was hampered by famine and civil war near Lake Nyasa and by constant delays for weeks and months. On top of that, six missionaries who accompanied him died from disease and starvation, including his wife, Mary, who was buried under a baobab tree.

Prior to that expedition, four of David's children were parceled out to relatives and boardinghouses. One of them, Robert, came to live with Janet. She remembered how he despised his own father for abandoning his family to be in Africa.

"He doesn't care about us, Aunt Janet."

"Of course he does. Don't say such things."

"Then why am I here? Why can't he provide for his own family?"

"He's a missionary. He has a different calling. You can't expect—"

He cut Janet off. "He has such compassion for the Africans, but what about us? Mother has now started drinking, and her health is not good. Why should his calling completely ignore us?"

"When he writes to me, he is always asking about you. He always thinks about his family."

"Words. Words. Empty words. Doesn't Christ say we are all children of the Lord?"

"Why, yes, yes, he does."

"And not just heathens, but everyone?"

"Yes. Yes, he does."

"Then why doesn't he treat us the same? Why doesn't he treat his own family as the Lord's children? That's all I'm asking. Why won't he help us achieve the very salvation that he allows to others?"

"He can only be in one place at a time."

"All I'm asking is for him to come home, or we could meet him in South Africa, once every two or three years. Is that asking too much? He won't even do that."

Janet remembered how she argued with Robert for weeks and how he was always getting into trouble with the authorities only to end up a volunteer in the American Civil War where he died in a Confederate jail under an assumed name. She remembered those hard and difficult years, years of doubt and confusion.

Nevertheless, she never wavered, never distrusted David's ultimate vision in the face of growing criticism, not only from his son but also from British politicians and his fellow missionaries. To them, he was a zealot, an extremist who had gone too far for his beliefs, no longer in touch with the goals of missionary work or with the tenets of

Protestant Christianity. Some even questioned his sanity, claiming that Africa had "touched" his soul.

The failure of the Zambezi expedition forced him to take a third trip in order to locate the source of the Nile River, without doubt the greatest river in Africa. If he could find its source, then steamboats would be able to ply from central Africa to Egypt, and the Mediterranean, a giant waterway far greater than the Zambezi, opening up trade that would benefit both the Africans and the British beyond their dreams. This he believed was God's intent.

What all of his critics didn't realize was that everything he did was but for the grace of God, that he truly believed he was put on earth to do His work. It was not his choice but his destiny to conduct his search. You could not convince the Africans of God's salvation unless the problem of income and economic resources could be solved. Slavery would not end until African people could find an alternative to the slave trade. Only then would Christian missionaries make any progress in Africa, and he was right.

But he also had another reason for going. He sought atonement for his wife's death. What most people, including his children, didn't realize was that Mary chose to be with him in Zambia. Despite the fact she'd had no permanent home in the last ten years of her life and came to stay with Janet—along with her children—on many occasions, despite the burden of raising her family when he was away, which led to her alcoholism and, at times, a real questioning of her own Christian faith, she was the daughter of a famous African missionary, Henry Moffat, and she had an intense desire to be with David in Africa, the same desire that Janet felt.

Part of who Mary was, her very identity, came from David, just as part of who Janet was came from him. Without David, Mary did not want to live. That's the kind of power he had over those who loved him. David went back to Africa to find the Nile and never give up. To do anything less would dishonor Mary and what she wanted him to do. This last trip was made in her honor.

Janet's brother had set off on that final mission in March of 1866 after his return from the Zambezi expedition. Before he left, Janet had seen very little of him. During those months in which he no longer basked in the public spotlight, he drew closer to his daughter Nannie, who was the last family member to see him off. After that, his letters came occasionally. Then she got word from John Kirk, the British consul in Zanzibar, that David was dead. A porter who traveled with him claimed he was murdered in an ambush along with his entire caravan.

That was the last she heard of him, five years ago when he went missing and his letters stopped. Rumors, however, persisted from various natives who claimed to have seen him. The government even sent out an expedition to search for him, to no avail. For Janet, her mission to find her brother was more than a sister's love for family. She knew what was at stake. She had to find out what had happened to his dream—his dream that began when they were children, when they labored under harsh conditions in the cotton mill, his dream that through dogged strength and determination he could rise up from his condition and do God's work. She had to find out if he still believed in those ideals that certainly still made her life worth living. And just like his wife, Mary, who died trying to redeem his beliefs, Janet had to reclaim him in order to reclaim herself.

Henry's caravan had reached the outskirts of Ujiji, and a crowd of nearly a thousand had hastened to meet it, energized by the roar of rapid rifle fire. The sight of the American flag they welcomed. Many had seen it before on the masts of ships in Bagamoyo or in Zanzibar and knew that it meant the same thing as the British flag—no slavery. Even the Arab sultans who bought and sold slaves welcomed them.

"Bindera Merikani," they shouted, "the American flag."

As the caravan moved in closer to the central square, shouts of "Jambo bwana" rose in a crescendo. The crowd drew even closer to shake caravan members' hands or grab their arms in a friendly grip.

This grand column of distant travelers had almost reached the very center of town, market center, amid the shouts and yells from the hundreds of Africans, their welcome cries now becoming a frenzy. The people had swelled to such an extent that they blocked the path of the caravan. They swelled even further as more and more Arabs joined them, for the news that a white man was coming had spread all around. The caravan managed to press forward finally into the center of the town, where it was greeted by a single black man, Susi. He was in his forties and dressed in a long white shirt, like the Arabs, with a turban on his head. He raised his hands.

"Salam." He addressed Henry, who was shocked to see a man of his bearing, his calm poise at odds with those surrounding him. Henry looked to Goma, expecting he would have to translate from Swahili or Arabic.

"Do you speak English?" Goma asked him.

"Yes. Good morning, sir," he said in a dignified manner.

"Who the devil are you?" asked Henry.

"I am Susi, servant to Dr. Livingstone."

At hearing David's name pronounced, Janet stepped forward. "Is Dr. Livingstone here?"

"Yes, ma'am. I leave him just now."

"And is the doctor well?" she asked.

"No, not very well."

"Run and tell your master we are coming," said Henry.

Meanwhile, in David Livingstone's dried-mud hut, a candle burned. Already woken from the sounds of guns firing, he pulled himself up from his platform bed, his ten-year-old daughter, Baraka, the offspring of a relationship he had with an African woman, helping him as she usually did. He sensed that something big was happening outside, so he pushed himself to hurry. As Baraka was lifting him up, Kalulu burst into the hut.

"Someone coming, a white man."

Upon hearing those words, his body began to tremble. He had not seen a white man in years. "A white man. Are you sure?"

Kalulu nodded his head. "Yes."

"Help me get dressed, quickly, quickly."

It was a moment for Western history books when the two groups met, Henry with his caravan surrounded by hundreds of Africans and Arabs, and Dr. David Livingstone with Baraka, Kalulu, and Susi, who had joined them. As these groups merged, voices began to hush until there was stone silence. All eyes turned on Livingstone, who, propped up by two African children, was pale with a white beard, looking tired and weary, with a bluish naval cap with a gold band around it. He had on a red-sleeved waistcoat and gray tweed trousers.

During this moment of silence, no one knew who should speak first. Normally, Henry would have barked anything out loud to demonstrate he was in charge, but for once in his life, he was dumbfounded, unable to speak, unable to believe he had accomplished his task. Janet didn't know what to say either. What she saw before her was a man she scarcely remembered.

When she last saw David, he was a medium-sized man, just under six feet, physically robust, his eyes shining and twinkling. Now, she could barely recognize him. He was thin, almost skeletal. His shoulders sagged with a slight hunchback. He looked like a shell of what he used to be, but then he smiled, and she knew it was him, for no one could smile like her brother David, a smile that reflected his absolute optimism, which he had carried with him from Scotland. She was suddenly reawakened.

Janet rushed to him and threw her arms around his neck.

"David, it's me, your sister Janet."

Livingstone at first just looked at her, her arms wrapped around his neck, her face running with tears. At first, he didn't believe it.

Who is this woman? Do I know her? My sister Janet? No! She doesn't look at all like the woman I remember.

He knew she meant him no harm, so he played along. But when

she pulled back, and he gave her a second look, her reddish-brown hair flying in all directions, he remembered back in Scotland, during their long walks near Blantyre and Hamilton in the countryside, her hair fluttering just as it did now. She would go with him after church to study the rocks and plants and try to identify each specimen. Then he saw the necklace around Janet's neck, the crucifix hanging on a silver chain.

Yes, it is Janet!

His prayers had been answered. God had brought her to him.

"You have brought me new life! You have brought me new life!" he repeated again and again. And then he collapsed, as soon as she released her arms from his neck, and fell straight to the ground.

18

—

ater, David regained consciousness. He lay in his hut, his
breathing heavy. Baraka stood over him, wiping his brow. Then
she bent down and gave him a sip of hot tea. Janet, Goma, and
Henry sat in a semicircle around him on rough, wooden stools. A few
Africans and Arabs, including Susi, and a large group of African girls
filled the remaining space in the room. Outside, hundreds of Africans
remained in place, their earlier excitement now dimmed.

This was not the first time they had seen Livingstone fall or lose
consciousness. Many of them had stood vigil outside his hut before, wondering if he would ever wake again. They had watched him
through his open windows and open front entrance, lying motionless
as if he were already dead, Baraka and Susi attending him. When he
woke up, he always looked weaker, and in recent weeks, he had grown
even more frail, remaining in his bed for days on end.

Sometimes, he'd sit up and lean his back against a dried buffalo
skin hanging against the wall. He'd ask Baraka or Susi to bring him
his pen and his diary. With shaking hands, he'd scribble a few notes.
Kalulu would then bring him food, meat cakes from the Arab cooks
nearby, that he always refused. He'd ask for some tea and continue to
write for an hour or two until he was spent.

He looked around the room and smiled at those whom he knew closest to him, the African girls especially, and Kalulu and Susi. He knew Kalulu would try to feed him whenever he woke up, but he was never hungry, and he couldn't chew with most of his teeth gone, fallen out from malnutrition in his prior travels. He turned to the sound of waves crashing along the shore of the lake. He knew evening would soon be approaching and wanted to sit up and look at the sunset.

Then, he noticed the strangers in his room sitting right next to him, a white man in a chalked white helmet, a woman with red hair almost breathing on him, an African man in long dreadlocks. He heard the sounds of guns firing from earlier and saw a procession of strangers floating toward him and waving an American flag. He looked at his clothes and remembered he had dressed and the sound of Kalulu's voice.

"Somebody coming. A white man."

No, this was not a dream. He didn't have the fever. And for once, he didn't have any pain. He sat up.

"David?" Janet whispered to him. "David?" she repeated. Then she bent down and fingered her necklace. "You sent this to me over a year ago."

It all came back to him. Kalulu had gotten through. His envelope had reached her. He had kept himself alive, hoping and praying for her to arrive, and deep down inside, he knew she would. He had foreseen this would happen, and now it was true. He straightened. His eyes flew open. Some of his strength began to return and he shouted.

"You have brought me new life! You have brought me new life!" Another surging wave of excruciating pain came from his abdomen, and he fell back down again.

The next thing he knew, he was sitting up, and his appetite had returned. Kalulu had brought food, three trays of hot meat cakes, which Livingstone was now gobbling despite his missing teeth. Everyone else in the room was eating, too, and drinking hot tea to wash it down. Evening was approaching. Someone had lit a candle. As he ate, more of Livingstone's strength came back and his memory, too.

KERRY McDONALD   131

"You have brought me new life," he repeated again.

Then Baraka stood up and wiped his brow and fed him another meat cake. He patted her head and turned to Janet. "What would I do without her?"

Janet looked at Baraka feeding him. "Is she your girl?"

"Yes. I knew her mother but we got separated. She disappeared one day. I never saw her again, and the others I brought them into my family." In a sudden burst of energy, with a half-eaten meat cake in his hand, he flung his arm toward the other children standing next to him, and then he tried to stand up but seemed once again to falter.

Janet took his arm and gently urged him back to the bed. "Don't talk, David. Save your strength. We have brought you some quinine."

As she turned to go outside and obtain the medicine, Livingstone held her arm. As weak as he was, he held her firmly, like a vise.

"Medicine won't help me. Not now. I have a malignant ulcer in my gut."

Janet dismissed any talk of his impending death. She tried to stand up again to get the quinine, but he squeezed her tighter.

"Sit down, Janet. I have something to tell you. We don't have much time." His face opened into a sad smile, a saintly smile, she thought, and she slowly sat back. He turned to the others, to Henry and Goma.

"And you, Mr. Stanley. Who are you?"

"I'm a reporter for *The New York Herald.*"

"That dreadful newspaper."

Livingstone spoke half in jest as if he were sharing a joke that everyone knew. He had read the popular publication but considered it substandard. Henry didn't mind, and he was even flattered that Livingstone had read *The Herald.* After the room was quickly filled with slight laughter, Livingstone continued. "Are you an American?"

"Born in Wales, but, yes, I spent most of my youth there."

Henry's American identity seemed to arouse Livingstone's curiosity and opened him up to a longer conversation, the subtext of which was for Livingstone to understand why Henry felt compelled to fly the American flag. Ignoring his childhood altogether, Henry spoke about his early work as a salesman in Arkansas, his brief enlistment in the Confederate army during the U.S. Civil War, his first newspaper assignment covering the conflict between the Cheyenne nation and the U.S. cavalry. At the end of his speech, Henry revealed how North America had shaped part of his character.

Livingstone remarked, "The British and Americans are the same people. We speak the same language and have the same ideals."

"Yes, we are brothers. Whatever I can do for you, you can command me freely as if we were of the same flesh and bone." Normally reticent and standoffish, Henry began to talk more, as though he were intoxicated, as though he were still touched by African fever.

His eyes shone when he said, "The Pacific Railroad in the U.S. has been completed and a telegraph cable was laid across the Atlantic, allowing instant communication between Europe and America."

"Is that right?" Livingstone was genuinely impressed.

Henry's eyes shone again. "The Suez Canal has opened and now ships can pass to the Mediterranean without sailing around the Cape."

"That's not good for Great Britain," said Livingstone, shaking his head. "It only helps non-British ships to compete. It's good for the French, though, and the Spanish and Portuguese."

When Livingstone revealed his admiration for President Lincoln and his devastation when he heard he had been shot, Henry announced that Grant had now been elected, and he would carry on where Lincoln left off. Then there was news about Crete, whose rebellion had ceased after the insurgents won, that a revolution in Spain had forced Isabella out, that Napoleon's revolution had finally been crushed by Bismarck's victories at Metz and Sedan, shifting the balance of power in Europe.

For a moment, Henry paused, realizing he had perhaps revealed too much and broken his carefully controlled exterior. He silenced himself and tried to recover his reserved dignity. In the middle of Henry's monologue, Livingstone had quietly glanced at Goma, who was sitting there next to his sister and Henry, not behind them as most

African servants did. He had rarely seen Africans who looked like him unless they were princes or chiefs.

Such poise, such pride. He looks educated. European trained, no doubt.

He wanted to know who Goma was and what he was doing there. Goma saw that Livingstone was staring at him.

"I'm Goma Foutou."

Livingstone suddenly raised himself up. He had heard that name from somewhere before. "Goma Foutou?"

"Yes." Goma was determined to tell as little about himself as possible. He would revert to one-syllable answers.

Livingstone stared at him with even more intensity. Something jarred his memory. Yes, he was certain he had heard or seen that name before. "I've heard of you. Where are you from?"

"It's a common African name." Goma cast his eyes down. Livingstone, with his deep-set eyes and bushy gray eyebrows, was making him nervous.

Henry, too, began to squirm. Tension mounted in the room.

"Where did I see your name?" Livingstone asked. "Was it in the newspapers?"

It was apparent from Goma's reaction that a nerve had been hit.

Henry scrambled to recover. "Maybe you saw it in *The Herald*."

"My God. I hope not." Everyone laughed as if Livingstone had just told a joke. When he was about to speak again, he was seized with another round of pain, and he cried out. Janet immediately ordered everybody from the room.

At last, she was alone with her brother. Normally, David would have been lying beneath his mosquito net sound asleep, but not tonight. With flies and insects buzzing all around him and a chorus outside of crickets and bullfrogs, he sat up, wide awake. For an hour, he had been talking to Janet, his memory and consciousness clear and bright. They talked about old times, their early years in Scotland, family members and people that they knew. He told her about the time when he poached a fish and how he got their brother Charles to hide it in his trousers.

"When I deposited it in the leg of his trousers, Charles told everybody he had a swollen leg. Are you sure I never told you this story, Janet?"

"This is the first I've heard of it."

"Well, there we were, me and Charles, who was limping with a 'swollen' leg. People passed us and asked what was wrong with him. So he says, 'My leg is badly swollen.'"

"You didn't."

"Oh, yes, we did. And then they'd look at him with sympathetic eyes and say, 'You poor thing.'" And then David laughed. Instead of the great bellowing sound that Janet remembered, a hollow sound came out of his chest.

Then, he poured out his heart about his family, his guilt about his deceased wife and his abandoned children. He wanted to know where his children were and who was doing what.

"You know about Robert?" she asked.

"Oh, yes. That was an awful way to die, like manure in a stinking Confederate prison camp."

"You know he came to stay with me before he enlisted in the army," Janet said.

"Yes, I received a letter from him just before he died," replied David.

"A troubled boy, complicated but genuinely a good person."

"You know he told me in his letter that he had many chances to kill the enemy in battle but he always aimed high. He never killed anyone." David briefly paused, then added, "Except himself."

"That was his Christian upbringing. He never lost it." For a moment, Janet remembered how Robert loved to sing Christian songs and had a talented singing voice.

She told him about his son Tom who was a student in medical school, and he told her about his daughter Nannie, how he tried to get closer to her before he had left for his last trip, hoping to atone for the neglect of his family. As the night wore on, Janet started to get up so he could get some rest, but he stopped her and told her to sit. He pointed at the crucifix around her neck, and then he asked her to give it to him.

After she slipped it into his hand, he said, "Janet, I want you to do something for me." He fingered the necklace and hesitated.

From the look on his face, whatever he wanted, she knew she wouldn't like it. Her response was muted. "What?"

"I want you to take all of my African children back with you to Scotland when you leave."

"African children? What African children?" She was shocked.

"Ten girls—those who were here earlier in this room. You saw them, including my daughter Baraka."

Her first reaction was to say no.

I don't want to do it. I can't do it.

It was impossible. It would be difficult enough to bring him along with his frail health, let alone ten African children marching through swamps and wilderness.

"What about you?" She spoke to remind him why she came.

"I told you. I'm not going to get out of here. It's a wonder I'm still alive. Can't you see this for yourself? I'm not coming back!"

His bluntness unnerved her and left her paralyzed. She wanted to tell him he was wrong. Hadn't he always told her not to give up, to keep on fighting no matter what? Her mind was a blizzard of emotions and thoughts.

"You must take them. They're all I've got. And Baraka is my daughter, your niece."

Here was a man who couldn't take care of his own family because of a calling that had come from God. But now he was asking her to take care of his Africans, something that God had not asked her to do. These Africans were his destiny, not hers. A feeling of resentment swept across her. She felt she had been used, manipulated, and even betrayed, drawn into his scheme without notice or warning.

Is this why I risked my life to reach him, only for him to die and for
me to be left with these children? It is unfair and unjust! Not to mention
the impossibility.

"Their parents were murdered, all of them slaughtered by slave
traders. I promised I would take care of them. You have to take them
with you!"

"No, David. No! I can't. I won't. It's unfair of you to even ask me!"

He leaned back and sighed a deep sigh that told Janet he had something he needed to say. She shifted herself on top of her stool. She was
going to be there a while.

19

—

"We left Mikadani in June—no, it was July, in 1866, with twelve sepoy guards armed with Enfield rifles, and thirty-five Africans. We carried the usual items for the trek, including scientific instruments so I could measure the land accurately. From the start, it was an ill-fated trip." David took a deep breath as he let his mind reach back in memory.

"We traveled up the Rovuma River, hacking through thick jungle growth, which broke the morale of my men. We had not gone far when they began to complain about the harsh conditions. Some accused me of strange practices—witchcraft and sorcery. They couldn't understand why or where they were going. I told them to find the source of the Nile."

Janet wanted to interrupt him. She didn't want to hear his story. She had her own story to tell. And yet, there was something about the tone of her brother's voice that gripped her. He no longer looked at her. He seemed to be hypnotized by some unseen power, and he kept nervously twirling the necklace in his hand.

"As we marched farther, the men began to desert, taking with them bales of supplies. Without these, we couldn't trade for food, and soon we suffered from hunger. As we neared Lake Nyasa, we entered the territory of the Mazuti, who had marauded other tribes to the north for slaves. They had destroyed all the villages in the region and taken all stocks of food, so we suffered even more hunger.

"More of my men deserted and I was left with only eleven men. I was sick and nearly starved to death with only my faithfuls. We walked for months in circles; we were lost. Do you know what it's like to be lost in Africa? I didn't know where I was. My compass had been damaged so I couldn't get an accurate reading of our position. And then we ran into a large Arab caravan who offered to help us."

David stopped, reached for Janet's arm. He looked deeply into her eyes, as if he were searching for her soul.

"I only did it because I was desperate. You must believe me. Without their help, I would have been dead. I had no choice. Please understand!" He spoke like a man driven by guilt. Then he settled back to resume his tale, his eyes drifting away again.

"This was December 1866. By then, I found out where we were and thought that the Nile began from Lake Bangweulu farther to the west, so I set out for it. But the winter monsoons came with heavy rain and swamps. The man who carried my medicine chest deserted and took all of my drugs. It might well have been a death sentence. I had nothing to treat my dysentery, and I was struck with rheumatic fever. And also some of the men got sick with nothing to treat them, causing more of them to desert. We ended up getting delayed and walked in circles for about a year to the end of July. I think this was, oh, about 1868." He broke off his narrative to allow himself to double-check the accuracy of the date. Once he was satisfied, he continued on.

"We ran into another slave caravan who felt sorry for us and gave us food and agreed to take my letters to Zanzibar, requesting from the British consul to send me more supplies. My group traveled on to Lake Tanganyika where we were supposed to cross it and come here to Ujiji to wait for my requested supplies, but heavy fighting in the region broke out between local tribes and the Arabs. That held us back again.

"In the meantime, I found out about the Lualaba River and was told that it ran into the Nile through the Congo, but by then I was down to just four men, my health failing once again with ulcers on my feet and in my intestines. My teeth were falling out from malnutrition." He stopped to open his mouth and show Janet his missing teeth.

"After time passed, another Arab caravan helped us get back to Ujiji, where I could rest and obtain drugs, but still, the supplies I sent for had not arrived. Yet, by the summer of 1870, I decided to gamble. With a few more men, including my faithful servants, Susi and Chumah, I set out for Nyangwe, a village located on the Lualaba River.

"We crossed Lake Tanganyika once again and had reached Bambarre, just a few days' march from Nyangwe, when I suddenly fell ill again, with anal bleeding and pneumonia, and the ulcers in my feet flared so I couldn't walk, so we were delayed a long time until around February—I think—1871. When we finally reached the village of Nyangwe, I tried to obtain canoes to continue my journey and confirm my theory about the Nile, but the villagers refused. They knew I was helped by the slave caravans. They thought I was one of them. Can you imagine that, me a slave trader? How could they even think like that?" His voice rose in indignation.

"So there I was, stuck in Nyangwe, unable to move. Soon, another Arab caravan arrived from the east, and they told me that my supplies from Zanzibar had arrived and were waiting for me in a storehouse in Tabora. With that information, I went back to Dugumbe—he was the leader of the slave caravan—and offered to trade my supplies in Tabora if he would let me travel with him along the Lualaba River since he was going in that direction anyway. All I was thinking about was I had found the source of the Nile but had to get more evidence. I overlooked that Dugumbe was carrying slaves. I didn't ask how he had gotten them. My only thought was to stay alive and to find the Nile.

"Dugumbe said he would think about it, so I waited in Nyangwe, dependent on him for everything, which I hated. As you know, we were taught never to depend on anyone."

Janet nodded her head. They both knew that the Livingstone credo was independence.

"Weeks passed. I sat around reading the Bible and writing notes in my journal while Dugumbe still had not made up his mind. One morning, I was walking in the marketplace. The local people were out shopping as usual. So far, the Arabs had not tried to enslave them. They assured the Nyangwe people they only wanted to use their village as a base for caravans going farther inland, and they were safe from kidnap or capture.

"Mostly women along with their children were shopping or trading that morning. It was a typical hot, humid day. But then around midday, I heard gunfire. I looked around and saw a group of slavers with rifles walking briskly. I thought this was strange, for they never carried rifles in the market. When they reached the upper end of the square, they opened up, firing volley after volley into the crowd." David paused and tried to stand up.

"They mowed them down, by the dozens, by the hundreds, blood and bullets everywhere. The villagers ran toward the river, hoping to swim across, but the slavers came to the bank and kept firing and killing many, many more. Those who survived the bullets were ripped apart by crocodiles before they could cross. The killing went on for hours and hours. It was horrible, horrible . . ." He struggled to contain his emotions. His eyes grew moist and wet. It took him a while before he could resume.

"For those weeks living in Nyangwe, and even before that, when I was first helped by a slave caravan and traveled with it farther north, I had compromised my principles. Perhaps, it could be excused when I was lost and helpless, when I had nearly starved to death, but when we reached Nyangwe, I had a choice. I turned my back on what I believed and cooperated with the slave traders. I allowed them to corrupt me, to forget about slavery, all for the sake of finding the Nile. After the slaughter, I realized I could not go on. My dream had come to its end. I decided there and then to go back to Ujiji.

"I stayed on for a few days more, helping those who survived to find bodies of their relatives and friends. That's where I found Kalulu, whose mother was shot and lying on the ground. We buried her—me, Susi, and Chuma. After that, my health broke down again. From the stress of the massacre, my blood pressure went up. My bowels broke down from dysentery, and the ulcer in my intestines flared up into pain. I also had a very high fever and had to lie up in bed. Again, without the help of Susi, I would have perished. I wanted to perish, but we gathered a few of the girls whose parents were killed. I was now determined to get them out before Dugumbe could make them slaves.

"We slipped away and headed east toward Ujiji, and as we marched, we passed so many Africans, so many, wandering along the trail, without family or food, running from villages that had been burned and raided. Most were children who ran from us because they thought we were slavers, except Makeda, who we found walking alone, talking to her black rag doll. We passed more villages as we trudged, all of them empty except for dead bodies and bones picked clean by vultures and hyenas. We picked up two more children along the path, Chichi— she's the one with a protruding belly—and Shali—she's the tall girl with the bald head—who were walking together. They came from a nearby village where their families were killed.

"Before we reached the western banks of the lake where I knew a tribe that would help us cross, we were attacked again by Africans in the bush, once again thinking that we were slavers. For five days, we were constantly set upon. Arrows were shot at us. Two spears narrowly missed my head. A huge tree that was felled with fire was purposely cast down on our path, just missing me. Two of the girls that came with us from Nyangwe were killed along with two of my men. Oh, Janet, I have never been so close to death, but it didn't matter to me. I was not afraid. The only thing that kept me going was getting these children back here to Ujiji, to save them if it were the last thing I would do on earth. So you see, I sent you this necklace, not for me, but for them."

He stopped again, his hands still fingering the silver chain and crucifix.

For several moments, Janet sat perfectly still. Midway through his narrative, she had lost any sense of shock. Rather, he had awakened in her an indignation she had experienced with the slave caravan that Henry's group had passed before Tabora. In a way, David had completed a picture that was already slowly coming to her. He had confirmed to a greater degree the full extent of the slave trade horror that she had briefly seen.

David was right. Everything else, the whole world searching for one white man while an entire race of human beings was being destroyed, suddenly became unimportant. But that did not obviate the difficult task he asked her to do. He had come so far with these children and survived against all odds, many times facing his death. He had succeeded so far. But she, a woman without his abilities, would surely fail. Her mind was overwhelmed with doubts.

"Mr. Stanley will never have it. I know what he thinks."

"Then you must force him."

"How?"

"The Lord always finds a way for the righteous. You must be bold as a lion." She bowed her head. Such comparisons only intimidated her. He had to try another approach. He began to recite Longfellow:

Tell me not, in mournful numbers,
Life is but an empty dream!
For the soul is dead that slumbers
And things are not what they seem . . .

Not enjoyment, and not sorrow,
Is our destined end or way;
But to act, that each to-morrow
Find us farther than to-day . . .

Act,—act in the living Present!
Heart within, and God o'erhead!

20

—

Another hot day. Spiders were crawling along the clay floor of Henry's room. Flies and wasps drifted in and out through the entrance. He was given this hut in order to store the most valuable equipment of his caravan—gold coins, the medicine chest, a few scientific instruments, glass beads and copper wire, calico and silk cloth. Henry had stacked these bags, boxes, and bales, along with his guns and rifles, leaving only a small space for his sleeping cot and a stool, where he could rest and eat and be alone. Janet had been with him since early morning, the sound of their voices spilling into the street that surrounded them. A few of the Africans stood outside, trying to fathom what they were arguing about.

"No, Miss Livingstone. It's out of the question!"

"We could do it. Ten girls do not need much food."

"But they get sick and scare easily."

"So do adults. So do men."

"Half of 'em will die before we get anywhere, and we'll never get through lion country. It's out of the question. It would be suicide."

"I'll take care of them."

"You're letting your faith get ahead of you."

"It's because of my faith that I know it can be done."

"And what about your brother? He has not died, even though you say he says he will, and he might not. As long as he is alive, we can't just leave him here."

"Come on, Mr. Stanley. He can't even stand up."

"My order, Miss Livingstone, is to bring him back. Nothing's changed. We'll carry him on a litter. You're his sister. You should be arguing about how we can keep him alive. We can't bring him back and the children, too." Henry paused. He knew this was not her idea. Livingstone had put her up to it the night before when she had spent those long hours with him. "If the good doctor asked you to do this, he's lost touch with reality."

"Perhaps it is you who has lost touch with your humanity."

Seeing that she could not get anywhere with Henry, her next step was to speak to Goma. He was staying in a separate hut in which the rest of the valuable supplies were stacked—cooking utensils, tools, some of the additional brass wires and beads. In his room, he had just a few large boxes, the beads were in bags, the wires on poles, along with his clothes, books, and two rifles. Otherwise, the room was simple, almost bare.

Like David's hut, the front door was an open space, and two windows were crooked, square gaps large enough to stick your head through. From the window space, he could see the silver waves of the lake crashing on the shore, and immediately in front of the door, the market square of the village with Africans and Arabs buying palm oil from vendors. Inside, Janet was more relaxed, and her voice more subdued than it was with Henry, but they both remained standing in the middle of the room. She had tied her hair back into a bun and let her shirttail hang out over her riding breeches. She began to pace the dirt floor as she tried to find words for her argument.

"You've got to help me convince him."

"He's not going to budge. Not with children."

"Why do you say that?"

"You know he has a thing for children, especially boys." It was true.

Many of his porters and guards were barely teenagers, which he pre-
ferred, young men who had nothing to lose. "You see, he's really still
a boy himself."

"Then he should understand."

"You know he's an orphan, don't you? His mother was a prostitute."

"Of course, I knew. He's not hard to figure out."

Goma stopped, walked to the front doorway, and looked out. He
saw the African girls playing in the street, Livingstone's orphans. He
gestured for Janet to come and look. She walked over. Some of the
girls were taking turns imitating the behavior of animals. The first girl
pranced like a lion, holding her head up as if she were the king of the
jungle. As she performed, the others watched and smiled. When she
was finished, they applauded and then the second girl got up. She
jumped and swung her arms about like a monkey or gorilla, jutting
her jaws out and scratching under her arms. She went around and
screeched into the faces of the other girls, causing them to laugh
with delight.

As the girls kept urging the monkey imitation on, Janet looked at
Makeda, who was short with thin, wiry braids, sitting apart from the
others on a log, playing with a black rag doll with patches of cloth
sewn onto its face to represent her eyes and mouth. Makeda talked to
the doll as if she were alive, her only friend. Janet also noticed another
girl sitting next to Makeda, Chichi, with a protruding belly. She sat
staring out into space with a dull expression.

Janet tried to imagine what it would be like with these girls—
wearing only goatskin cloth—next to her, tramping through dense
jungles hundreds of miles on their way back to Bagamoyo. She couldn't
see it. *Maybe Mr. Stanley is right,* she thought. How were these children
going to make it through all of the difficulties ahead, and what if they
were attacked by men with knives and spears? Yet, she also reflected on
how resilient these children were, playing like normal youths in front
of her. Just a few months ago, they had lost their loved ones, perhaps
they had even seen them murdered. Their villages were burned or

pillaged and they were left by themselves to wander along a wilderness trail without anyone to assist them.

Except for the two girls sitting apart, the one talking to a rag doll and the one with the big belly, these girls showed no outer signs of emotional disorder. Janet wondered if she could say the same thing about herself had she experienced what they had. Perhaps these girls were tougher than she thought. *Perhaps my doubts are more about myself.*

"I don't know if I can do it."

"Do what?" he said.

"Take them back with me."

Just then, Baraka got up. She had a slightly lighter complexion than the others, the most obvious sign of a mixed-race child. Janet wondered about her mother, who and where she was. Then it occurred to her that it didn't really matter when all of the girls had both of their parents missing or dead. Baraka pretended she was a bird, imitating a beak with her thumb and forefinger placed near her mouth. She lifted her arms as if they were a pair of wings flying above the ground. Everyone smiled at the grace and ease with which she moved. Janet also smiled and looked at Goma. Baraka turned to Janet and Goma. Janet waved to her.

"How can I convince Mr. Stanley when I haven't yet convinced myself?" Janet's eyes were still fastened on Baraka.

"You don't want to take them?"

Baraka continued to fly and soar. The girls laughed with glee.

"It's a huge burden."

"There is another possibility. Tell Henry the truth, that Baraka is David's daughter, and the others will be sold as slaves after surviving their parents' death. And make no mistake about it. They will be sold."

"Mr. Stanley doesn't care about Africans. He cares about Anglo-Saxon supremacy."

When Baraka had finished, another girl, Shali, who was taller than the others and had her head shaved almost bald, began to strut like a camel, bobbing up and down and making grunting sounds.

Goma turned away and looked seriously at Janet. "Then tell him you won't go back to England unless they do. He's not going to leave you here," said Goma.

The next day, everyone awoke to the sounds of an iron bell ringing from the Christian church near the village square. For those who lived in Ujiji, they knew this bell was never rung unless it was marking a special occasion, like Christmas, the New Year, or other important ceremonies. Otherwise, the bell remained silent unless there was an emergency. From the bold, clear way in which it rang, the bell was summoning the entire village.

Many people were still sleeping when it began. They knew something was wrong. Janet lifted her head inside her hut. She got up and looked out onto the square. Already dozens of Africans and Arabs were running, but not toward the church. They were running toward David's hut. She jammed her legs into her riding breeches and threw on her cotton shirt. Henry put on his holster, pistol inside, and ran. Goma put down his coffee and the book he was reading and joined the crowd.

Within minutes, the assembly grew to the same size that welcomed Henry's caravan when it first arrived. This time, hundreds, perhaps even thousands, streamed toward David's hut. Outside, Susi and one other African man kept everyone back, only letting some through the entrance, including Henry, Goma, and Janet.

As Janet entered, she saw Henry, Baraka, Kalulu, and a small group of African men she had never seen before. One of them, dressed in Western pants and shirt, was bent over David's body to examine it. He lifted David's lifeless arms and turned him on his side, where Janet saw her brother's face, his eyes closed. Goma stood in one corner, whispering gravely to Susi.

"Tell me again, Susi, what happened, so I can tell the others."

Susi began. He told Goma of how Dr. Livingstone spent his last hours. The pain in his abdomen had grown worse.

"Susi. Susi!" Dr. Livingstone had shouted.

"Yes, bwana."

"Get me some clean cloth. I'm bleeding again, and bring the medicine chest closer." Susi ran and returned with three towels. He turned Dr. Livingstone over and lowered his pants. Blood was oozing out of his rectum.

"I'm sorry you have to do this, Susi. I'm so sorry."

Susi took a towel and wiped Dr. Livingstone's buttocks and legs until he cried out in pain.

"Water. I need some water." Susi poured water in a cup. Then, realizing that the end was near, he left the medicine chest where it was and gave the cup to Dr. Livingstone.

"Thank you." As he drank, the bleeding slowed and the pain eased.

"Who is that shouting outside? Can you hear it?"

"No one shouting, bwana. No one outside. Just you and me."

"You're a good man, Susi. You can go now. I'm going to try and get some sleep."

Susi remained standing nearby, watching Dr. Livingstone's every move.

A few hours later, Dr. Livingstone crawled from his sleeping platform, lit a candle on the ground, and prayed on his knees. "Thank God for His great mercies so far. How soon I may be called to stand before Him, my righteous judge, I know not . . ."

Dr. Livingstone stopped and turned to Susi once again. His pain had returned. "Calomel. Get me some calomel. Hurry."

When Susi returned, Dr. Livingstone was dead.

Outside the elevated window slots, the faces of Africans looked into the somber room lit by two candles burning more for ceremonial purposes than to provide light. Everyone looked morose amid the utter silence. Janet sat down on a stool next to David's head and began to weep, the only sound that could be heard save for the tolling of the bell. Goma turned from Susi and addressed all those in the room. He pointed to Susi as he spoke.

"Susi says Dr. Livingstone asked him to get his bottle of calomel, and when he got back, he was gone, passed on to another world." Silence persisted in the room, aside from Janet's weeping. The bell continued to toll.

In the afternoon, a meeting was called at the Christian church. Janet didn't know who had arranged it. At first, she was too grief-stricken to notice much of anything around her. She cried because she had to, driven by emotions that had been building inside her over which she felt she had no control.

For one thing, despite what David told her of his impending death, following her last conversation with him, she was hoping he would re-cover. She wanted him to live because she needed him. She needed his words of guidance and his personal support. Even if they had to carry him a thousand miles, she needed someone to talk to, someone who could comfort her on the long trip back. Perhaps she was being selfish, but that's how she felt.

She also cried because now she was truly alone in the face of her responsibility to carry on his legacy, the first part of which was to bring back his ten African girls. It was not sorrow for her dead brother that kept her tears falling. It was her loneliness and fear that she was now going to fail, that everything he had fought for would be destroyed by her inabilities. She cried because she had never felt so helpless in her life.

Inside, the church was little more than a larger dried-mud hut with a conical roof, the center of which was supported by a long stake that upheld a tower. Buffalo hides were spread around a circle on which Africans and Arabs sat listening as Henry spoke in the center of the room. Many of those in attendance she hadn't seen before except the African man in Western clothes who had examined Livingstone's body earlier and another man—Chumah—who had stood next to Susi out-side David's hut, allowing only a few to get in. He was now whispering to Susi. He was dressed in a long white gown that covered his torso and legs and a black jacket.

Indeed, many of the men and women in the room were covered with greater amounts of cloth than usual, and Susi was wearing a white

turban. She thought they dressed more like Arabs, though their skin
color and mannerisms were that of tribal Africans, but she had seen
Africans like this before in Tabora and on the slave caravan they had
passed. She thought it was odd that nothing in the room pointed to it
being a Christian church, no icons of Christ or Christian saints. Before
her brother died, he asked her to save his African children, but what
about his Christian converts, Africans who had accepted his faith? She
didn't see any evidence of them.

In the middle of Henry's delivery, Susi jumped up. "We embalm."

"Embalming? Are you kidding me?" Henry replied.

"We embalm. It good. Chumah, Fallajah, and me." He pointed
to the African examiner in Western clothes and the man sitting next
to him. "Fallajah and Chumah is with Dr. Livingstone from start.
Just like me."

As Henry continued to shake his head in disbelief, Goma stood
up. "It's okay. They've both embalmed many bodies before. They know
what they are doing."

"What're their credentials?"

"Fallajah was a doctor's assistant in Zanzibar and has extensive
training. Chumah has performed the operation many times. Both of
them have worked for the doctor for many years," Goma said.

"I have no idea what they're talking about." Henry threw up his
hands in frustration.

"Africans have been embalming for thousands of years. It preserves
the human body," Goma replied.

"You mean like a mummy?"

"Precisely. Fallajah will make an incision at David's abdomen and
remove all of his internal organs. Then they will put salt on the body
and put it in an open trunk."

"Wait a minute. Slow down. What happens to the organs?"
asked Henry.

"They bury them separately," answered Goma.

"Then what?" Before Goma could answer, Susi walked over to

him to confer, whispering in his ear. Henry didn't like them talking by themselves. "What are you talking about? Can you share it with all of us?"

Goma leaned into Susi's ear until he had finished, then he turned to Henry. "The body is exposed to the sun and dried for two weeks. After that, they bathe the face in brandy as a preservative. They put the body in calico, wrap it in sailcloth, and sew it. Then, they encase it in tar to make it waterproof and place it in tree bark like a tube. After that, two men will carry it suspended on a pole to Bagamoyo. From there—"

"Wait. " Henry interrupted Goma. "What's this about Bagamoyo? Do you mean to say—"

"Yes," Goma quickly replied, "they will transport his body in a caravan back to Bagamoyo, and from there, his body will go by ferry to Zanzibar for his trip home."

"Bagamoyo? You're joking. No! He should be buried here where he died."

Susi intervened. "You bury him with own people. He want that."

"How do you know what he wanted?" Henry snapped.

"We embalm, take body to Bagamoyo and Zanzibar. English take him to English country. He bury there."

Henry continued to look dumbfounded. "This is all a joke. How the hell are they going to get him to Bagamoyo?"

Goma disagreed. "It's no joke, Henry. They know this country better than anyone, better than you or me. They will get the body back. They will march in a caravan, an African caravan."

"We take body. You take book, you take journal," said Susi.

As this debate went on, Janet became more concerned and drawn toward the discussion, and she began to feel flashes of resentment because she had been left out. After all, they were talking about her brother.

That is why I came to Africa. Yet nobody asked me what I thought. I wasn't even told about this meeting.

For a moment, her old insecurity returned, her inability to speak up for herself. She raised her hand to be recognized and even tried to call Henry's name, but everyone acted like she wasn't there. She suddenly remembered in Tabora when the door was shut in her face at the Sheik's house: "No women." She remembered her sister, Agnes, telling her she must not let others trample her. Janet grew angry, angry at herself.

Enough mourning, she thought. *Enough silence and timidity. I must stand up. I must speak out. I must be as bold as a lion.* She stepped forward and addressed them.

"It makes sense. They take his body back to the coast. It crosses the ferry at Bagamoyo to Zanzibar. From Zanzibar, he can be shipped back to Southampton. They take the body. We take the book. We take his journal and papers with us." She turned and looked directly at Henry. "There's your story and your evidence, his written diary. You don't need anything else."

Henry merely laughed at her, but she was deadly serious. "Who's going to make the arrangements in Zanzibar?" he asked.

"John Kirk. He's the British consul. It's his job." There was a moment of silence in which Henry stared at her. Janet thought she might have convinced him to change his mind. But she knew him. She knew he wouldn't give in that easily. More moments lapsed. Henry continued to stare at her. *What is he thinking?* she wondered.

"I'll agree, but on one condition."

She already knew what he wanted before he spoke again. She preempted him.

"No! If the children must stay, then I will stay with them!"

This caused murmurs to spread around the room. Except for Goma, no one even knew what she was talking about. Henry, too, was thrown off guard by the force of her voice and tone. She had seized the moment and gained the upper hand. Unable to speak, Henry turned and looked at Goma, hoping to draw his support, but Goma, like Janet, had also seen it coming.

"If she stays, then I stay."

"And one more thing," Janet continued. "I want to see a map!"

In the evening, Goma, Janet, Henry, and the guide, Asmani, were back in David's hut, looking at a map of Tanganyika spread out on top of an empty crate over David's sleeping platform. His body had already been removed by Susi, Chumah, and Fallajah to begin the embalming process. Candles were burning as insects swirled. Eerie shadows danced along the dried-mud walls, reflecting the somber mood in the room. Janet took notice of David's journal, a large, thick book set inside a tin box sitting atop a stool in the corner.

For a while, they had been arguing about the best way to get back to the coast. Henry was still fuming that Janet had outplayed him, that she could even question his authority.

How dare she, he kept telling himself. *How dare she demand anything from me.*

His anger was so acute he wasn't even listening. He made up his mind that anything she said, no matter how useful, he would reject.

"Why can't we keep going south to the Rufiji River? From there, we build rafts and float down it. The river would take us to the coast, to Kilwa." Janet bent over the map, using her forefinger to trace out a line from Ujiji to the river.

"That's uncharted territory," Henry snapped.

"To us, but not to them."

By "them," she meant the Africans. She remembered what Goma had said earlier, that the Africans knew this country better than he did. If so, why not use their expertise? She looked at Asmani.

"Do you know that country?"

"Yes. Two tribes up north—Kimbu, Sangu." He pointed on the map. "But we go south. No see them. Kimbu tribe, many fight with Mirambo. We go south, avoid."

"What's in the country? Jungle? Mountains? Flat?" Henry asked.

"Flat. Very dry. Sometimes no rain."

"I don't like it," Henry repeated.

"Can we take the river?" Janet asked.

"Yes, river good, slow, deep."

"There's a small settlement in Kilwa, a Jesuit missionary if we can get there," Goma added.

Not to be left out, Henry spoke. "Yeah, I know it. I've been there before, by boat from Mombasa. It's an old slave-trading post."

"I say we should go there. We have an African guide." Janet had made up her mind.

"And what if Asmani deserts us? We're lost. You can't trust them. The plan is reckless."

"Henry, we can't go back the way we came. The farther north we go, we run the risk of Mirambo's people, and now that Tabora is gone—" Goma moved closer to Janet's side.

"I still don't like it," Henry said.

"What *do* you like?" replied Goma.

"I like certainty. I like to know where I am. That way, I can fight."

"Don't forget about the lions," said Goma.

"Why do you keep reminding me about that? Dammit!" Henry kicked one of the stools.

"What do you say, Asmani?" asked Janet.

"Go south."

Janet and Goma nodded their heads in agreement. Then they turned to Henry.

"Now I have to listen to the bloody blacks! My answer is no! No! No! This is my expedition. We are going to stick to my plan!" With that, he stormed out of the hut.

The next day, as Henry's caravan began to prepare for the long trek back, a short Christian funeral service was held for David Livingstone. By now, Fallajah and Susi had removed his internal organs, including his heart. They found a tall palm tree on the outskirts of town. They dug a hole three feet deep and called on Janet, Henry, and Goma to attend. Janet brought along the African girls and Kalulu, who would soon be joining Susi and others to take her brother's body back to Bagamoyo.

The ceremony was short and without fanfare. Susi read from several passages in the Bible. Janet quoted a few lines from the Book of Psalms. She remembered, just before David left for Glasgow to take the steamer for his first trip to Africa, the family had gathered early in the morning. After breakfast, they said their goodbyes and called on her to read Psalm 121, which she now read again as a memorial:

I will lift up mine eyes unto the hills

From whence cometh my help . . .

The Lord is thy keeper:

The Lord is thy shade upon the right hand.

Janet's reading was almost perfunctory. It was not until the final passage that she actually felt what she was reading, that she felt the words connected to her brother's passing away, and as she read it, she was moved to tears.

The Lord shall preserve thee from all evil: he shall preserve thy soul.

The Lord shall preserve thy going out and thy coming in

from this time forth, and even for evermore.

Already, Susi had carved on the tree: DR. LIVINGSTONE MAY 1, 1873, just above the hole where his remains—contained in a small tin box—would be placed. Susi and Chumah lowered the box by a cord of cloth wrapped around all four corners of it from which another cord like a rope was attached, allowing them to lower it, ever so gently and slowly. On top of the box, they placed a palm leaf, a symbol of Africa. Next to the leaf, they placed some of his personal items: his toothbrush, his drinking cup, his fork and spoon. These things they believed would be needed for when he entered the afterlife.

Then Susi, Chumah, and Fallajah took iron spades and covered the hole with dirt, tamping it down with their feet.

A fitting end, Janet thought.

Her brother would be buried in two places. His heart was buried here in Africa, where he spent his entire adult life. The rest of his body would be buried somewhere in Great Britain, no doubt enshrined in a concrete tomb with his name etched in stone for posterity.

21

—

The caravan was finally moving out of Ujiji, a somber procession, the opposite of how it went in. The pace was slow, a funeral march, no American flag flying, no gunfire, no horns, no drums, just a steady, slow trickle moving away, moving toward the Ukaranga hills. The size of the train had been reduced to just over forty men, Henry still up front. Instead of walking as he usually did, he rode on a donkey. Behind him trailed Selim, the Palestinian guard, and behind him, Asmani the guide, with Livingstone's diary in his backpack.

Many of the same guards and porters were still traveling with them: Saburi the long distance runner, Ferrari the cook, Mkati the porter with bulging muscles, the porter who told hunting stories, the two superstitious men from Wajiji. In addition, they had picked up three fresh donkeys, which helped reduce the weight each porter had to carry. They also had more supplies, canvas bags filled with meat and fish, palm oil, cassava, and sweet potato. Otherwise, they carried a reduced amount of cloth, copper wire, and beads, having used some of them for local trade.

The caravan moved slowly because many of the porters and guards had attended a huge funeral ceremony that lasted two days.

More like a festival or celebration, Janet thought.

After they buried Livingstone's organs underneath the palm tree, the tribal Africans conducted their own funeral in their own way. Henry sat it out, but Janet attended some of it with Goma.

Tribes from the area descended upon Ujiji early in the morning to pay tribute. They first assembled at the palm tree near his burial inscription. Some of those who knew Livingstone well gave short testimonials about his kindness and how he had helped them. One of the village elders slaughtered a goat as a sacrifice and sprinkled its blood on the burial site to prevent Livingstone's misfortune in the afterlife.

Soon, the crowd began to swell into the hundreds, so they moved to the village center where they held tribal ceremonies and sporting events. Many pails of beer were brought in, and people began to drink. Drums began to beat, and the people began to dance. They danced all day until they reached fever pitch, followed by a huge feast and more singing and dancing to the steady throb of drums. Upon their faces Janet noticed smiles and laughter, no signs of the somberness that, in her experience, death usually evokes.

"It bothers me," she said to Goma.

"What bothers you? The funeral?"

"Not the funeral, but the way it's conducted—the carefree, casual attitude, not to mention the absence of any Christian customs, which my brother believed in."

"Janet, they have already mourned, when he died, but now they are celebrating his passing to another life."

"What other life?" She was thinking about heaven, but she knew that's not what he meant.

"To the world of dead ancestors whose spirits remain alive in the here and now."

Was it for this that her brother died? These were pagan beliefs that he fought against his entire life. "Aren't these people supposed to be Christian converts? There's nothing Christian about them."

"Janet, they all loved and respected Dr. Livingstone because he treated them kindly, not because he was a Christian."

"Then it seems hopeless to me." Janet frowned as she watched the Africans getting drunker and drunker. She felt they had betrayed her brother.

"What's hopeless? I don't understand."

"Look at them. They act like heathens and savages. And these are the people he tried to help? How ungrateful they are. Such lack of respect."

Goma sighed. He had heard all this before many times, both in Africa and Europe. "Many of these people you see here—they are torn between three religions—Christianity, Islam, and their own tribal traditions, taking ideas and tenets from each."

"Christianity doesn't work like that. It's not some meal you can nibble on, tasting from different dishes. It's a commitment. You should know that."

"Your memory is short, Janet. I'm no longer a Christian."

"Then what are you, Goma? What do you believe?"

"I believe in Africa, where we are right now, not Europe or Oman where one is Christian or Muslim. Here, the idea of a single and absolute conversion is foreign. You expect it to happen, all or nothing, and you expect it to happen at once. Remember, Dr. Livingstone just got here a few years ago. Islam has been here since the ninth century, perhaps even before, and our tribal beliefs we've had for thousands of years. We're sick and tired of outsiders telling us what we should believe."

"But still, one must make a choice. Otherwise, what's the point? You might as well believe in nothing."

"It's unreasonable for you to think Africans can convert in such a short time. That's all I'm saying. And even if we do convert, we'll never give up our African traditions. We will never give up our funerals. You're just going to have to accept that."

The caravan stumbled on, tramping in silence, more out of awkwardness, still adjusting to carrying packs on their heads, or rifles, contemplating the trials that lay before them. Goma, as before, stayed in the rear, guarding against any attack from behind. Janet, however, walked with the girls even farther behind Goma, a position she thought was not safe, but the girls couldn't really keep up.

From the beginning, they fell behind, just as Henry had said. To speed them up, she had them hold each other's hands, but that didn't work. Part of the problem was that each girl was different. Some could walk fast, others more slowly, especially Makeda and Chichi, both of whom seemed to drift. Janet had to slow all the girls down to keep them together. She didn't want to separate them. Otherwise, she would lose the slower ones. If she had a problem or needed advice, Goma was close enough, so she felt somewhat safe, but still, Chichi and Makeda kept lagging, and no matter what she did, she couldn't change that.

When they got to chimpanzee country, dozens of friendly chimps descended on them as before, but up in the front, Henry kept on moving, as if they were part of the exterior scenery, a rock or a tree or a waterfall. After a while, a large female chimp approached the children. She had two dashing young chimps behind her that hooted and called out to the African girls, who hooted and called back like they were talking to each other. Then, Baraka took out a banana and fed it to one of them, which jumped with delight. As the mother chimp held back, she lowered her head and lay on the ground, as if she were going to take a nap, but the young ones kept dancing around the girls who were now feeding them fruit and peanuts. Baraka took another banana and gave it to Janet and pointed.

"Ndizi. Banana, ndizi." She instructed her on how to pronounce it in Swahili.

"Ndisi," Janet repeated.

Baraka shook her head. "Ndeeezzi." She emphasized the rolling z.

"Ndeezzi," Janet said, this time correctly. "Ndeezzi," she repeated.

Baraka gestured for Janet to feed the little chimp, waiting for her to offer the banana. Janet hesitated. For a moment she feared the animal might bite off her fingers if she held the fruit out, but Baraka gestured again that it was all right. Janet fed the chimp, who jumped and danced with glee. After eating the banana, the same chimp came back and held out its hand to Janet, as if she wanted to get picked up. Janet looked at Baraka, who again gestured to her that it was okay, but Janet held back again.

This time, she was afraid the chimp wasn't clean, that her black fur might contain parasites or bugs that would rub off, and she was worried about an odor. To feed the chimp was one thing, to hold it in her arms was another. The chimp was persistent, threw up its arms, and began to scream and make a racket.

By now, the caravan had stopped. The porters and guards encircled the girls and chimps, delighted to be relieved from marching. Everyone seemed to relax, seemed to be enjoying the moment. Baraka went up to Janet and told her to pick up the chimp. If she didn't do it, it would get angry and scream and cry again, so Janet picked it up and then, when she did, she didn't want to put it down. The chimp did not smell nor did its fur display any crawling parasites. All of Janet's fears and concerns had suddenly vanished. Then the mother chimp got up from the ground, and the two young chimps rejoined her, dashing up into the trees, never to be seen again. The caravan moved on.

As midday approached, Lake Tanganyika was still visible west of them, the steep mountains forming an escarpment along the shore, the trail winding below through a narrow valley on which small ridges and hills rolled one after another through thick jungle growth. The girls kept struggling to keep up, and now they were tired. They didn't have the stamina of the men. Makeda and Chichi and one or two others constantly lagged behind, making the procession longer and more spread out. Henry, up front, couldn't see what the rear was doing. It soon became a separate train.

Janet grew more and more concerned, so she ran forward to Henry and told him to slow down, told him to stop so the girls could catch up, but Henry ignored her. When she ran back to the girls, who were now traveling in clumps of two and three, frightfully exposed to the wilderness, she frowned and grew afraid. The caravan kept moving.

At sundown, unseen by the travelers, three lions dashed along the mountain slopes above them, two lionesses and a male with a black mane. Leading the group was the lioness whose cubs had been shot by Henry, his bullet still lodged in her shoulder, her other wounds visible on her face. For hours, the big cats had been tracking the group, keeping out of sight. Now, they dashed forward almost parallel to the caravan, their eyes focused on the girls.

22

—

The caravan made camp on a clearing along a small plateau. Within an hour, they had put up their tents and started fires. Ferrari cooked dinner, fish stew in three steaming pots. He also roasted meat cakes given to him by the Arabs in Ujiji, a favorite meal among the porters. After dinner, everyone retired.

Some of the guards and porters wrapped themselves in blankets on the ground. The rest of the guards remained on duty, protecting the meat rations. Janet told one of them to stand by the children as a precaution. There they would stay posted until relieved by one of the guards who started the night sleeping. Henry was nowhere visible. He had disappeared inside his tent as usual. Once Janet was satisfied that the girls were protected, she sat by a smoldering fire drinking coffee, next to Goma. After a long silence, she spoke up.

"Mr. Stanley hasn't said a word all day. He's got a strange look in his eyes."

"Not for long. He's going to have to speak soon. The going will get rougher when we leave the lake region."

"That's what I'm worried about, with the girls. You saw them. Henry's got to slow the pace down. There's no need for him to push so hard."

"He can't help it. That's the way he is. He's not going to slow down unless he has to."

"That's what I'm afraid of."

"Or if you admit to him that you were wrong. Then he'd slow down."

Janet shook her head in disbelief. "Wrong about what?"

"About the girls. That you shouldn't have brought them."

"Of course not. I would never do that." She paused. "He's the one who's wrong."

"I know."

"It's too late anyway. We can't go back."

Janet stared into the dying flames in silence. All was quiet save for the sound of night owls and bullfrogs. "How did you meet him, Goma? Mr. Stanley." She looked at him and waited for an explanation. She had wanted to ask him that question for a long time.

Goma continued to stare into the fire, realizing that he owed her some account for why he was here. Now was as good a time as ever. "I killed a man. That's why I left Oxford."

Janet was completely thrown off. "Excuse me?"

"I murdered a white man in London. A man who disrespected me. It was in all the papers. I'd do it again if I had to." He turned and looked her in the eye.

"That's where David saw your name. He must have read about it."

"Maybe, but back then I was going by my Christian name, Jacob Wright. I never used my African name unless I was around my own people."

"What happened? Why did you do it?"

"I was invited with some of my fellow students to the home of an Oxford graduate who didn't know one of us was black. When I got to his house, I refused to eat dinner with the servants, as is your custom."

"Yes, if you're not of the upper classes."

"The dinner was extremely awkward, and my host was livid with anger, but I was determined to eat with everybody else no matter what.

After dinner, the man confronted me and called me a bloody nigger who should learn his place. I strangled him on the spot."

"So what happened after you killed—"

"The police looked for me. I was wanted. I ran away. For weeks, I survived in the sewers of London in various disguises, only coming out at night. I pretended I was a sailor and hung around the docks. That's where you find more blacks than anywhere, so I didn't stick out."

"How did you escape?"

"Henry got me out."

Janet's eyes widened. Once again, she was stunned. "You mean Mr. Stanley?"

"He smuggled me out of England."

"How? Why?"

"He was assigned to go to Abyssinia to cover the British campaign against Theodore. He found me in a bar, and I told him my story. He needed me to help him in Africa. Sort of like a guide."

"And you had nothing to lose."

Goma nodded. "I've been with him ever since."

"But what's forcing you to stay with him now? There are no white police here."

"When I killed the white man, my people found out. The elders said I disgraced them. They told me not to return."

"Your people, meaning . . .?"

"My tribe here in Tanganyika. My people still uphold British ways and my village sacrificed so much for me—going to Oxford and all. I was being groomed to be the leader of our clan. To go from that to a wanted criminal . . . to be banished from your people is a fate as bad as death."

"So assisting Henry in finding David will earn you pardon. They will know you were part of a noteworthy event."

He nodded again. "And I can go home."

Unknown to Janet and Goma, the trio of lions had been watching as they talked by the fire. Watching and waiting. Biding their time.

The following day, Henry's group descended into the Great Rift Valley. To the west, more mountains formed an escarpment along the rim of Lake Tanganyika, which was now fading behind the caravan. Ahead of them, on the northeast side, were great mountains like the slopes of craters on the moon, with brown and gray rock formations made from volcanic rock patterns when the earth was formed. Rocky ravines and plateaus intersected with protruding masses of disintegrating bleached sandstone. A closer view of these cliff-like hills gave the appearance of granite fortresses and embattled towers, boulder resting upon boulder and immense columns of solid pillars holding up the sky. Underneath the surface, masses of iron ore popped up at intervals, an unsettled and ancient land of thorn clusters and gum trees.

Below these rock formations, stretching south, there was a lush valley, ridge upon ridge of low hills rising and falling, wave after wave as far as the eye could see, stretching farther south, covered with blue-black belts of thick timber forests and woods. The group descended into this valley, the high peaks lording over them from two sides. The skies above were alive with eagles, pelicans, and pigeons. Bird and animal sounds echoed everywhere.

By now, this train of voyagers was moving faster, the children barely keeping up. Janet did her best to maintain them in a group. She tried again to get the girls to hold hands and stay together. She grasped the hands of Baraka and Shali, both of whom helped to set a pace for the others. Chichi continued to fall behind, but slowly she began to close the gap, slowly she began to wake up from her long slumber.

Only Makeda with her rag doll fell dangerously behind, and Janet had to stop at times to pick her up and carry her forward until she grew too heavy. Makeda would then march with the group for a time, but eventually drop back again while holding another conversation with her rag doll. When Janet tried to take her doll away, hoping this would force Makeda to concentrate more on walking, she would scream and make an awful fuss as though Janet had stolen her only companion.

They came to a fast-moving river, the Rungwa. Henry got off his donkey and waded in to cross it. Midway through the rushing current, the water flowed up to his waist, but it reached no higher and he crossed safely to the other side. His guide, Asmani, followed him, carrying the tin box of Livingstone's journal on his head. He was almost completely across when he slipped and juggled the box in his hands. When Henry saw the box about to fall in the knee-deep water, he ran to Asmani, pulled his revolver from his holster, and pointed.

"If you drop that box, I will shoot you through the head."

As Asmani worked to regain his footing, the box teetered again and plunked into the river. As it fell, Henry cocked the trigger. This spurred Asmani to leap forward and grab the box before it could float away or be submerged deeper. One of the guards, Selim, jumped in the water and pulled Asmani out, helping him get back on his feet. The box was saved.

They made camp beneath a tall sycamore tree, a favorite choice of Henry's. Whenever he found a small clearing underneath a sycamore, or if he found a similar large tree, he would make camp. This was a pattern he had established during the trip.

In the evening after dinner, campfires smoldered. The girls had gone to bed, all of them sleeping under two separate tents. The guards were posted around the camp. The porters and others turned in, exhausted by their long day of marching. Goma rolled in his blanket. Janet sat sipping tea by the fire. Henry, as usual, remained in his tent. All was quiet and calm when suddenly from nowhere came the loud roar of a lion. The whole camp jumped as if the lion had already descended upon them. Rifles and pistols were drawn. Henry flew out of his tent. Janet dropped her tea and ran over to Goma.

"Did you hear that?" She balanced her pistol in her hand.

Then another lion roared. This time, Makeda jumped up and ran to Janet, who took her hand and led her back to her tent. Janet took Makeda's rag doll, now lying on the ground, and placed it back into the child's arms, which helped to soothe her. Janet then turned to the rest of the girls, who were all awake and sitting up. She tried to calm them by smiling and repeating, "Everything's okay. Go back to sleep. Everything is fine."

"I scared, Mamma," said Shali. She stood up, but Janet walked to her and urged her to go back to sleep, gently pulling her down and rubbing her bald head.

Once Janet got the girls settled, she went to one of the guards and told him to stand near the children's tents, after which she walked back to Goma.

"The girls are terrified. So am I."

"They won't attack tonight. They'll wait for a better opportunity."

When the group began to march again the next day, from the thickets and heavy jungle growth on both sides of the winding path, lion roars came at staggered intervals. No doubt, these lions were tracking the procession and using their horrible bellows to intimidate the group without having to attack it directly.

Henry now slowed the pace, and their forward movement began to lumber as heads darted side to side, each person scouring the thick foliage, expecting to be attacked. This made the procession more compact and tighter. Although the girls still trailed the main caravan, one of the guards hovered next to them with his rifle ready. Goma and Janet also surrounded the girls, making sure they stayed together, including Makeda.

Evening came again, another night at camp. By now, the caravan members showed greater signs of anxiety and fear. Normally, after they ate dinner, they would listen to the Wagogo storyteller delivering yet another exaggerated hunting tale, or the two Wajiji men—who looked like brothers—would make predictions about the future, or the porters would sing their tribal songs, sometimes loud and sometimes soft. Some of the porters would say their evening prayers. Now, not even the Wajiji men spoke—no stark predictions about the evils that lay ahead—they were too scared. The men sat around in silence. Some smoked their pipes. Others picked meat off of bones left from dinner.

It shouldn't have surprised anyone when another roar rattled the night air, but of course it did. Chichi and Shali screamed. The guards scrambled for their rifles, pointed their barrels toward the surrounding woods. Janet and Goma hopped to their feet, scanning the darkness for shining eyes. Henry perched on a stool inside his tent, his rifle stretched across his lap, beads of perspiration clinging to his brow.

Part of their terror was their confusion. The lions' bellows reverberated through the night, seeming to come from all directions at once. A single lion's roar could sound like a whole pride.

The cacophony continued for several minutes before it eventually stopped. But even after the quiet returned, nobody slept deeply.

The next day began with drizzle in the morning, but later it became steady rain, the first the group had seen in a long time. As the caravan members walked, the packed-dirt path turned to mud, and they had to navigate the slippery and sticky terrain more slowly. Janet found pieces of cotton cloth and tore them into smaller strips to wrap around the girls' heads to shield them from the rain.

As they marched through the sludge, one of the donkeys froze. It refused to budge, and the luggage on its back fell into the grime. Four porters flanked the donkey's rear and pushed together until it finally took a plodding step and begrudgingly began moving again. Some of the men began to grumble because, despite the rain, despite the fear of a lion attack, Henry forced the caravan onward.

That night, the rain turned into a downpour. Even though Henry chose a dry space surrounded by tall trees with thick leaves to pitch camp, large amounts of water dripped down, making campfires impossible. The men soon tried to rest, wrapped in blankets wherever they could find a sheltered area. One tent was up. Janet and the girls slept under it next to the two guards posted nearby. Henry and Goma, neither of whom could sleep, stood on patrol. Their instincts sensed they were in danger.

The downpour shifted irregularly, coming down in heavy spurts, then falling lightly, then again in sheets.

During the heaviest cascade of the night, the wounded lioness charged through the camp without making a sound and leaped through the tent for one of the children. Before anyone could get a shot off, she sprang into the darkness with one of the smaller girls dangling from her jaws.

Janet ran to Henry in tears as the rain flowed down.

"We've got to go and find her, Mr. Stanley!"

Henry could hardly hear her through the crash of rushing rain. "What?" he yelled.

"I said, 'We've got to go and find her!'"

Henry half-smiled at the absurdity of her request. "Negative, Miss Livingstone. I'm sorry, we can't. Look at this rain. We'll never find her."

"We've got to do something!"

"I'm sorry. She's gone."

The girl was gone, and no one had foreseen the attack. The lioness used the rain as cover. Janet and Henry continued to argue back and forth through pelting drops, until Janet let out a roar of her own and spun around in disgust and dismay and stomped off to soothe the remaining terrified girls.

The rain-soaked days flowed into each other, an endless dreamlike state of trudging through mud and setting up camp, punctured with nightmarish bellows that made it difficult for anyone to sleep or even rest. Eventually, the rain stopped, and the convoy picked up its pace, moving relentlessly and without breaks. Since the lion attack and the killing of one of the girls, the group's spirits had plummeted.

Everyone was demoralized, anxious, afraid. Despite Henry's attempt to set a vigorous pace through the heavy jungle dripping with wet leaves and smelling of decaying trees, caravan members marched as though they were drifting in space, silently and alone. Everyone was wondering when the lions would attack again. Janet, too, lost some of her resolve. The fact that the lioness could get to the girls despite their precautions and protections, despite the posting of armed guards, dejected her, made her less vigilant and less careful.

The girls were now traveling in scattered clumps, spread out, scared and confused. Janet held on to Baraka and Chichi, who by now had gained some resolve. The rest of the girls fell farther behind. Heavy vegetation made it impossible for Janet or anyone to see the lagging girls, to keep track of each person. The lioness could have attacked again and carried any one of them off, and no one would ever know until it was too late.

Makeda was at the tail end of the caravan, zigzagging along the path, smiling and talking to her black rag doll. She didn't see or hear the lioness in the nearby thicket, creeping along silently, stalking her.

Suddenly there was a tremendous roar. Makeda screamed and ran into the dense foliage away from the path. She screamed again and both Janet and Goma heard her; so did the rest of the caravan.

Janet cried out, "Makeda, Makeda!" as she scanned the dense jungle for any sign of the girl. Henry ran back with some of the guards and porters and they dashed into the forest on both sides of the path, shouting Makeda's name over and over. The drummer beat the drum. Someone blew a horn in part to scare away another attack, but also to make noise so Makeda might hear it if she was lost.

But it was all to no avail.

After an hour of searching the woods, the group found no trace of the missing child and reassembled at the trail. Goma and Janet were the last to return, where they met Henry standing near the rest of the men. Janet's clothes were torn and her face bore small cuts from thorns and branches. As she drew closer to Henry, who stood waiting for her with his rifle slung around his shoulder, her anger spilled out.

"We need to stop here and do another search."

"No, Miss Livingstone. I'm sorry, but she's gone. The lions have gotten her."

"How do we know that? I say we do another search."

Henry pointed to the ground. Makeda's black rag doll lay on the dirt, its face smashed, its lifeless limbs akimbo. Janet gasped, quickly pivoted, and ran full tilt back into the bush. Henry gave his rifle to a porter and dashed after her. Goma followed. When Henry caught up, he grabbed her by the back of her shirt and spun her around.

"Let me go, Mr. Stanley!"

"She's gone!"

Janet fought to wrest herself from his grip, but Henry held on, almost forcing her to the ground.

"She's gone, Miss Livingstone!" Henry shouted. "And if you go back there, you're next!"

At these words, the fight went out of Janet and she stopped struggling, so Henry relaxed his grip.

"Well, then, I'm next!" she retorted. "So what. We're all next! We're getting picked off one by one." She stood up and faced him. "Of course, you don't have to worry. You're way up front, riding a donkey with your rifle!"

"I told you, Miss Livingstone. They couldn't keep—"

"You won't let them keep up! Why are you pushing us so hard? Are you willing to kill us all because you want to make a deadline and get your story out before anyone else? Does your career mean that much to you?"

"You said you'd take care of them."

"You're pushing us so fast they can't keep up. You ensured her—"

"You said you'd take care of them!"

"You ensured her death. You murdered that girl!"

Goma stepped in before Janet's rage led her to say or do something she would regret. He wound his arm around her waist and pulled her toward him, and she began to stagger. Then, she broke away to walk by herself, leaving the caravan in a daze. As she swayed forward, she ran right into a tree as if she were blind. She rebounded and continued to lurch unsteadily forward.

Henry turned to Goma. "She's got the fever."

"Are you sure?"

"No, but she's got something. You'd better get a hold of her."

Goma followed Janet until she crumpled. He picked her up and carried her back. Henry walked the caravan a short distance up the trail to a small clearing, where he ordered the group to stop and make camp. Goma spread a blanket on the ground for Janet, who was now breathing heavily and trembling, and ran back to Henry.

"I'm going to put up her tent. We might be here a couple days. We can't go on like this."

"Do what you can. As soon as she's better, we're moving out."

"Make sure you post a guard by the children," Goma said before he went back to her.

23

—

The rain started again. Everyone huddled. The girls clung to each other wet and shivering in their tents. The porters and guards were once again wrapped in their blankets. This was the hardest part of their journey, when they had to stop, unable to do anything but sit around. Boredom and inactivity further eroded their morale.

Henry sat alone in his tent, wondering how long he had to linger, how long it would take before Janet got better, strong enough to walk again. He hated delays. Already, there had been a slow trickle of deserting porters, and the more they waited, the more the caravan ran the risk of even more desertions.

In Janet's tent, Goma lay her down on a cot, took off her wet clothes, and dried her. He put on her dry trousers, a shirt, and a woolen sweater, then he wrapped her in two heavy blankets so she could sweat. All the while, she remained conscious, but delirious, and shouted, "Goma! Goma!"

He wiped her brow loaded with moisture. Her thighs and spine shook and shuddered and were wracked with pain. Her eyes filled with terror and popped out as she clutched Goma's hand and shouted his name.

"Goma! Goma!"

He pulled back to pour quinine into a cup and tilted it into her mouth. He took out two rouser pills and forced her to gulp them down along with a large dose of water. He measured out a few grains of calomel and fed them to her on a spoon. After many minutes passed, perhaps even an hour, he stood up to leave her tent, but she grabbed hold of him and pulled him back down.

"Don't leave me, Goma! Please don't leave me." He bent down and touched his cheek to her forehead.

Eventually, the rain stopped, and Janet fell asleep. Goma spread his blanket out beside her, and he, too, took a nap. Outside, everyone began to sleep except for some of the posted guards. The sun came out with the dawn. Patches of bright yellow light flashed through the trees and the canopy overhead.

Once again, Ferrari made breakfast, mixing some of the meat cakes with thick porridge and coffee. The porters and guards were up, looking nervous and anxious. They wanted to move out but knew they would be here at least one more day. Henry was soon talking to Asmani, trying to get a better understanding of where they were, trying to plan his next move. He thought about building a stretcher so, once Janet woke up and the fever had broken, they could carry her. For now, all he could do was wait.

Baraka, Chichi, Shali, and the other five girls were chasing snowflakes that were floating down all around them. The girls twirled and flung their arms with delight. More and more white flakes fluttered until it looked like a snow shower. Shali snatched at one flake and examined it. It wasn't a flake but a flying ant. There were thousands and thousands of flying white ants.

Janet continued to sleep, but soon she started to mutter to herself, and she began to toss. Images and faces flashed before her, scenes from long ago. Distant voices came and went. She saw long moments of total darkness and then instant light. She was inside her tent, dreaming:

She's lying on her cot, fully awake, looking around the tent. She can see her clothes and all of her belongings, her backpack and toothbrush, her comb and hairbrush, David's necklace and her Bible resting on top of a box. She's alone. She tries to sit up but can't. Her body is paralyzed. Try as she might, again and again, she's stuck. Hours seem to pass.

Night comes. She can hear the porters and guards outside, talking and laughing. She wants to talk to them, so she tries to get up again, but she can't. She remains paralyzed. Then she tries to shout for Goma, but words will not come. She cannot move, and she cannot talk.

Soon, the voices outside disappear. She is alone for a time, no sounds at all. Then she hears the voice of Mr. Stanley. He sticks his head through the tent entrance.

"I told you to get ready. We're moving out. Why are you still lying there? If you don't get ready in the next five minutes, I'm going to leave you here."

She opens her mouth to protest, but again no words come. His face fades away. She hears more voices from other caravan members, but their sounds soon die out too. She tries to cry out, to shout Goma's name again, but she can't.

Another night comes. She lies in the dark. The sounds of wild beasts and dogs torment her from outside the canvas, screaming, snarling, grunting. Terrified, she strains to get up but again cannot. Then she hears the pitter-patter of bare human feet running up to her tent. A little black girl sticks her head inside. It's Makeda! She walks slowly with her rag doll in her hand and stares at Janet with hostile eyes.

"You said you'd take care of me."

Janet tries to speak, to tell her how sorry she is. She tries to say that she did her best. She wants to beg Makeda to forgive her, but Makeda looms over her trapped body, glaring at her with menacing eyes.

"You said you'd take care of me." The girl whirls around and vanishes through the flap. Janet tries to shout and yell, tries to tell her to come back, that it won't happen again, but she cannot speak. She cannot move.

Janet kept dreaming. She dreamed she was back in Blantyre, standing in line at the butcher's shop:

She has been waiting for a long time, and she starts to sweat. Her sister, Agnes, stands next to her, and behind them grows a long line of women and girls. The woman in front of her pays for her meat. Now, it's Janet's turn.

"One pound of the braising steak," she says.

Without looking up, the butcher starts to cut from a carcass, thick blobs of nothing but fat. He keeps slicing until a small mountain piles up in front of him. Janet tries to object but can't. The man, with his hovering mustache, lifts his gaze and sneers, trying to stare her down and intimidate her. When Janet looks at his face, she sees it's not the butcher. It's Mr. Stanley!

"Hurry up, Janet. Place your order." Agnes nudges her, but Janet can't move, nor can she open her mouth.

"You must be strong, Janet. You've got to stand up for yourself," says Agnes, but Janet remains frozen.

Mr. Stanley barks, "Hurry up and place your order. You're holding everybody up!"

Then the women behind her begin to complain. They yell at her to hurry up and pay for her order, but Janet can't. Soon, everyone is screaming at her and calling her all kinds of names: idiot, imbecile, stupid and slow. She is admonished for not knowing what she's doing. She's a moron, a dummy, a complete disgrace. They keep shouting at her till she can't take it anymore, so she turns on her heel and runs from the shop. She runs, and she runs and runs and runs.

Suddenly, she is younger, in her early teens, strolling along a beach on the Scottish island of Ulva, the island of the wolf, where her grandfather lived in the eighteenth century, before he moved to Blantyre. She's wearing a blue dress with long sleeves and a petticoat that brushes the ground. Her reddish-brown hair is long and is tossed around by the ocean air. She walks behind David along the shore of green ferns and small, smooth pebbles. The strong breeze also tousles his hair. He has on a plaid shirt and corduroy pants and plods in front of her with heavy, lumbering steps. She feels at peace to be with her brother, young, carefree, and full of optimism. She likes being in the land of her people, steeped in Celtic traditions, where families live free in the open air and are contented and happy. David will soon be in medical college in Glasgow. She knows their future looks bright.

As they continue to stroll, as far as she can see a range of huge rocks and boulders border the shoreline just inland. Farther up the coast, a large basalt cliff known as Rocky Mountain rises up. David points to it and to a group of rocks below.

"That's Kirsty's rock. Once a woman was put in a sack and bound there till she drowned at high tide."

"For what?"

"She accidentally killed a girl she only wanted to frighten for stealing some cheese. The woman was devastated for what she had done and begged the islanders for mercy, but they were deaf to her remorse."

"That's terrible."

"The world is full of such incidents, so much pain and suffering."

"I wish we could do something about it." Janet speaks too soon, not realizing what she has said.

David slows down and turns to her. "We can. We must. Let's make a pledge together to devote our lives to ending human misery, to alleviating human suffering wherever we are."

"What good would it do? We are only two people."

David stops walking and faces her. "Christ was only one man and look what he accomplished." His eyes grow wide, his words tumble out excitedly. "All you need is faith, real faith, and guidance from the Holy Spirit."

She is not convinced. He takes her hand. "Come, Janet. Let's pledge."

He pulls her to the ground by the arm until they are kneeling, facing the sea. Janet tries to push to her feet, but he drags her back down.

"Maybe for you, David," she protests. "You are so much stronger than I am. I can't do anything. I'm not Christ." She tries again to stand, but his iron grip keeps her on her knees. He pulls her closer.

"Yes, you are. You're just as strong, even stronger, only you don't know it yet." He releases his hold and, with outstretched hands, looks to the sky and recites a prayer: "For the Lord shall vindicate his people and have compassion on his servants."

Janet scrambles to her feet as soon as David lets go. He breaks his prayer and also rises, putting his hands on her shoulders. "You have no choice. God has chosen you. You must!"

"No!" She tries to flee, but he holds her in place, clutching her shoulders.

"Pledge with me, Janet. Pledge!" He is shaking her like a rag doll. "Pledge with me, Janet! Pledge!"

Finally, she frees herself and sprints down the shoreline. David chases after her but he seems to be moving in slow motion. As she gathers greater distance from him, he screams out, "Janet! Janet! Janet!" but she keeps running. She runs, and she runs and runs and runs.

24

—

Janet woke up. The tent was a flickering reality, dark then light, insects swirling, early morning sunrays pouring through the canvas seams, slanting beams of floating dust, voices outside, Ferrari the cook, the donkeys braying. She was shocked that she could move again, that she could sit up, that she was no longer dreaming. Then she felt a surge of energy, like a bolt of lightning from an African storm with clouds piling up into mountains. She leaped up, just to see if she could. Yes! She could do anything she wanted.

She jammed her feet into her boots and picked up her pistol. Where she was going, she didn't know. Something inside was driving her, pushing her, something she could feel, but somehow didn't want to control. She felt invincible. She was tired of sleeping, tired of lying down and holding herself back. She crashed through the tent door. Early-morning dew and mist, the smell of roots and grass and sweet flowers, bean pies baking, coffee, leather, and urine.

She ran through big flapping leaves that cut into the side of her face, broken branches, spider webs, bush rodents scampering out of her way. Where she was running, she didn't know. She didn't care. She had no future and no past. No place to go to. No place called home. The only thing that mattered was now, her body bursting through an

African field of tall, wet grass and patches of mud, her boots trampling on worms, caterpillars, scurrying black ants, beetles and centipedes, rocks, black soil, fallen leaves, twigs, fruits, and nuts.

Janet heard David's voice pleading with her again. "Pledge with me, Janet, pledge!"

But it wasn't David. Someone else was running after her, shouting, "Janet, come back!"

Ahead of her, a large brown rock was propped up by four pillars. As she charged toward the peculiar rock formation, it moved slightly, and then it moved again. *What was it? Not a rock. Were those eyes?* Staring her down, waiting for her to get closer.

No, not just staring. The eyes narrowed into the purposeful gaze of a patient predator. She had seen those eyes somewhere before. *Where? Where?!* Eyes that wait for you to falter, to fall down or tire or make a mistake.

Janet's legs slowed and she stumbled to a stop. Standing directly before her was the wounded lioness, dried blood caked to the fur on her shoulder. Janet looked for her pistol, but it wasn't in her grip or tucked into a pocket. She must have dropped it along the way.

For a moment, she thought she was dreaming again, but then Goma's voice called out from behind.

"Janet! Janet, come back!"

As she turned to him, from the corner of her eye, she saw the brown rock flash huge white teeth and the pillars fold into a spring-loaded crouch. The wind in Janet's lungs suddenly drained. She was gripped by fear, a fear that numbed her and spread quickly throughout her limbs; her legs and arms grew stiff.

Once again, she was paralyzed. She couldn't move. Only this time it wasn't a dream. A tidal wave of dread swept over her. Everything turned red.

Henry had seen Janet rush out of her tent, while he was arguing with a porter who complained of stomach pain. Instinctively, Henry yanked his rifle from where it was resting on a tree and followed her.

Goma was ahead of him, also in pursuit. Henry ran behind them, trailing but catching up. He reached a large field, where he found Janet standing in front of his lioness, her hands raised as if she were being held up by a robber.

Henry charged past Goma, who had slowed down upon encountering the standoff, and raised his rifle. The lioness bent low, her shoulders near the ground. Henry aimed his barrel at her, but just when he was about to pull the trigger, the sun's rays shined into his eyes, and he couldn't see. His head went dizzy.

In that split second, the lioness leaped for Janet. As she arced through the air, her legs raised to strike, Goma stepped in front of Janet and fired his rifle from his hip. He got two shots off before the lioness landed on top of him. She raked his face and chest with her massive paws and mauled his shoulder with her teeth. She bit into his leg and hip and was just about to clamp down on his throat when Henry finally fired a shot, and she ran off into the tall grass and disappeared, wounded further but still alive.

Janet ran to Goma, who lay on the ground, a bloody mess. Once she saw he was still breathing, she immediately set to work. She would use all of her knowledge and skills to try and save him. His right arm and shoulder looked splintered and his chest and throat deeply scratched. The lioness had also made several gashes on his chest, and she had bitten deeply into his right leg, possibly breaking the bone.

Janet shouted to Henry, "Get the medicine chest!" but he didn't move at first, as if he hadn't heard her. He just stared agape at Goma's mangled flesh.

"Get the medicine chest. Hurry!"

Henry blinked twice, then focused on Janet and nodded his head. Before he ran back, she untied a small cotton towel from around his neck, then used it to swab Goma's body. She daubed his wounds again and again, trying to slow the flow of blood. Soon, some of the porters brought up the medicine chest. Janet took out more towels and dipped them in alcohol to keep Goma's wounds from getting infected. She fished around for what she needed to suture the wounds—a metal clamp, a curved needle, and some thread—all the while swabbing the gashed areas with the towels.

Although she had some medical knowledge learned mostly when her brother attended medical school in Glasgow, she had never sutured before, but she had seen it done. Her mind was now clear, and she got to work. As she began, most of the caravan members caught up and surrounded her.

She shouted, "Everyone get back, except Baraka."

Janet didn't have to tell Baraka to get a pail of water from a nearby stream for cleaning the wounds, and the girl held the metal clamp as Janet pushed the needle through the two layers of torn skin, pulling it out on the other side. Janet tied a knot and cut off the thread, then repeated the process until a series of knots closed the gash. The suture looked awkward and fragile, but it would have to do. She moved to the next laceration and stitched again and again and again, then the next wound and the next. As Janet worked, Baraka used cotton balls and water to daub and clean the wounds, making sure any debris was removed.

Meanwhile, Henry stood behind her, pacing back and forth, muttering to himself and to Janet over and over, unaware that his presence was a distraction. "I don't know what happened. I blacked out."

Janet ignored him. She had no choice. For now, Goma received her only attention. After she sutured all of the wounds, taking care to sew all the gashes and close the skin, a procedure that seemed to take hours, Henry continued to pace behind her.

"I blacked out, I tell ya. I don't remember anything!" Mumbling to himself and to the wind, his voice was the only sound on the field except for the screams of high-flying falcons that seemed to be admonishing him.

Janet began to work on Goma's arm and shoulders. Baraka got behind and lifted Goma up so Janet could see the large swelling on his skin and the black and blue marks indicating that his shoulder bones were dislocated, not broken. She would have to reset them.

Once again, she had never done this operation before but had once watched it demonstrated at David's medical school. She remembered the instructor pushed and pulled the bones until they were back in place, making it look easy from a student's point of view. Now, she thought she might make a mistake, but somehow, she was not worried. Her mind was sharper than it had ever been. Using Goma's facial gestures as a guide, she pushed the bones back into place, taking pains not to sever or damage any arteries. As she pushed and sometimes pulled, Goma screamed out in pain, but she had no anesthetic to calm him.

For his leg, she turned to Baraka. "Go find two forked branches or sticks, a short one and a long one."

"How long?"

Janet stretched her arms, indicating the length needed. "As straight as possible. Hurry!"

Goma's leg was broken, no doubt about it, a closed fracture with a large swelling lump on top of the skin. With the help of the other girls, Baraka returned with two straight sticks stripped from tree branches. Janet took the longer stick and placed the fork under Goma's armpit, aligning it with the side of his body, chest, waist, and right leg, all the way down to his feet. Then she turned to Baraka again.

"Cut strips of cloth so I can tie the sticks to his upper body. Quickly."

Janet took the shorter stick and put the fork near his groin where his leg joined his hip and made it parallel with the left side of his leg to his feet. She straightened the leg and wrapped cloth strips tightly around both sticks pressed against two sides of his leg. She had formed a splint, two sticks that kept his leg in place so the bone could hold firm and possibly heal.

While Janet was struggling to save Goma, the day continued on. The rest of the caravan had moved toward her, bringing up all the equipment, tents, and bags. Some of the porters set up a tent. Baraka continued to assist her. Baraka, too, knew something about medicine,

having helped treat Livingstone before he died. She helped Janet hold
the splint while Janet wrapped bandages around Goma's leg, and she
fetched clean water to wash the skin. Everyone else stood around,
watching and waiting as the sun continued to blaze in the sky. Henry
was useless, his mind still lost in a daze, his legs still pacing back and
forth, his mouth still muttering futilely.

"I don't know what happened. I couldn't see. I blacked out, I tell ya."

After they helped Baraka find the two sticks for Goma's leg, the
girls stood on the sidelines like everyone else, watching and waiting.
When it became clear that Goma would live, at least for now, they
broke away among themselves. They found the small stream where
Baraka had drawn water and waded in, not to play but to wash and
clean each other. Imitating Janet and Baraka, they used washcloths to
wipe any dirt that had formed on their skin, and they looked for ticks
and leeches under their arms and in their hair.

Some of the girls had fungi or rashes, extensive insect bites, bruises,
and skin inflammations. Shali went to each of the girls and examined
them. If a girl was clean, she moved to the next one. The girls were
imitating Janet and Baraka in the way children imitate adults in play,
but, at the same time, they were helping each other keep themselves
clean and healthy.

Near the end of the day, it turned cloudy. The air remained hot and
humid, but the unbearable sunlight had softened, filtered by haze. The
porters put up more tents and Ferrari set up tripods to hold pots for
boiling soup—fish soup from crabs and snails purchased in Ujiji. He
fetched water from the nearby stream. He smiled at the girls as they
washed and examined each other.

"This is good. Take care of your sisters," he said.

Saburi talked in Swahili with Selim, just to while the time away.

"Where you from in Palestine?" asked Saburi.

"I was an orphan, raised by a bishop at Christian school. That's all
I know, all I remember. And you? You said you were from Bagamoyo."

"No. I live in Bagamoyo because of my job, but I was raised in my village farther up the coast in the north. I am Waswahili."

"Waswahili? What's that?"

"My people are black, African."

"That's where you learn how to run?"

"In my village, everyone is good at something. Some because they can hunt, some because they have skill with wood, some are great speakers. I am a runner. What are you good at?"

"All I know is how to shoot rifles. I can hit anything from one hundred yards out."

"Who taught you to shoot rifles?"

"I taught myself. I practiced many times till I was good."

As Ferrari cut the crabs and placed them into pots and stoked the fires to boil the water, he worked in silence, not his usual smiling and talking self. The porter with the bulging muscles—Mkati—who had challenged Henry near the Makata swamps, smoked a clay pipe and looked at Goma. Mkati hadn't forgotten that Goma sided with him in his argument with Henry, and he was grateful that Goma kept his word and paid him higher wages back in Tabora. Mkati also remembered how Janet removed a musket ball from his leg after the fighting in Kwihara. He decided that no matter what, he would stay with both of them to the end.

The rest of the caravan grew restless. The guards kept watch on the edge of the camp, their rifles cocked and ready should the lioness attack again. The porters were getting hungry and kept looking at Ferrari, wondering when he would call them to eat. Some of the men were thinking about the future. With Goma wounded, what would happen next?

The porter from the Wagogo tribe, who was usually full of stories to tell, stayed silent. His face was glum. Now was not the time for storytelling. The two porters from the Wajiji tribe who looked like brothers or twins had long ago decided that the trip was doomed, that an evil spirit had descended upon them. When darkness set in, just after sundown, they took advantage of the disarray caused by the lioness attack and slipped away into the bush, taking a few valuable cloth bales with them. Two other porters who saw them go also decided it was time to leave after they had been fed Ferrari's fish soup. They, too, slipped away when it grew dark. By dinnertime, Henry had stopped his rambling and retired to his tent to brood. The last thing on his mind was the thought of deserting porters.

At night, Janet slept on the ground next to Goma inside his tent.

How ironic that just one day ago, I was the sick one and Goma lay on the ground taking care of me as I writhed with fever and nightmares.

How quickly she had recovered. For a moment, she thought about the mentality of diseases, how people can sometimes recover or grow worse because they do or don't have the will to go on, a belief that David upheld. When David was alive, he once told her he would have been dead in Africa long ago if he didn't have the will to live on. In effect, Mr. Stanley had said the same thing in Kwihara when he took an oath: *While the least hope remains in me, do not break the resolve. Never give up the search until I find Livingstone, dead or alive. I shall not die. I will not die. I cannot die.*

Janet realized that if people lived or died because they wanted to, maybe Goma had a chance to live, if he willed it so. She knew he had too much to live for, so she would try and do everything possible to give him hope, to make him want to live. And then there were the girls, two of whom were already dead.

Independent of their will, I neglected them. It was I who caused their deaths.

Just before Janet fell asleep, she vowed it would never happen again.

In the morning, Janet and Henry were up at dawn's first light, arguing like there was no tomorrow.

"He needs a doctor. He's lost a lot of blood, but he's still alive. And look"—she paused as she pointed—"at the scratch marks across his throat. He's unable to speak."

"What does that mean? That he's going to die?"

"No, not right away."

"We must turn back, take him back to Ujiji."

For the moment, Janet kept silent. She herself was unsure what to do. As the caravan began once again to get assembled to continue its trek, Janet looked around. The group was now down to twenty men. A staggering twenty to twenty-five porters, including one guard, had fled since they had left Ujiji, taking much of the supplies with them. Of course, they had been diverted by these lion attacks, and Janet realized there would probably be more of them. The lioness who mauled Goma had been wounded but was still alive out there somewhere, and there were one or more lions with her. Whether they returned to Ujiji or kept going south, or even if they turned back toward Tabora, the lions would assault them again. Who would be the next to die?

The girls by now seemed to be adjusting, especially Chichi, who was carrying herself with a new determination, and her protruding belly seemed to have flattened, perhaps because she was eating. She no longer stood apart from everyone. Indeed, in recent days, all the girls had come together as a group, looking out for each other, taking care of each other. Janet had also drawn closer to them, especially to her niece, Baraka, whom she relied upon for help, just as David did when he was alive. Baraka knew instinctively what people needed, and she always fulfilled those needs if she could.

What really worried Janet was Goma. He needed a doctor, and he needed to rest somewhere and recover. Being carried on a stretcher was precarious, and they had to pass over difficult terrain. Despite that Goma's bleeding had stopped and his leg was set for recovery, she worried about infection and what would happen if his body was suddenly jolted. Something deep inside of her said that they should continue on to find help. They had to risk it. She went back to Henry.

"He'll never make Ujiji. There's no one behind us to help him."

"Many of my porters have fled, as I knew they would, and they took supplies. We've got to go back, for Goma and for us."

"Not all of them left, and we still have the guards. I say we keep going south." Janet spoke just as forcefully.

"Miss Livingstone, there's nothing down there!" he shouted.

"How do you know?"

"We could lose even more, and what if we run out of food?"

She grew even more determined to make her case. *No matter what, Mr. Stanley will tell me no.* "Goma will die if we go back to Ujiji. If we go south, we might be able to get help."

"From who?"

"I don't know, but there's a chance! We owe Goma at least that much."

"Look, Miss Livingstone, I know how you feel. He saved your life, and you feel you owe him, but now you must look at the bigger picture. It's not just Goma but—"

"He will certainly die if we go back to Ujiji," Janet said once again, cutting Henry off, "but we still have our guide who knows the way to the Rufiji River. If we go south, we know where we're going."

Henry spat on the ground. "Across an unknown country to build rafts and float down an unknown river infested with who knows what."

As Henry and Janet continued to argue, Goma, who was lying on a stretcher close by, struggled to speak but could not. He could only make soft grunting sounds, and he tried to lift his left arm. He managed to draw Janet's attention, so she went over to him. Goma looked in her eyes and lifted his left hand. He wriggled his fingers.

"What do you want? Something to write with?"

She fetched a pencil and writing tablet and helped him move his hands and fingers up and down. In a very rough pattern of letters, he had written one word: *SOUTH.*

25

—

Miles and miles of flat, dry prairie land, enormous sheaths of low-lying grass, shrubs, sandstone, rocks. They passed tamarind and acacia trees growing in low-lying gulches that ran with clear streams during the rainy season, but it was now late November 1873 and the sun continued to scorch the earth. Any day now, wet clouds would roll in, but, until then, the heat wave persisted with a vengeance.

They passed whistling thorns found in heavy clay soil. The holes in the galls that covered their branches created a humming sound, a chorus that tried to lull the caravan to sleep as it trudged wearily into nothingness. They passed baobab trees that looked upside down with their swollen trunks and branches twisting like roots. Sometimes, their trunks shined silver-white, making them look like ghost reflections of themselves, some of them thought. Sometimes, an anthill rose up into a pointed cone. Sometimes, a fox or jackal trotted by underneath the fever trees with dead leaves painted in copper-red colors. Sometimes, they passed a few scattered huts, abandoned villages with no signs of life.

Against this background, the caravan members moved slowly along a brown, rutted road. They had just crossed the Great Ruaha River, now reduced to a bare trickle. In two months, it would roar again, flooding the plains. Now, it was just another dried-up riverbed on which antelopes, leopards, and gazelles traveled, searching for another source of water.

As the sun poured down day after day, Henry stopped riding his donkey. They needed it to carry supplies, especially now that everyone's energy had drained. He still walked in front of the group to show he was in charge, but otherwise he seemed detached, as if he didn't care anymore. Behind him, Asmani tried to keep up, his white loincloth now stained with brown dust. Livingstone's journal was still strapped to his back in a tin box. The flag bearer and drummer had long since deserted, along with the flag and the drum.

Since Goma's mauling by the lioness, more porters had deserted, so many that Henry had given up trying to stop them. The caravan was soon reduced to eight porters and five guards, excluding Ferrari the cook, Mkati with bulging muscles, Selim the Palestinian guard, Saburi the runner, and the Wagogo storyteller. The remaining porters continued to carry their loads, thirty-pound packs of glass beads and cloth, copper wire, the medicine chest, tents, and equipment. The guards still carried their rifles, cocked and ready should any lions reappear.

Goma lay on a crude wooden stretcher, dragged by a donkey ridden by a guard at the very end of the procession. Janet still attended him when she could. She had wrapped a blanket around his body to shield him from the sun and wind. Otherwise, he remained barely alive, fully conscious and able to communicate. Whenever he wanted to express himself, he would signal for someone to bring a pencil, usually when they had set up camp, and he would write something out, but that was rare. For the most part, he kept silent as he was dragged along.

Janet drew closer to the girls, who continued to walk in the rear, just in front of Goma. There were now eight of them, including Shali, whose long legs often set the pace for them all. Saburi sometimes lingered and talked to her in Swahili.

"You should be a runner like me. You tall and have strong legs like a man."

"Yes, I like to run when I know where I'm going. I don't know where we're going now."

"No one knows but the kubwa mkuu. The big white chief."

Janet always walked with Baraka at her side. Baraka knew some English that she had learned from Livingstone, and Janet needed her for translating, especially now that Goma was disabled. As she walked, she asked Baraka how to say certain English words in Swahili.

"How do you say 'peace' in Swahili?"

"Amani."

"Just like the name of our guide." Janet pointed ahead to the guide walking behind Henry.

"No. He is Asmani with an 's.' Amani means peace, not Asmani."

"What does Asmani mean?"

Baraka shook her head. She didn't know.

Janet continued. "How do you say, 'Go in peace'?"

"Nenda kwa amani."

"Nenda kwa amani. Go in peace."

They went on like this for hours on end, trying to keep their minds away from the harshness of their journey, their burning throats, their tired legs. Among the other girls, Chichi still struggled to keep up, but she had come a long way, her former brooding self all but dead. Her protruding belly had extended again, now that the group lacked food and water.

Yet, they trudged on, dragging their feet, now sleeping at night under an open sky. Tents were not needed here with no rain in sight and the ground looking scorched and exhausted. During the day, Janet became increasingly worried that they would never find help from anyone.

Perhaps Mr. Stanley was right. Perhaps we will never find help. We need assistance and soon. If not, Goma will die in a few days, and the rest of us will also be jeopardized.

The caravan members had been marching three weeks since Goma's attack. They had a brief flash of hope when they saw a village ahead of them one morning. Dozens of thatched-roof huts lined the road. As they drew closer, they discovered the huts were empty, no signs of human life except for hundreds of bleached bones scattered on the ground. Many of the huts were burned down, the grass around them black from fire, and the village water hole was completely dry. In the surrounding trees, vultures still perched, looking for any trace of flesh they might have missed from prior pickings. As the procession passed through the town center where people once gathered to sing and dance, Janet felt she needed to talk to Henry.

"Mr. Stanley."

He ignored her and kept walking.

She wanted to ask him what had happened. "Mr. Stanley."

He kept ignoring her.

"Mr. Stanley!"

Finally, he turned. "Slave raiders, Miss Livingstone. Slave raiders!" He was annoyed, angered that she couldn't figure it out for herself.

After another four days of moving farther south, the caravan's food supply was nearly gone and animals to shoot for meat had nearly disappeared. To make matters worse, they were almost out of water. To preserve what they had, Ferrari rationed each person two cups per day, which was not enough to sustain them in such blaring heat. This prompted Chichi to walk up to Janet.

"Maji, Mamma, maji." She used her hand to imitate a cup raised to the mouth for drinking. "Maji, maji."

Janet still did not understand, so she turned to Baraka, who interpreted. "She says she wants water."

Then another girl spoke. "Ni enye njaa. Mamma, ni enye njaa." Once again, Janet looked at Baraka.

"She says she's hungry."

Janet smiled at Chichi and all the other girls and tried to assure them. "Soon we find water. Soon we find . . ." Janet didn't know the Swahili word for "food."

Once again, Baraka spoke up. "Chakula. Tell them, 'hivi karibuni chakula.' Soon food."

Janet smiled again as she addressed the girls. "Hivi karibuni chaku-la." Behind Janet's smile, her face was grim.

The road dipped, and they entered a valley with very tall grass. For the first time, they could see a mountain range in the distance, rising a few thousand feet above the plain. These were the Mbarika Mountains that Janet recognized from the map. Somewhere inside of them lay the Rufiji River. This gave her hope that at least they were headed in the right direction.

Through the pink haze, she could barely see the forests that covered the peaks ahead where they might find water if they could make it, but the hills looked so far away and, unbeknownst to them, there lay another danger. The lioness, riddled with bullet wounds, and two other lions—another lioness and a male—ran through the grass parallel to the caravan, following it. Some of Henry's group believed the lions had gone, chased off by the dry climate, but Janet knew they had not gone away. She kept the guards vigilant to protect the girls.

And still, they kept moving. Everyone staggered ahead toward the distant Promised Land. They looked like zombies, the walking dead, which prompted Janet to liken their caravan to that of slaves. She remembered the slave caravan they passed near the Marenga Mkali—the female stragglers who trailed behind the rest of the slaves chained or tethered to slave sticks.

We look just like them, wandering with glazed eyes and emaciated bodies like ghosts.

In a flash, Janet decided she wouldn't die like that, not like a fallen slave, eaten by jackals and hyenas.

No, that's not how I'm going to die!

She gathered all of her energy and ran ahead to Henry.

"Mr. Stanley."

He ignored her again, his eyes peering straight ahead.

"Mr. Stanley!" she shouted again.

Finally, she gathered every ounce of her power and leaped directly in front of him, blocking his body from going forward. He would have to knock her down or push her out of the way. "I know you don't like me. And I don't like you. But this has got to stop!"

"What?" He spoke as if he didn't know what she was talking about.

"Look at me!"

He turned slightly to see her face.

"We've been walking for weeks and you don't speak. You ignore me. I don't even know where we're going."

"We're going south, Miss Livingstone, just like you wanted."

"If you don't start communicating, we're all going to die and not because of lions or anything else. We have to work together to find a way out!"

"We are working together." As he spoke, he turned his head away from her, unaware that his action had the opposite effect of what he was saying.

"No, we're not! I can see it in your eyes!"

In a fury, he turned to her directly. He had to let his anger out, anger that had been slowly building. "See what? What do you see? What do you see?" he shouted.

Just then, a large male lion with a black mane bounded out from the cover of the grass. Henry saw it immediately and, pushing Janet out of the way, he lifted his rifle. All of the guards lifted their rifles and aimed. The lion came forward as if unsure whom he should attack, and then he stopped. He was ten yards away from Baraka. The lion crouched down to leap, but Baraka stood her ground and didn't move, unafraid. The lion hesitated. In that split second, a barrage of gunfire opened up from everyone who had a rifle. The lion dropped dead in his tracks.

26

—

The killing of the lion gave caravan members a new sense of hope and determination, their first good break since Goma was mangled. Through the hot blaze of the afternoon sun, they surged ahead toward the mountains, emboldened by their momentary victory. Everyone now believed they just might live. If they could kill a lion, they could do anything.

The procession came together in tighter formation, a more compact line. Now, the children, along with Janet, walked in the front. Not only could the girls keep up, but they were setting the marching pace, almost running, with Shali in front. They looked like child soldiers dashing forward to the front lines of a battle, leading their men on to victory. Even Chichi, who usually straggled, walked with a new sense of purpose. The porters, too, walked faster with their thirty-pound packs on their heads. And Goma, who remained on his stretcher, balled his fists and held on.

Toward evening, they were within range of the Mbarika Mountains, medium peaks with lush green vegetation. Henry raised his hands and called out. The caravan stopped. He took out his spyglass and looked ahead. Then he turned to Janet and Asmani.

"Up ahead, if we can get to the forest, there will probably be a stream. Also, I think I can see the outlines of fruit trees. The growth is very thick. That might keep the lions out. We've got to get there before dark."

The next morning, the caravan woke up. Dew dripped from the trees. Insects crawled—beetles, centipedes, worms, ants, even lizards. The night before they had made it to the mountains and crashed to the ground, exhausted, at the first clearing. They felt like they had slept for twenty hours. With the morning sun hidden behind dense jungle growth, they felt the first signs of relief. They had made it.

As the caravan awakened, Henry walked ahead through the dense foliage alone. Using a hatchet, he chopped away vines, branches, thorns, and dwarf trees, forging forward and clearing the way. Soon he discovered a thin footpath that zigzagged farther into the brush. He followed it for a half mile. When he returned, he found Janet talking to Asmani using sign language and one-word syllables. If she got stuck, she turned to Baraka to convey her meaning. Goma lay next to them on his stretcher, listening.

Then Janet turned to Henry. "Asmani says we're close to the river."

Henry used his hands to ask Asmani the exact distance. "How far away is the river?"

Asmani shook his head. "I don't know. River close."

From his pocket, Henry pulled out an unripe mango. "I found some fruit trees ahead, bananas, papaya." He gave the mango to Janet, who gave it to Chichi. She devoured it until nothing was left.

"They could be planted," Henry said. "We could be close to a village."

Soon, the entire caravan followed the zigzagging path to the fruit trees that grew inside a small grove—four trees laden with bananas, some of them riper than others. Everyone climbed up to pick and eat. They ate greedily until their stomachs were full, so full that some of the girls threw up. Janet pulled down a few bananas to feed Goma, and then she fed bananas to the donkeys.

The fruit helped, but still, the group was hungry. They had eaten just enough to sustain their energy and keep walking. More vigor was produced because everyone's hopes had been revived—the footpath and fruit trees were signs of human life close by, so the caravan furiously chopped its way through the thick growth that blocked the path as it twisted and turned. The going was rough but steady, the vegetation so thick it blocked the sun. Monkeys and birds screamed high overhead, announcing to the forest that they were coming.

At the bottom of a hill, Henry spotted a sign on the path, a straight stick that poked up from the ground about five feet with the skull of a buffalo with horns, clearly put there by someone. With renewed momentum, he pushed on.

Within minutes, they came to a young African who stood on the path, calmly as if he were waiting for them. He was tall and thin with long, wiry ringlets hanging down his back. He wore a green wraparound cloth that covered his torso. "Jambo," everyone said as they smiled and waved. Even Henry was on his best behavior.

"Do you speak English? Swahili? Portuguese?" Henry asked.

The young man shook his head no and bypassed Henry, walking down the line of the caravan, taking care to carefully examine each person and the packages they carried. He smiled at the girls, who smiled back. He looked at the bales of calico and cloth. He fingered the canvas tents, glass beads, equipment, and utensils. To Janet, he looked like a customs official checking the baggage of travelers.

He continued to walk until he reached the very end, all the while being addressed with smiles and jambos. Finally, he came to Goma. They stared at each other. Goma nodded his head with conviction and authority. The young man turned, walked to the front, and gestured for Henry to follow him.

They came to a village gate, a wooden entranceway with a high fence on each side that spanned about twenty feet across. More skulls stood on top of the posts that held the fence together. Upon crossing through the entranceway, a wooden statue appeared anchored on a wooden box in front. The statue was the face of a man painted white with blacks eyes and Negroid features. The young man bent down before the statue and folded his hands in tribute and proceeded to lead the caravan into his village. Everyone knew they were going into a tribal village with traditional ways, neither Christian nor Muslim.

They entered a clearing with about fifty brown huts arranged in an irregular pattern, conical in shape and made of wood with dried mud or clay to keep the walls firmly in place. Dozens of villagers came out to greet them. When the villagers saw the utensils and tools, the hatchets, guns, spades, and ropes, the bales and boxes of cloth and other goods, when they saw the faces of the caravan members, emaciated and lean, worn from hunger and thirst, they turned around and came back with food for trade, baskets of ground nuts and cassava, millet, bean pies, and an assortment of cakes. They also brought out carved masks, hoes, and knives, anything that they thought they could barter. They looked like they were used to trading.

They beseeched the weary travelers, offering their goods for food, for whatever items they saw and liked, until a tall, imposing African man came over with long, unruly hair flaring out like a bush. He was in his late forties, and, across his shoulders, a blue calico toga was tied, and he carried a long walking staff elaborately carved and decorated.

"Get back!" he yelled in Swahili. "Get back!"

As he pushed them farther, the villagers retreated in deference. The caravan members surrounded him in a semicircle. Janet stood next to Henry but also looked at Goma, still lying in his stretcher tied to the donkey. She wanted to see his face in case his eyes flashed danger signals. She anxiously squeezed Baraka's hand.

"I am Zaid." The man addressed Henry. "I am griot. Mimi sema Klingereza. I speak a little English. Also Portuguese."

"What's a griot?" Janet whispered to Henry.

"A storyteller."

Then Zaid frowned, raised his hand, and shouted, "No slave here. No brutu!"

Henry gestured by waving his hand. "No slave. No brutu! We come in peace." Henry bowed and folded his hands, imitating the young man who paid tribute to the statue at the entrance gate. "Peace. No brutu! We hungry. We trade." He gestured with his hand the act of putting food into a mouth. Then he pointed to the bales of cloth and beads.

Zaid understood and relaxed. He brought his arms down. "This Wanyamwezi tribe. Mbariki." Then he moved toward Henry, stretching his arms. Henry responded by holding his out. As the two men drew closer, they interlocked, grabbing each other's forearms in a tight embrace. Zaid bowed slightly and said, "Wakey, wakey, wakey. Waku, waku," a kind of chant or ritualized greeting.

Henry, still holding firmly to Zaid's arms, bowed his head and chanted back, not knowing what he was saying, "Waku, waku." He had been in Africa long enough to hear the rhythm and sound of words to figure out their meaning. Zaid smiled broadly and released his hold on Henry's arm, and then he grunted twice. "Huh, huh."

Henry also grunted twice. "Huh, huh."

When the introductory ceremony ended and the villagers and caravan members exchanged similar salutations, everyone scattered into small groups. Food and water were brought out, and they ate for the first time since they killed the lion: fish, goat meat, sweet potato, corn cakes, millet, fruits, and vegetables. They were also served a thick porridge made of garden leaves, cucumber plants, and beans mashed up with ghee, which they wolfed down with their fingers and hands.

As they ate voraciously, the Wanyamwezi villagers stared at them, wondering why they were here. Because of their isolated location, the Wanyamwezi people rarely received any visitors. They did most trading by traveling to other tribes or lands. They carried their goods from one place to another and brought back their proceeds after a few weeks or months. Their young men were known all over Tanganyika as traveling salesmen. Their specialties included iron products, especially hoes and ax blades. They also traded in musical instruments and dyed cloth.

The Wanyamwezi was a very large tribe scattered throughout Tanganyika, with many subtribes and branches of various names, such as the Ukongo, Usukuma, and Ukawedi. Most famous among them was the Ruga, a group of mostly teenagers well trained in warfare. They sold themselves to the highest bidder as mercenary soldiers and were known for their ferocity. Mirambo had employed many of them in his army that attacked Tabora and Henry's group in Kwihara, but the Ruga were hired by others throughout the region as long as they got paid, except by the Arabs, whom they hated.

Other offshoots of the Wanyamwezi tribe hired themselves out as porters to various caravans, including the Arabs. The Wanyamwezi were found in all of the major towns in east-central Africa—Bagamoyo, Kunduchi, Dar es Salaam, and Kilwa. Sometimes, they waited to be hired as sailors on ocean voyages.

The present king of the Wanyamwezi was Mkasiwa, who lived far away. Zaid was not only a griot, but he was also the chief of this small village, and he had a hierarchy of sub-kings and chiefs to whom he had to answer in the region. Within his realm, he governed his people according to mutual consent. Everything they did was by consensus. If a dispute emerged that required a judge, he would make the final decision but not without consulting the entire village, unlike other chiefs who only consulted a small group of elders. Anything of importance was put to a vote with the majority ruling accepted. As a result, the village was a model of democracy, free from the ugly effects of slavery and despotism.

After caravan members finished eating, everyone dispersed. Many of the porters and guards, including Selim and Saburi, went off with the men to see their iron smelting operation. The villagers also showed them how they made musical instruments from bamboo, exquisite flutes and drums, guitars that looked like a small bowl with one or two tight strings and a long handle. They also made a variety of horns. Among other things, the Wanyamwezi men were well known for their musical abilities and traveled to distant villages to play.

Asmani and a few others were shown the public assembly, or Wanza. Here, men gathered to socialize and talk, smoke pipes filled

KERRY McDONALD   201

with strong tobacco and other substances, and discuss regional politics, war, and social events, such as the fighting near Tabora, the white man, and the Arab slave caravans. It was here that the caravan members heard about the fate of the deserted village it passed a week ago in the Kilombero Valley, the burned-out village with bleached bones.

"That was a Wanyamwezi village," one of the village men said in Swahili.

"What happened to them?" asked Asmani.

"They were attacked one night by slave kidnappers. They killed all of our men and anyone who couldn't walk and took just the women and children. One of these women was my sister. They took her a few days after her wedding day. Now she's gone."

"But why did they live way out there, cut off and separated, without defense?" Asmani asked.

The village man replied, "They were a renegade village. They argued with us and with the big chief here in the mountains. We told them not to go, but they did."

The women went off by themselves to drink tea and gossip. Janet and the girls watched them, as each mother sat on a stool while one of her daughters fixed her hair by plaiting it or turning kinky locks into ringlets and twisting them. The Wanyamwezi women were heavily ornamented with red, blue, white, and green beads hanging from necklaces or wrapped around their waists like a belt. Brass and copper wire dangled from their wrists or accentuated their ankles. Some of them nursed babies while little girls ran around in short, cow-skinned kilts.

As with the men, the women usually talked—not about politics or war, but about family matters and personal experiences. But now, the women plied Janet with many questions in Swahili, Baraka translating.

"Where do you come from?" one of them asked.

"From Scotland," Janet replied, looking at Baraka.

"Where is your family?"

"In Scotland."

"Where is this Scotland?"

"Far away. You reach it by sailing ship."

"We have sailing ship, too," another woman said.

"You have ships?" Janet was surprised, and for a moment, she didn't believe her.

"Yes, long ago. We have ships on the coast. They row boats all the way to islands in the sea, far away. To trade. Now not so much."

Janet had read about how blacks in the South Sea Islands in the Pacific could row large canoes for thousands of miles using nothing but the stars to guide them, but not in Africa. She hadn't read that Africans could sail ships, too.

"How do girls get married in Scotland?" a third woman wanted to know.

"In a church."

"What do you mean church?"

"By a priest. The girls get married by a priest."

"Oh, priest. Like medicine man."

"Yes. Like medicine man."

"How many wives each man can have?" asked a fourth woman. As she sat on her stool, a young girl combed out her hair.

"Just one."

"Only one wife?"

"Only one."

"Do you have bride price?" she asked.

"No, but the groom always pays."

"How does he pay?"

"In fedha, money."

The woman smiled at Janet. They both understood.

Everyone else who was not with the women or the men, including Henry and Ferrari, stood inside the center of town, trading cloth and beads for food: grain and dried goat meat, groundnuts, corn, and potatoes. Henry made sure the caravan had plenty to eat, at least enough food to feed them for a week. The Wanyamwezi were also curious about tools and gadgets such as scissors and can openers, needles, thread, candles, and matchboxes, and they also sought to trade their goods for these items.

The day rolled on, the sun still hidden behind a thick jungle canopy that surrounded them above. Janet stayed close to the children, who began to play with the Wanyamwezi young girls. For the first time since they left Ujiji, they were laughing and smiling, enjoying themselves and having fun, as they swung on enormous vines suspended from tall trees. She watched as Shali wrapped her long legs around a vine and lowered her body to swing upside down. More Wanyamwezi girls joined them, and they soon became such a large group that they broke into two. Some of them continued to swing on the vines. Others began to carry each other on top of their shoulders.

They would take one of the girls and place her on the shoulders of two others where she would sit between them with outstretched arms. With a small crowd surrounding the sitting girl, the girls would travel around the village, stopping before each hut to sing a pretty song about oranges and bananas while the rest of the girls clapped their hands.

Ndizi machungwa
Ndizi machungwa
Nani yutaka
Nani yutaka
Ndizi machungwa
Nani yutaka

Janet was pleasantly shocked that they chose Chichi to sit on top of their shoulders. She remembered when she first saw Chichi in Ujiji, sitting on a log by herself. Now she smiled and waved her hands above a small group of children. For a moment, Janet almost wept.

How many times had these girls faced certain death? Now look at them. And what about the others, like Makeda, those who didn't make it this far? No, I will never let that happen again.

Late afternoon arrived. It was time to think about the next day. Janet slowly turned away from the girls and spotted Zaid talking to Henry, Asmani, and Goma next to his stretcher, which by now had been raised on a steep incline where they could see his face. They were examining a map, so Janet walked over.

"One march away. Rufiji River, in Mbariki." Zaid held up one side of the map and pointed.

Henry gestured with his arms the action of using poles to steer a raft. Zaid nodded yes. "Yes, boat allow. Must get from chief. Big chief."

"You take?" Henry asked.

"Yes. We go tomorrow."

Goma raised his hand to try to speak. Zaid saw him and bent down his head to listen. While they were talking, Henry turned to Janet. "Zaid says we have to get permission from their chief to build rafts. He says the river is in their territory."

"So we go to their chief tomorrow?"

"Yes. Zaid will take us there. It's not far. We have to paddle by canoe downstream."

"What do you think?"

"I think it's okay. Zaid will help us."

In the background, Zaid and Goma faced each other, communicating through gestures, written pictures, and occasional sounds. Since the caravan arrived, Goma had spent much time with Zaid, who communicated with him through animated motions, and Goma was even smiling again. They seemed to instantly take to each other. Zaid made sure that Goma was comfortable by lifting his stretcher up almost to shoulder height and leaning it on a tree or any upright structure so that Goma looked like he was standing up, almost like his normal self, except for his bandages and splints. Both Janet and Henry were delighted to see him making progress.

"Goma's beginning to speak again," said Henry.

"Really? That's wonderful."

"Well, he's able to speak in small words, a little."

"Maybe the Lord is answering our prayers, Mr. Stanley."

"It's about time," Henry replied, with a look of scorn on his face.

They both turned from Goma and Zaid and began to walk. As they moved, strolling in silence, Janet kept trying to think of something to say to him but could not. She couldn't engage in minor conversation with him. When she tried to do so at the beginning of their journey, he had told her, *I'm not here to make friends or chitchat. Go do that with the Africans.* Ever since then, most of their conversations were decidedly hostile. What could she say now after everything they had been through? That's why she refused to call him anything but Mr. Stanley. *He is not my friend.*

Meanwhile, a young African woman came up to them. She saw Janet's necklace and pointed to it. She touched the silver chain. Janet pulled out the crucifix so the woman could see it better. The woman wanted to trade.

"No, I am sorry. I can't. No trade."

The woman persisted. She took Janet's hand and put her own necklace into it, a polished stone at the end of a leather string. Then she pointed to Janet's crucifix again. She wanted it badly, but Janet shook her head no. The necklace was the reason why she had come, and it was her only physical connection to her deceased brother. The woman smiled and pointed again. Janet was about to say no again but stopped.

The necklace was the means, the vehicle that spurred this trip, but now she had accomplished her mission, and David was no longer alive. She had the African girls to keep his memory alive. David had always said true Christianity was not expressed through symbols but only inside the human heart, only inside the human soul. Faith and actions, not words or empty deeds or outward symbols for display.

Janet took her necklace off and gave it to the Wanyamwezi woman, who put it around her neck and ran off, smiling with glee. Janet put the leather string around her neck and fingered the polished stone, which looked like turquoise but with a deeper color, and it was heavy, a material she had never seen before. The stone seemed to cling to her skin.

Henry nodded. "Never thought I'd live to see you do that."

"There's a lot of things I've done here I never thought—"

He stopped and looked at her directly in the eyes, something he seldom did. "Why *did* you come here?"

Janet wavered, surprised by his sudden question. She knew what he meant but decided to evade him. "I've told you many, many times before, Mr. Stanley."

Henry knew she knew she was dodging him. "I mean, why aren't you like most other women?"

"I was once someone's fiancée. That's what you really want to know. Why I'm not married."

In one moment, it all came back to her, her years in Blantyre, her relationship with boys. She was not an unattractive girl when she was growing up, and as she got older, young men did try to flirt with her, even try to kiss her, but she was always so devoted to her religion, which turned the men off, and she kept close to David's side. This caused those same men to whisper among themselves. Many people thought her devotion to David was unnatural, including Agnes, but that's the way she felt. She couldn't help it. All the young men of her town she couldn't respect. They had no ambition, no desire to learn, no sense of destiny.

When she got older, once David had gone away to Africa, she did court one of David's friends from medical school, Jonathan Younger. She met him through David when she attended some of his classes. Indeed, he was David's best friend. He, too, was a devoted Christian and a serious medical student, though he had no desire to be a missionary. He and David would often study together, and he supported David when others criticized him. She and Jonathan drew even closer together in part because many had pressured her to find someone to get married to before it was too late. After she and Jonathan got engaged, and it looked like they actually would get married, she realized she was living through the expectations of others and not herself.

As Janet's mind wandered back through the years, Henry continued to stare at her. "Something is driving you, Miss Livingstone. Something I don't understand."

"You're driven by your ambition," she said. "That's why you're not married. I'm driven by my belief."

"Just like your brother."

Mr. Stanley, at last, is beginning to get it.

"That's what my sister says all the time."

"And what do you tell her?"

"When I was younger, David and I made a pact. We dedicated ourselves to ending suffering in the world. We gave up normal lives to do God's work and, like you, I couldn't do both." She continued to walk ahead, hoping she didn't need to say anymore. As she walked, she left Henry behind, looking at the ground, deep in thought.

27

—

Evening came. Torchlights burned. The entire village, including all the members of Henry's caravan, assembled at the village center before a platform stage. Drums were beating in anticipation of a big event. The faces of men and women were beaming. Children smiled. Everyone from Wanyamwezi knew what to expect.

Goma was propped up to a standing position near Janet, who sat close to Baraka. The rest of the girls sat in front, giggling and pointing to the Wanyamwezi girls they had befriended earlier. Mkati, the porter with bulging muscles, sat next to Ferrari and Asmani. Saburi sat next to Selim. The rest of the porters and guards sat in small groups scattered throughout the audience. Henry stood up in the back behind everyone else. The audience grew restless as the minutes passed and there was no sign of the impending show. Janet, who was growing a little impatient, turned to Baraka and smiled.

"Wapi?" She asked Baraka when the performance was coming.

"Hivi karibuni" Baraka replied. "Soon."

The drums stopped beating. The audience became silent. After another minute or two, Zaid emerged on stage with ceremonial headgear draped around his face and a blue calico robe that covered his entire body. Behind him flowed a blue cape that fell to the ground. As soon as he stepped out, the audience exploded with applause. He smiled and stepped toward the crowd.

"Wakey, wakey, wakey!"

The audience shouted back, "Wakey, wakey, wakey!"

"Waku, waku!" he shouted, and the audience repeated again.

He stopped for a moment to collect himself. He spread his arms wide and walked to the center of the stage. He turned to face everyone and came even farther down. After another moment, he began to speak softly in Swahili.

"A lonely, isolated man, not yet human, carved himself a female and placed her upright in the sun." He mimed the action of a man carving wood.

"And so she came to life, but when night came, she died. Twice he conceived her, and twice she died." He mimed the motion of a child being born and a child dying.

Janet sat with Baraka in rapt attention. She couldn't understand everything he was saying, but through his actions on stage, she got a basic understanding.

"And so he moved to higher ground," Zaid continued. "From the lowlands in the south, he walked to the Mbariki Mountains in the north." Zaid mimed the action of a man walking. "And then he carved a third female, and this time she lived."

Zaid continued to narrate his creation tale, not unlike Adam and Eve, and how the Wanyamwezi people were formed and how they grew and developed in the early years of their inception. Janet was drawn to the story because he emphasized the survival of women, and he never mentioned slavery.

After the performance, the entire village came out to party in the same area where Zaid's performance took place. On the platform stage, instead of Zaid, a lively band of musicians played bamboo flutes, banjos, and reeds. Surrounding the musicians, everyone danced to the sound of drums, whistles, and tambourines. Men and women were drinking beer. People were getting drunk. Even the women and children danced.

Chichi was shaking her protruding belly, Shali lifting her long legs. Baraka also danced, though somewhat modestly. She kept looking over at Janet, who stood by herself, watching them.

As the party got wilder and more raucous, Janet remained on the sidelines with a drawn face. Even from the beginning, she refused to dance. It wasn't because she frowned on dancing from her religious beliefs. She simply did not know how to dance and was self-conscious about it. In her lifetime, she had attended very few parties, and so she never learned, and even if she had learned, the kind of dancing in Scotland that she knew differed from what she saw here, where bodies swayed and flowed so naturally like the currents of a river. She wanted to dance, but her pride held her back. *No, I can't go out there. I'll just make a fool of myself.*

The Africans wouldn't have it. A group of men, including the young man whom the caravan members first encountered before they entered the village, came over to her and pulled her in. She resisted by insisting, "I cannot dance. I couldn't. I really don't want to. I can't." The more she resisted, the more they pulled her. She would dance. She must dance.

Everyone was dancing. More relaxed now, Janet moved with the beat. The pent-up emotions so carefully held down inside her came bursting out. The porters, the guide, the cook, and the guards, they, too, were dancing as if there were no tomorrow, sometimes alone, sometimes in a group, sometimes with one of the African girls. Even Goma, propped up on the side, rocked his head to the rhythm of the beat.

Everyone danced, deep into the night, except for Henry. When a group of African women tried to pull him in, he, too, resisted. Unlike Janet, he wasn't afraid to make a fool of himself. He had danced before when he was younger in America and England. If he wanted to dance, nothing could hold him back. As the African women kept pulling and pushing, trying to get him into the fray, he stood firm. He would not dance no matter what, simply because he didn't want to. And if he didn't want to do something, no one was going to force him. After a while, the women backed off, realizing he was hopeless. Everyone in the village was dancing except him, and Goma, of course. He stood off, looking lonely and unhappy, the way he always looked.

Morning soon came again. The cock crowed; the village stirred. Stiff and bleary-eyed, people rose from a night of joy and celebration. Ferrari awoke to make breakfast and coffee. The caravan slowly began to assemble. Today was the day.

Janet got up as usual and had her coffee. She had eaten so much the day before. She wasn't hungry. Instead, she sat by the campfire, twirling the polished stone around her neck. She rubbed it.

Maybe it will bring us some good luck, she thought.

She looked at the girls. They were rolling up their blankets. Their faces looked sad because they had to leave. They had to go back and face the unknown. Henry was up as usual, talking to Zaid. Both of them strolled over to Goma. Their faces dropped as they talked to him.

What's going on? Janet asked herself. She strolled over.

"Good morning, Goma," she said in a cheerful tone, the lingering effects of last night's festival.

He barely smiled. Zaid and Henry looked away.

"What is it?" she asked. They wavered. Her heart jumped. She sensed bad news was coming. "What is it?" she said again, louder this time.

"Goma is staying here. He wants to stay."

Janet suddenly jolted. "What?"

"Like I said," replied Henry, "he's not coming with us to Kilwa."

At first, she didn't believe it, so she looked at Goma. His eyes avoided hers. She wanted to ask him directly, but his answer was written all over his face.

"But why?" She kept looking at Goma.

"Zaid has offered him medical attention. He really shouldn't be traveling. It's the right decision," said Henry.

Zaid also spoke up. "Goma stay. Goma heal."

Janet froze all emotions and went back to her tent. She had to get ready for the journey ahead. The full import of Goma's decision had not made any impact yet. She continued to believe he was coming with them.

By late morning, Henry's group was on the move, laden with packages and parcels, boxes and bags of all kinds. The porters put their packs on their heads and lined up to march. Janet and the children walked up front, just behind Zaid, Henry, and Ferrari. Henry gave the order, and they started to march down a steep path, dozens of villagers following behind them. Two young men carried Goma on his litter. They proceeded down the path to a small rivulet lined with a fleet of canoes. The people from Wanyamwezi said their goodbyes with last-minute hugs and handshaking. The girls clapped and sang goodbye songs. Then, the caravan boarded four large canoes. Some of the village men got in with them to paddle.

Janet was now about to board, but she stopped and looked back at Goma. His stretcher was lying on the ground, lifted up by the steep incline. She walked back to him. She reached out to shake his hand. Her heart raced as she drew closer. She could feel him pulling her.

"Thank you, Goma. I owe you my life."

He reached out to her, tears forming in his eyes.

And then a strange thing happened. Just as their hands touched, Janet felt as if someone pushed her from behind, and she fell on top of him. Some huge uncontrollable force pulled her down, and she couldn't get back up. She grabbed his head and kissed him hard on the lips, kissed him like she had never kissed anyone before. She pulled back, gasping for air. She grabbed his head and kissed him again and again, but this time much harder, her fingers buried inside his dreadlocks, and she began to sob, so loudly that everyone could hear.

"I'll never forget you! I'll never forget you!"

She felt love for a man other than her brother, love for a man for the first time, the kind of love that makes you dumb, that renders you helpless in its grip.

"I'll never forget you! I'll never forget you!" she kept repeating over and over.

She collected herself and got inside the canoe.

Then it was Henry's turn to say goodbye, so he gave Goma a hug, fighting to hold back any display of emotion, and yet, under the watchful eyes of everyone, they could sense his voice cracking as he spoke.

"I'll see you again, ol' buddy. When you get better, I'll be back. We'll do another march together."

The caravan shoved off, Zaid's canoe leading the way. Inside were Henry, Janet, Baraka, Chichi, boxes of supplies, and two village men paddling. The rest of the girls followed immediately behind in the second canoe. Everyone was silent except for Janet, who was weeping uncontrollably, filling the dark forest with her echoes. The girls stared at her, watching her every move. Henry kept turning his face away, struggling to hold back tears.

As the caravan moved farther from the shore, the Wanyamwezi people shouted after it, waving their arms and yelling goodbye. "Kwa heri! Kwa heri!"

Goma stood up, lifting himself from the stretcher. He couldn't speak but flapped his arms back and forth. Then, the canoes rounded a bend and the Wanyamwezi people could no longer be seen, but their voices still cried out.

"Kwa heri! Kwa heri! Bye-bye."

28

—

fter the canoes rounded the bend and the Wanyamwezi goodbyes receded, the caravan floated down the stream in silence,
except for the cries and screams of birds and monkeys. Janet
had stopped weeping, though her eyes remained wet and sore, and
the Ujiji girls continued to stare at her. For the moment, each person
was alone with their thoughts, saddened by the loss of Goma. There
was some thought about the previous day, when they were happy for
a brief time, the best moment of their trip. Now, everyone wondered
what would happen next. Henry kept his eyes straight ahead. He was
thinking about his meeting with the big chief.

Ahead of them, as the oars from the paddlers dipped and splashed,
amid the throaty chirping of unseen toads, they could see a steep hill
on which stood an imposing fortress, rising like a cliff on top of a
mountain. Zaid pointed to a landing below, a small area of cleared
space along the riverbank with small wooden wharves at which several
canoes were already moored. Each of the caravan canoes drew into
separate stalls. Zaid and Henry got out.

"Everyone wait here. I'm going with Zaid. I'll be back." Henry was
about to take his rifle with him, but Zaid shook his head no.

Janet stepped out of the canoe and wiped her eyes. She looked at the girls, surrounded by porters and guards.

They'll be okay if I leave them here.

She straightened herself and walked up to Henry. "I'm going, too."

Without hesitation, they walked up a sharp path winding through boulders and small trunks of trees. From a distance, the trail didn't seem that long, but up close, the climbing was hard.

No wonder they built their fortress here, Janet thought.

It was nearly impossible for individuals to climb because it was so steep and windy, let alone a group of warriors. Most of the smaller trees and shrubs had been cleared away so that anyone on top could see them coming, could even see their canoes as they approached.

It took nearly an hour before they reached the top of the summit, and Janet was out of breath. They stopped to rest on small platform seats built from wood for those who wanted to look out at the vast Wanyamwezi territory. The view of the surrounding countryside was breathtaking—undulating blue-black hills to the north and south. In the west, Janet could see the vast plains the caravan had crossed just days ago stretching infinitely.

I can't believe we walked that far, Janet thought.

Immediately before her, opposite the panoramic view, stood a large plateau of rock and sandstone, at the end of which stood the fortress walls made of teakwood stakes sealed with clay and mud, about forty feet tall. Along the wall, arranged in two tiers, dozens of muskets poked through portals aimed at them. Janet could see some of the gun barrels moving, a clear sign they were being watched.

After they drank water and rested, Zaid spoke. "I go talk to big chief now."

Zaid approached the entrance door, tightly sealed. He walked slowly and with great deference as if, behind those walls, there lived some great deity with special powers. The imposing presence he had displayed the night before during his performance was now completely gone. When he reached the fortress door, a small square slat opened, and he spoke to someone inside.

"Who is he talking to?" Janet asked.

"The big chief of the Wanyamwezi clan, the leader of this area. He's responsible for protecting the surrounding villages."

"There are more villages?"

"Oh, yeah, scattered all around these hills close by. Zaid's village is just one of many. If we hadn't found Zaid, we would have eventually run into another group."

"How can the chief protect his people when he is here isolated in a fortress?"

"There are soldiers inside who could come out quickly and assemble down by the river in canoes. And they probably have paths on the other side leading down in different directions. The people could also come to the fort for protection, but that would only happen with a major . . ."

Henry broke off his conversation to watch Zaid turn around. He was now walking back, much faster, his face looking solemn and stern.

"Such as Mirambo?" Janet resumed their conversation.

"Yes. Mirambo's army couldn't breach these walls."

"So they're safe from the slave raiders and caravans?"

Before Henry could reply to her, Zaid returned. Henry asked, "What did he say?"

"River near. I show you, but . . ." He looked at Henry with apprehension. "You must pay honga for river."

Henry was expecting this and didn't look surprised. "How much?"

"Guns. You must give up rifle."

Henry's face suddenly fell. "You mean he wants us to give up our rifles?" He shook his head in disbelief. "Absolutely not! Let me talk to him."

He started to walk toward the fortress by himself, but Zaid ran after him and spun him around. "No talk. Rifles for river."

"All rifles?"

"All rifles must give up."

"Why won't he come out? Why can't I talk to him?"

Up to now, Janet had been listening and trying to make sense of the chief's decision.

A smart move, she thought. *If I were he, I would have done the same.* She drew closer to the two men. "If it means we get access to the river, I say give them up."

"But these guns and rifles are our only hope. Our only weapons," said Henry.

"So is the river. We are so close to Kilwa I can taste it." Janet didn't think they needed guns if they went down the river to Kilwa. They would probably not face any more hostile tribes.

And then Henry hit a nerve when he said, "I'm worried about the lions."

Janet hadn't thought about the lions since they had arrived in the Wanyamwezi village. It was as if Henry brought her back to harsh reality again.

Yes, he's right. The lions have not gone away. The lions will never go away, but I believe we might still be able to get to Kilwa if we stay on the river. If we don't give up the guns, we'll face not only lions but also the hostile warriors of the big chief who won't let us pass.

"I still say we give them up, but if you don't want to do it . . ." She would leave it in Mr. Stanley's hands, knowing full well her opinion didn't matter.

After a long pause, Henry said, "If we're gonna build rafts, we'd better get started. Looks like rain is coming."

Zaid led them down to the Rufiji River, less than a mile away. The rivulet that had taken them to the fortress now took them to a slow-moving tributary flowing from the Mbarika Mountains. The Rufiji River was wide enough to hold floating crafts, and it was slow moving enough, which was good, but it seemed shallow with many rocks and boulders sticking out to hamper movement.

For Henry, who had traveled many times on rafts in North

America when he was younger, the river seemed too shallow, barely deep enough. Yes, they would be able to launch their vessels, but the caravan's ability to maneuver farther downriver depended entirely on what lay ahead. Despite any possible difficulties, everyone from the caravan, including Zaid and the Wanyamwezi men who had paddled the caravan members from the village, set to work.

"We have to work fast before it rains!" Henry yelled.

First, they set out to chop down trees to make the logs. The logs had to be of equal length, so they looked for trees of the same size. Fortunately, they found a group of medium-sized cottonwoods clumped together, chopped them down with axes, and stripped off the limbs. After enough tree trunks were gathered, they stripped them of bark and knots and cut off the ends to make them all around the same length. This process took several hours.

Then, they took two logs and made them the connector logs. Since they were building four rafts, they had to get eight connector logs to build a rectangular frame—two connecting logs tied by rope to two floating logs. Once the frame was tightly secured, they placed more floating logs inside the frame and tied each one to the outer connecting logs and to each other.

This process proved to be the most difficult because they had little rope to spare, having bartered much of it earlier for food and supplies. They did have enough rope, but the rafts were not as compact and sturdy as they would have liked. When they tested the rafts in open water, the vessels were able to float and hold heavy loads, but, as they looked up at the sky, they wondered how they would float against the incoming heavy rain and rapidly flowing water.

They loaded the supplies on top of the logs, first the trunks and bags with clothes and food, then heavier boxes and remaining bales of cloth, then the canvas tents, beads, and bracelets, some of which they had to leave behind because they wouldn't fit. The caravan was now down to four guards, three porters, eight Ujiji girls, Ferrari, Asmani, Saburi, Selim, Mkati, Janet, and Henry.

Even with their low numbers, their bodies took up most of the raft space. Ironically, the big chief's decision not to allow them to keep their guns helped them. Had they brought the pistols and rifles, including ammunition, more of their important supplies would have had to be left behind. As it was, their guns and rifles lay piled up underneath a cottonwood tree, where they would remain to be taken by Zaid and his men.

When the rafts were finished in the late afternoon and the supplies were loaded and ready to go, Zaid, Henry, and Janet assembled near the shoreline. Zaid crouched down to draw a map with his forefinger in the sand. He drew a long winding line to represent the river and pointed to it.

"From here, river good, but here"—he pointed to his drawn line four inches farther up—"river rough." He wiggled his finger to suggest agitation. Henry and Janet nodded.

"Rapids," Henry said.

Zaid nodded in agreement and continued to point until his finger reached the end of the line. "Here river drop." He took his hand and pointed in a sharp downward motion.

"Waterfall." Janet took a guess, but she was right, judging by Zaid's response.

"No raft here. Get out, walk. Kilwa here. Very close."

Suddenly, Zaid stopped and looked up at the sky. Janet and Henry, too, looked up. It was raining, a heavy downpour. Through the oncoming cascade, Janet and Henry reached out and embraced Zaid. They thanked him for his life-saving help and warm hospitality. Then the four rafts floated downriver with all the caravan members holding on to the boxes, luggage, and each other.

Henry, using a long sturdy tree branch as a pole, steered the first raft ahead of the others. On it were supplies, a few of the girls, Selim, and Asmani. As Henry steered the raft against pounding raindrops and thick haze, he kept his eyes on Asmani, who carried Livingstone's journal in a tin box inside his backpack. If anything should happen to their craft, he would secure the journal above all else.

Janet sat on the second raft, commandeered by Mkati, the porter with bulging muscles, who also used a long tree branch as a pole to steer. On this raft sat the rest of the Ujiji girls, including Baraka, Chichi, and Shali, clumped under long strips of canvas to protect them from the torrent. Behind Janet, who sat in the stern, two more rafts came floating down filled with porters and guards. On the remaining rafts, the guards, who no longer carried guns, shivered next to the porters and worked with them as if they were one. Now, it seemed their earlier differences didn't make much sense.

The river began to swell. Water swilled and rushed more rapidly and with a rougher flow. Haze soon turned to fog, which made it harder to see ahead. Then, they entered rapids; this made the rafts harder to control. Henry thought about trying to steer everyone to the shore where they could bank and wait out the storm, but it was too late. The rafts began to spin around, and some of the supplies fell off. They hit rocks but soon got clear, only to keep dashing forward, driven by the current they couldn't control.

As they bobbed and bounced together, the rain still falling furiously, falling to make up for the months of dryness, Janet's raft fell behind the third raft, but Mkati used his position to try and steer ahead, to try and follow the others who had already floated before him—clearing a path—in a certain direction. Then, right in front of him, the raft ahead hit a rock and flipped over. Everything fell out, all of the men and supplies. One of the porters was Saburi, the young runner. He would have to use his swimming skills to stay alive.

Mkati tried to steer his raft closer to Saburi, whose arms thrashed to keep above water. Several times, Mkati got close enough only to be pulled back by the current. Finally, they got within range for Mkati to thrust out his pole for Saburi to grab. Saburi had it in his hands but failed to keep hold. Meanwhile, the two guards who had fallen with him were also drifting downriver, but they were holding on to floating

boxes that kept them buoyant. One of the porters who was also floating had made it to the riverbank and crawled out onto the land.

Mkati kept trying to reach out to Saburi, again and again, as the
rain pounded them, making it more difficult. Finally, Saburi grabbed
the pole and climbed onto the raft next to Janet. The two guards floating on boxes paddled near the last raft in line and were lifted up, saved,
but the rain kept pelting down; the rafts kept lurching down the river.

Eventually, the rain began to ease and the rapids bottomed out.
The river current remained strong, keeping the rafts propelled, careen-
ing from side to side, but steady enough not to tip over, and the river
grew deeper. All three rafts were still in sight of each other with Henry's
raft still in the lead. Then the river broadened wider and wider. As it
did, the current picked up with a force that made the rafts difficult to
control again. They would soon be approaching the waterfall. As he
floated toward a broad bend, Henry took advantage of a swathe of land
jutting out and steered his raft to the shore, the others following.

By day's end, the rain had stopped. The caravan, what was left of it,
made camp inside a small clearing, surrounded by thick jungle growth,
just along the river. Fast-racing clouds churned across the sky like the
current of the river they had just crossed, and on one side of them,
they could hear a great crashing sound that was the waterfall beyond
the bend. Henry had pulled in his craft just in time. Between them
and the falls, a broad strip of an unkempt field wrapped around the
thin line of trees and dense foliage that surrounded them.

Once all the rafts had been moored, the guards and porters carried
most of the remaining supplies to the campsite thirty yards inland.
Since there were now more guards than porters in the group, and since
the guards no longer carried rifles, they were enlisted to carry the packs,
something they would not have done ordinarily, but all those differences were put aside.

The caravan members were thankful to be alive, guards and porters, and no one complained about their assignments or tasks. They
all worked together with singular purpose, something that took them

months to achieve. Perhaps it was the killing of the lion, or the brief blissful stay with the Wanyamwezi people. Perhaps it was because there were so few of them left, the majority of the porters having deserted. Perhaps it was because of their last ordeal battling the rain and rapids of the Rufiji River. Perhaps it was their sense that they were close to Kilwa, and soon, their journey would be over. Whatever it was, a mood of unity now brought the caravan survivors together. As they ate dinner, soggy biscuits and beans, they smiled and talked with satisfaction.

After dinner, everyone pulled closer to the burning fires and dried themselves out by the warm flames. Some were already sleeping on their mats or with damp blankets wrapped around them. The girls had already dried each other with the remaining cloth from an opened bale. Ordinarily, these small, tightly bound packages would not be touched. They were used only for trading purposes, but the caravan had to use whatever it could to keep itself living and healthy. Janet sat next to Baraka with a dry cotton cloth she used as a towel to wipe her arms and legs because she was drenched in sweat.

Baraka touched the towel as Janet dabbed her eyes and face. "Towel. Tualo." She pointed to the towel that Janet held.

"Tualo." Janet imitated Baraka's Swahili pronunciation.

Janet continued to dry her, but Baraka wanted her to speak more Swahili. "Your towel. Ku tualo."

Janet smiled but changed the context of meaning in English. "Our towel. You and me."

"Etu tualo. Our towel," Baraka translated.

"Etu tualo." Janet pointed to Baraka and herself. Baraka smiled.

Henry got up and walked around the camp, satisfied with everything. Then he walked farther up toward higher ground near the break where the line of trees along the river ended and the broad field began in front of them. He took out his spyglass to look around. Night was coming, but there was just enough light to see a short distance. On one side of the field, it sloped, and he saw the river turning into a waterfall with great white mists and froth-like smoke. As he spanned the glass to the right, he saw the field, and beyond that, about ten miles away, a few scattered lights, torches, and kerosene lamps from a distant settlement. As he pondered the lights ahead, smiling to himself, Janet walked over. He gave her the spyglass to look through.

"Over by the lights." He pointed. "That's Kilwa."

"It's not far. Not far at all."

"Tomorrow our nightmare will be over."

She handed him back the spyglass. "It's hard to believe." She thought hard for something meaningful to say to him. It was difficult.

"When we get there, we can catch a ship. Either south to the Cape of Good Hope or through the Suez Canal. It might take weeks or even a couple months." He paused. He, too, was fishing for something to say. He, too, felt awkward in Janet's presence. "How are the girls?"

"Tired but happy, like everyone else." There was another long silence. She didn't have anything more to say to him, so they listened to the waterfall that seemed to be singing a chorus of ancient melodies. "We lost another porter on the river."

"Yes, but he made it to dry land. He'll be okay. So will all the others who left us. Don't worry about them."

"What happens now, to the porters and the guards? All the men you hired in the camp? To Ferrari, Mkati, Selim, Asmani, and Saburi? What will happen to them now?" She almost included Goma on her list, but she left him out. It was too painful to think about him.

Henry leaned his arm against the trunk of a tree and hooked his thumbs inside his pants. "They'll get paid, go back to their villages, wherever. Until the next caravan. Some of them have been doing this their whole lives." And then he changed the subject. He didn't want to talk about the porters or the guards anymore. "And you, what will you do?"

"Go back to Scotland."

"I miss England."

Janet was a little shocked given that he was so insistent on carrying the American flag to Ujiji. She saw him as more American than any-thing else. "But you're American."

Henry was used to these comments. Livingstone, too, before he passed, had raised a similar question about Henry's identity. Henry always thought such comments carried a hint that his American self brought with it a legacy of inferiority. "Yeah, but I miss England," he rejoined. It was true. From his perspective right now, England seemed like the Promised Land.

"What will you do when you get back there?"

"I want to go back, but when I get back there, soon I'll want to come back here."

"To Africa?"

"It becomes a part of you, your bones, your blood. I hate it, but I love it."

As Janet listened to him, she realized the enormous difference be-tween them, why it was difficult to talk to him. "I don't hate it, but I don't love it either."

"Then what?" He looked at her in confusion.

"It is what it is. Like any continent. I don't find Africa fascinating."

"Well, I do. There are parts of Africa we've never seen, laden with resources the likes of which Europe can't imagine—gold, copper, silver, rich agricultural land for raising crops. You don't find that fascinating?"

"Those resources don't belong to Europeans. They belong to the people here." Janet suddenly remembered her long conversations with David in which he argued for African self-development, but even he believed they couldn't do it without help from Europeans. And she remembered her discussions with Goma, who told her something else: "The people here don't realize what they have. I am fascinated by Africa's potential. What it could accomplish if it had our help."

"I respect it," she told Henry. "I respect Africa for being what it is— different. I hope it never gets to be like England or Scotland. I hope we don't come here and take what's not ours in the name of help."

29

—

Early the next morning, the sun came out quickly, drying what was left of yesterday's rain, but then it soon turned to a cloudy gray. The caravan members got up earlier than usual to prepare for the final stages of their march. Since yesterday, everything had been brought from the rafts to the camp and readied for carrying, mostly boxes and trunks with clothes, tools, utensils, bags of food—rice and beans—canvas tents, the medicine chest, and a few bales of remaining cloth. Many of the guards still had their backpacks, loaded with personal items, and, of course, there was the tin box containing Livingstone's journal, guarded closely by Asmani and Henry. Otherwise, most of their supplies had long since disappeared with the deserting porters, had been lost, or had fallen from the rafts during the rainstorm.

Janet was dressed. She wore her usual riding breeches and cotton blouse, which had dried overnight. She put the polished stone, which she had traded for David's necklace, around her neck. She fingered the stone and kissed it. Then she helped the girls get ready, brushing their hair, rolling up and tying their blankets, and wrapping cloth tightly around their waists and loins. She made sure everyone ate breakfast.

"Chichi, kula kiamsha kinwa. You must eat breakfast."

But Chichi just looked at her, her bottom lip pouting.

"You must eat to stay strong."

Janet looked at Baraka to help her communicate. Baraka glanced at Chichi and so did the other girls to reinforce Janet's advice. Chichi picked up a sodden biscuit and began to nibble. For a moment, Janet thought she had that forlorn look again, but she dismissed it as the lingering effects of their grueling river ride.

Shali seemed to be walking with a limp from a foot injury. "Inashida gani, Shali? What's wrong?" said Janet.

"It's nothing," Shali replied.

"Are you okay?"

She nodded her head yes. It didn't look serious, so Janet dismissed it.. Soon, they would be in Kilwa where she could get treatment.

Saburi saw them talking and walked over. He picked up Shali's foot and ran his finger over her heel.

"It is nothing, Mamma." As he spoke, he turned to Janet to reassure her. "Runners get foot hurt all the time."

Shali playfully protested. "I no runner."

"Soon you will be." Saburi smiled.

Henry was once again looking through his spyglass across the field. With the daylight, he could see much more. Ahead of them, the width of field ran its course for about sixty yards until it seemed to end abruptly, probably due to a slope or hill that he couldn't see. Beyond that, he saw a rope footbridge that appeared to span the gorge that led to the Kilwa settlement. He folded his spyglass and went back to Janet.

"I'm going to cross the field. There's a rope footbridge at the end. It looks pretty sturdy but I want to make sure."

"We'll stay here. When you come back, we'll go."

Henry crossed the field, wearing his Wellington boots. He had put them on instead of his cheaper, ankle-length boots in order to look good when he got into Kilwa, but the Wellingtons were heavier and made him walk slower than usual; his steps were firm, leaving imprints on the ground. The field was still wet from yesterday's rain with patches of mud and puddles, which he avoided. The grass was not tall, and it bent into clumps. That was good. He could see clearly in front of him. As he walked, he drew in deep breaths, feeling buoyant and upbeat. He felt for the first time in a long time that he could relax a little.

He reached the end of the field, and then it sloped down steeply for three hundred feet, and there was another small field just before the bridge. On both sides of the field, there were woods and trees. It looked like he was walking a naturally cleared area that led to the bridge. Henry kept walking. He looked up. The sky was still cloudy but the wind was picking up, and suddenly he felt himself shuddering. Why? All of a sudden something seemed wrong. What? He couldn't place it. He couldn't identify it. Something in his gut was telling him to beware.

He crossed the footbridge, taking care to test the ropes to see if they could carry his weight and the weight of the porters and guards with packs. It could. It seemed in proper order and didn't need repairs. He walked all the way across to the other side and rested for a moment.

He remembered he had half a cigar in his shirt pocket and took it out. Just when he was about to light it, he suddenly realized what was bothering him.

It's too quiet! No sounds of animals or birds in the vicinity, the same silence just before the siege at Kwihara. Yes, something is wrong. He threw down the cigar and hastened back across the bridge. *If only I had my rifle. Do we have any weapons left? Yes, swords and knives and a few hatchets. How could I have forgotten to bring them? How careless of me. I must get to them.*

He crossed the bridge and began to walk across the small area before the slope that would take him back to the field and the caravan, when he heard a sound, a rustle, and from out of nowhere, the lioness came from the woods, directly in his path. Behind him, another lioness emerged, blocking his path to the bridge.

It was his lioness. She had the bullet wounds to prove it—streaks of dried blood on her body, a scar across her forehead, and two large lumps on her shoulders where two bullets had lodged. Her body was also badly bruised with numerous cuts and scars from traveling through jungle growth.

For several moments, they stared at each other as Henry kept telling himself, *Stay calm, don't panic. Don't let her know you are afraid.* But he was afraid without his rifle, fear creeping slowly over him, fear he had not felt for a long time, not since he was captured as a rebel prisoner in the U.S. Civil War. There, too, he did not have a weapon. Without his firepower, he was lost.

Back at the camp, Janet sat waiting for Henry's return. So was everyone else. She kept looking across the field to see him walking back.

What's holding him? she said to herself. *He's been gone for fifteen minutes.*

"Is Mr. Stanley coming soon?" asked Baraka. She, too, called Henry Mr. Stanley in imitation of Janet.

"Yes, Baraka. He's just checking the bridge. Or maybe he's talking to someone." She thought about going after him, but she knew Mr. Stanley. *How many times during the trip had he said he would be right back and didn't return until much later? That's the way he is. Remember the time he got lost wandering around the woods in his pajamas? Give him a little more time.*

More minutes ticked by. Asmani approached her.

"We are ready. We go now, okay?"

"No, Asmani. We will wait until he returns." She knew everyone wanted to get moving, but he really hadn't been gone that long. *The one thing I have learned in Africa is to be patient. There are always delays.*

On the other side of the field, beneath the slope, Henry looked around for a weapon, a tree limb or a stick. Anything. Then, he saw a tree about ten yards away.

Maybe I can run for the tree and climb up it before she gets to me. It's a long shot, but what other choice do I have? He started to walk toward the tree. The lioness crept alongside him until he broke into a run. Just as he reached the tree, the lioness leaped, sank her teeth into his shoulder, and shook him like a rag doll. She growled and backed off.

He lay prostrate on the ground, shaken and bleeding. He clutched his mangled shoulder and breathed heavily.

She's playing with me. She wants to kill me slowly. Can lions think like that? What to do now? I'm going to die. He gathered himself and tried to stand. *Keep trying for the tree. Not going to die without a fight.*

He rose, blood pouring from his shoulder. He was almost standing when the lioness charged him again, using her front paws to knock him down. Then, she backed away again.

Why doesn't she kill me? She's playing with me. Maybe I can buy time. Maybe the caravan will come like Goma at Kwihara. He rolled to the side. *No, let's get it over with. Try again.* Using his one good arm, he pushed himself up.

The lioness drove her head into his chest, knocking him back to the ground.

The sun poured into his eyes. He could taste his own blood and sweat. He could feel the flies buzzing in his face. One of his boots had fallen off; black ants scurried up his leg. The lioness stood in front of him, waiting for him to get up again, but he couldn't this time.

For a moment, Henry looked away from her. He knew he would never make it, but he would try one more time.

I have to get up. As long as I have my mind and my breath, I will not die. I will not go down without—

As he turned to try and push himself up with his good arm, the lioness charged him again, using her paws to knock him down, and she flipped him over, conscious but on his back.

So this is how it ends, he thought, *mauled to death by a lion. On some dirt field in East Africa. Maybe I deserve it. Maybe it is just. But I'm not ashamed. I don't regret it. Nothing I did in life I regret, except my momma. Look where your boy is now. The boy you never wanted. Remember that time you came to visit me at St. Asaph's, and when I came out, you pretended you didn't know me. I shouted at you, Momma, but you got up*

and walked away. I begged you to take me, but you didn't. Take a good
look at me now, Momma. This is where your boy ended up. And it was all
because of you.

Janet kept looking across the field but saw nothing. The girls began
to recite silly rhymes to pass the time away. She could hear the heavy
sighs of the guards and porters behind her. More minutes ticked off.
She expected Mr. Stanley any moment to show himself. *Just a little lon-*
ger, she kept saying. *Patience, patience. In Africa, one must have patience.*
Pretty soon she could hear the voices of the men complaining. When
she turned around to look, she saw Asmani standing up. Before he
could move toward her, she turned to the caravan and the girls.

"I'm going across. Everyone wait here."

She hurried across the field, alone. When she got halfway across,
she heard the sound of feet running up behind her, swishing through
the low grass and mud. All of the girls were running after her. She
turned and knelt on the ground, reaching for their hands and for
hugs. They smiled. They wanted to be with her. They would cross the
field together.

When they reached the end of the field, where it broke into a
downward slope, they saw Henry lying on the ground below. By then,
the lions had retreated because they'd heard more people coming. Janet
waved at him and smiled. From a distance, he waved his arms and
shouted to her.

"Go back! Go back!"

She didn't understand. It looked to her like he was greeting them.
She walked down the slope, the girls skipping behind her, as if they
were still back at the Wanyamwezi village having fun and playing
games. When they reached Henry, the two lionesses came out, surrounding Janet and the girls.

"I tried to warn you," he said.

Janet looked at the wounded lioness, standing in front with her battered body, and it looked like she hadn't eaten. Her ribs were showing

beneath her skin. The girls next to Janet clung to each other and were afraid but remained quiet, just like Janet.

"Are you hurt?" she asked Henry.

She saw the blood on the ground. One of his boots had fallen off, and his right shoulder was mangled. Probably some of the bones had been crushed. She didn't see any injuries to his legs.

"Not as bad as it looks," said Henry, "as if that makes any difference now." He laughed.

Janet looked around again, deep in thought. She looked at the lioness blocking the bridge and realized it was the wounded lioness who held the key to their survival. The wounded lioness who had traveled all this way and followed the caravan for weeks driven by vengeance for her fallen cubs, a powerful motive not unlike the emotions of humans. *There's got to be a way out, but what?* Something inside Janet began to emerge, a mere hint of hopefulness. The fact that the lioness had not killed Henry instantly or attacked her or the girls gave her a ray of hope. *There's a reason she's not attacking us now.*

"They want me, not you. I'll run to the hill, drawing them out. You take the girls and get across the bridge. That's our only chance."

Henry's words seemed to fade as Janet kept looking at the lioness, who now seemed to be eyeing the girls sitting next to her, their arms around each other. Baraka was holding Janet's hand. For once in her life, Janet knew everything depended on her. She held the key for what would happen next.

She reached a decision. *I have to face the lioness. I have to show her I will defend my family no matter what. If she attacks me, I shall die. Lord, I hope and I pray that you have mercy on me.* She stood up. As she did so, she reached down toward Henry and pulled his left arm. "Get up."

Henry was shocked, taken aback. "But—"

"Get up!" She shouted this time and yanked his left arm with incredible strength, leaving him no time to argue. "Get up!"

Henry pulled himself up from his knees by holding on to her hand for balance until he was standing next to her.

"Hold on to my shoulders. We're going across the bridge."

He reached out with his left arm and placed it around her left shoulder. He had to hold on or he would fall.

"Girls, come around me in back. Hold each other's hands. Stay together tight. Don't spread out."

They inched toward the footbridge as a group, not looking as the other lioness looped around them to join the wounded lioness at the entrance to the footbridge, blocking their path. Henry was limping but clinging on. The girls were holding Janet's blouse in back. One step at a time, they kept moving until they reached the entrance to the bridge with the lions in front of them. They stopped.

Janet looked directly at the wounded lioness, ready to sacrifice herself. They stared each other down but not in any hostile sense. Janet knew her stare had to show the lioness she wasn't afraid to look her in the eyes, nothing more.

I am ready to sacrifice myself. I am prepared to die.

They continued to stare at each other. Silence. No one moved.

Then Janet took her right hand and placed her fingers on the leather-bound necklace around her neck. She fingered the polished stone hanging on it. She rubbed the stone, making sure the wounded lioness could see her. As the lioness shifted her eyes to the stone, Janet balled her fist around it and lifted it toward the lioness as if she were offering it to her. She could feel the sharp edges of the stone cutting into her hand.

Let it bleed, she said to herself.

She started to walk directly toward the lionesses, and got just feet from the wounded lioness's face, where she could see the bullet scars and dried blood from Henry's rifle shots, where she could hear the lioness breathing, deep and unsteady inhalations and exhalations.

At the last moment, the lioness abruptly stepped aside, followed by the other lioness. They let them pass. Janet, Henry, and the eight Ujiji girls walked across the footbridge. The lions disappeared among the weeds.

30

—

Janet leaned across the wooden railing on deck of the large Blackwall frigate *Carina*, staring out upon the dark gray Atlantic Ocean. The *Carina* was a fast-moving sailing ship with three masts and a crew of thirty. It was carrying silk, spice, pepper, and tea from Murat in India to London via the Cape of Good Hope. The ship had stopped briefly on the African coast to pick up a supply of ivory, where Henry, Janet, and the African girls had boarded after a two-month stay in Kilwa. Henry had used Livingstone's journal as collateral to pay for their passage, promising that Gordon Bennett would compensate the British East India Company upon their arrival in England. Of course he kept the journal close to his side and would not let anyone take possession of it.

It was twilight. The sea was calm and moving like a night sky filled with tufts of clouds, their silhouettes rolling evenly through moonlight. But there wasn't any moon, nor stars to speak of, only the sound of the wind and the sails and the great rising masts creaking. A few sailors worked on deck, pulling ropes, repairing sails, or keeping watch for anything that lay ahead. From one of the corners in the bow, a few of them crooned a sea melody.

Farewell an' adieu to you fair Spanish ladies,

Farewell an' adieu to you ladies of Spain,
For we've received orders for to sail for old England,
An' hope very shortly to see you again.

We'll rant an' we'll roar, like true British sailors,
We'll rant an' we'll rave across the salt seas,
Till we strike soundings in the Channel of Old England,
From Ushant to Scilly is thirty-four leagues.

Janet turned to listen to them and thought she heard some re-semblance to the work songs the caravan members sang with a leader, usually the loudest voice among the men, who sang a line while the rest of the group or crew repeated it. She remembered when she first heard the Africans singing, and how she soon grew bored by their con-stant repetition and unchanging pattern of sound. She didn't feel that anymore, not with the Africans, not with the British sailors on deck.

I am in my second life. Everything is sharper now and more alive. Even a small song reminds me of how grateful I am to be able to be here and have use of all my senses. From now on, I'll take nothing for granted. Live every moment as though it could be my last.

She had left Henry below deck, talking to the young sailor appren-tices about Africa. She had left him in the midst of a crowd of boys like him, poor street urchins who dreamed of adventure and travel to exotic lands, and they clung to his every word.

"What is it like to hunt and kill lions?"

"Why, there's no greater sport on this planet, and no greater chal-lenge to the hunter who kills them."

"Did you, yourself, kill a lion?" one of the young sailors asked.

"I bagged one near Lake Tanganyika, just as he was about to leap at me."

"Were you afraid?"

"Let me tell you, the man who says he's not afraid is either a liar or a coward."

He bragged on and on about how he found the lion—he used the male name—alone in the bushes, how the lion crouched and leaped at him, how he pulled out his rifle and shot it twice, killing the lion instantly as it arced through the air.

"And as he came down, he fell on top of me, his body knocked me down, and he bit into my shoulder before he died."

Henry showed them how he crouched, and he fell back on the deck, holding his right arm still bound in a sling, while the young sailors watched with complete attention.

Janet thought of Goma as Henry talked, how Goma was also a master showman, that first day in Bagamoyo when he mocked Henry in front of a crowd. She remembered how she loathed Goma then. *Just as I loathe Mr. Stanley now. I wonder where Goma is. I hope his leg will heal completely. I hope he will walk again.*

Ever since they left Cape Town, the ship's first and only stop, where Henry found out that his discovery of her brother had already made headlines in England, on the front page in both *The Herald* and *The Times*, that is when he began to change. That is when he reverted to his former self, leaving any talk of the injustice of slavery far behind, but Janet was not surprised.

He is not the kind of man who can change his habits and personality, no matter how hard he tries. His own personal ambition always comes first.

She left his performance down below to breathe in fresh air from the top deck. Before they had left East Africa, they paid off the porters and guards, and said their goodbyes. They had entered Kilwa shaken and humbled—yes, even Mr. Stanley, who had suddenly become a different man. When he stared death in the face, he felt he had to atone.

I was not afraid. I looked into the soul of the lioness, and she looked into mine.

It had been three months since the caravan had entered Kilwa on that fateful day after Janet faced the lioness that let them pass.

Kilwa was a small seaport town like Bagamoyo, only smaller and more isolated. In Kilwa, seafaring ships came, but rarely, usually bringing in commodities to trade for ivory or slaves. Kilwa was the assembly center of the slave trade in southern Tanganyika, a starting and ending point for caravans in the region. The traffic was not as large as Tabora. Nevertheless, Kilwa housed hundreds of slaves imprisoned in pens, guarded by soldiers and surrounded by fences, leaving the slaves to sleep under open skies.

"See these slave pens," Mr. Stanley said. "We should tear down these fences and walls. Let all the slaves free." He spoke out to the African Muslim governor of the town, to the Catholic priests, to the fishermen and sailors.

It started immediately on the day they arrived, after the porters and guards helped him walk from the footbridge, after Henry found a local doctor who dressed his wounds and put him into a hospital, the only one in the town. While he was recovering, he spoke out to anyone who came near him, anyone who would listen, as though he were on a mission or crusade.

"It's unjust, I tell you. Slavery is killing and destroying the African people, leaving lost children wandering in its wake. It's evil and it's wrong, this filthy trade of human beings."

No one believed what he said. Indeed, to others, he looked crazy, and they avoided him—just another white man who had lost his mind, just another white man trying to spread his Christian faith.

A few days later, after she and the girls had found food and shelter and received medical attention at a Jesuit mission, Janet noticed Henry avoiding her. True, he lay in a hospital bed for days, but even when she went to see him, he wouldn't talk to her. Even after she had saved his life, he withdrew whenever she was around and avoided her eyes.

She realized he did this not out of arrogance or disrespect as before, but because he was completely baffled by what she had done, so he was frightened, troubled, and anxious in her presence. He was unable to speak to her, as though he were traumatized, not unlike the symptoms of African fever. One day he got up his nerve and spoke, but only once, their last real conversation in Kilwa.

"Back there near the footbridge."

"What do you want to know?" she asked as she sat by his bedside.

"What happened? I mean, I have never seen anything like it before. What did you do?"

"I did nothing, Mr. Stanley."

"Come on. You did something to stop the lioness. What was it?"

"I didn't stop the lioness. She let us go. She held all the cards. She decided to let us pass."

"But why?"

"For reasons, Mr. Stanley, you'll never understand. You see, lions are like people. They have their pride, and they love each other like we do. Mothers love their children, and they love their families. All I did was to show the lioness, the same lion we had been trying to kill, I tried to show her I understood her, and, like her, all I was trying to do was to protect my family as she had done. We both had lost children, so she believed me. You see, lions are sentient beings, not mere beasts to be shot and killed; they do not harbor evil inclination. I told you once I respected Africa. Now I hope you see what I meant."

"I wish I could say I do—that I do understand—but I don't."

"You won't let yourself understand."

"No. I only know one thing, how to survive through force. A man is nothing unless he fights, fights for what he wants in this world. If not, he will surely die. There's only weakness or strength, nothing more."

"But what about belief? What about love? What about faith and hope? What about forming relationships with others: men, women, animals? You see, how we treat the animals depends a lot on how we treat ourselves. And how we treat ourselves depends on how we treat animals."

"I don't know about those things. Maybe I never will."

"I was once like you in some ways. I feared anything and anyone different. It is possible for people to change, even you."

Now on the deck of the ship, Janet stood, leaning against the railing, watching her life go by as quickly as the waves on the ocean. The light had faded but she could hear the ocean whispering all around like a sky with invisible angels.

She had left Mr. Stanley below, bragging to the sailors. She also had left the girls down below in the mess area, studying for an English lesson she would be giving tomorrow, but it was difficult to study, for they were crammed in a small space, eight of them inside ten square feet with water leaking down and cockroaches and rats and a foul odor wafting in and out.

Every day now, since they left Cape Town, in the morning from eight o'clock till ten, she taught the girls English, speaking and reading. That is, when days were calm. If a gale or storm came along, all they could do was find something to hold on to as the ship pitched and rolled, causing the girls to vomit. Now that the girls no longer had seasickness, were no longer fighting off dizziness and dysentery, she intensified their lessons to prepare them for what was to come.

As soon as they got to Scotland—and it would be soon—the girls would have to adapt to new ways. They were no longer Africans. They were two weeks away from London. The girls knew it. So did Janet. All of them thought about what it would be like, eight African girls in British streets, fresh from the African jungle. What would the British people think of them? And when they got to Scotland, how would Janet's people in Blantyre treat them?

I know how I thought about Africans before I left. Will my relatives and neighbors be able to change like I did? Will Reverend Ewing help me with the girls?

All of the answers to these questions were still unknown, like traveling through Tanganyika for the first time.

31

—

When they first entered Kilwa and Henry was undergoing his phony transition, born from guilt and remorse, from brutal caravan leader to anti-slavery crusader, the girls had stayed with Janet at a Jesuit mission, under the care of Father Baertz who had founded a school for African children. Father Baertz and his mission were a throwback to the days when the Portuguese government had a presence there and controlled the buying and selling of slaves.

For nearly two hundred years, the Portuguese held sway all along the East African coast until the Arabs from Oman reestablished Muslim control in the eighteenth century. The Arabs from Persia and Oman united with black Africans, who had become Muslims, so-called Moors, along the East African seacoast to reestablish Islamic control.

When the Portuguese were forced from the region, it was mainly the black Muslims who took over Kilwa and let the Catholic missionaries stay, using them as props to show the tribal Africans they were doing good, to show they didn't treat all their African brothers and sisters as slaves.

While the African Muslims had embraced an Arab religion, they knew their success in obtaining slaves depended on keeping close ties with those tribes who would help them. It was the conflict among tribes that kept the caravans coming, and some of those tribes the Muslims needed as friends and allies. Yet, in truth, any African who was not a Muslim was vulnerable to slavery, so these alliances were often broken.

Janet finally began to understand these tensions without asking Goma or her brother David. She finally understood how deeply entrenched the Muslim religion had pervaded the coastal towns from Kilwa to Mombasa in the north. On the day she said goodbye to Saburi and Selim, she asked them where they would be going now that the caravan had ended.

"We travel together back to Bagamoyo," Saburi said. "Arab and African, Christian and Muslim together." And then Saburi told her that he was a Muslim, but she would never have known it from his past behavior.

And Asmani, too, when he left to go back to his village with the Yao people in the south, spoke of being a Muslim, even though he never showed any signs of it during their travels together. He never mentioned his religion, but she never asked, and she never paid attention to him when he prayed.

Like with the others, Ferrari and Mkati, the Wagogo storyteller, she assumed they were tribal Africans, but now she couldn't be sure. But it didn't really matter. They were all human beings together despite their differences. Ferrari found work as a cook with Father Baertz, so she saw him every day. Mkati and the other porters and guards just disappeared. One day, she saw them, and the next day, they were gone. She never saw them again. She didn't know what happened to them. She didn't know where they had gone.

The Ujiji girls started right away to take classes with Father Baertz himself, who was the head teacher. He taught the girls, along with one hundred African children from the interior, Latin and Greek grammar. He also taught them Portuguese and French and classes in Christian catechism.

At first, the girls were stellar students. After living with death and constant danger, they burned with the desire to study and learn, to live in peace, to think and pray, but after a few weeks, after they were forced to wear Western skirts and blouses and taught how to sing pretty Portuguese songs, they grew unhappy. They became homesick and didn't want to change their ways. Baraka was the first to protest, but she spoke for all the others.

"We not African anymore."

"Don't be ridiculous," Janet replied.

"I don't want to wear dress, to speak white language, and eat white food."

"You must change and adapt. You are going to live in another country. Do you want to stay here? Or go back into the bush and be sold as slaves?"

Janet would have to persuade the girls. She managed to convince them whenever she mentioned slavery, but still, the girls looked unhappy and lost. Nevertheless, they continued their Jesuit education and learned how to study through discipline.

While Janet took issue with some of Father Baertz's beliefs and practices, such as his boxing lessons for the boys and drinking wine with dinner, she thought his focus on education was good for the girls. It was better for them to learn about white folks' customs and ways here in Africa. Once they reached England, their concentration might get lost in the face of institutional living and industrialism. Even Blantyre might be too overwhelming for them with its railroads and cotton mill.

And so the *Carina* sailed on, bearing its exotic commodities, a Scottish woman, a British-American reporter, and eight African girls dressed awkwardly in Western skirts. As the ship drew even farther north following long, established trade routes to England, the weather grew colder.

It was now late February 1874, and they would arrive in London in early March, a time when the winds began to pick up, not as bad as January, but still, there remained some frost and cold. Then, one morning, they passed the Dover Straits. The girls ran out on deck to see the great white cliffs. Even Henry came out to watch them in awe, a spectacle he once thought he would never see again.

They arrived in London and sailed up the Thames until they reached the huge complex of docks at Surrey, where the ship finally moored. Already a large crowd of reporters and government officials had gathered, waiting for them. It was early morning. Janet and the girls had just eaten breakfast when she heard the voice of Gordon Bennett on deck. To Janet, he didn't look so impressive anymore. Maybe it was because he was not wearing a suit, or she couldn't smell his cologne. Bennett went directly to Henry to hug him and burst out with greetings in tones of glee.

"Come, Henry. We have a large group of reporters who want to talk to you. You have to say something. Your discovery has shocked the world." Then he saw Janet and forced himself to smile. "Miss Livingstone! How are you? How was your trip? You look so well." He spoke as if she were a tourist coming back from holiday. He barely touched her in his embrace as his eyes took in the African girls. "And what is this?" He continued to force himself to smile, trying to be polite because it was his duty. Already, he was thinking about getting Henry down to the reporters.

"These are my brother's children."

She proceeded to introduce them, one by one, making sure she pronounced each girl's name distinctly. She knew he didn't have the patience to meet them.

By God, he will stand there and listen whether he likes it or not. I will not be rushed.

"And this is Shali from Ujiji."

Gordon smiled and tipped his hat.

"And Baraka, my niece." She made it a point to say *niece* loud enough for him to hear, and knew that he did when he raised an eyebrow.

"Your niece?" he asked.

"My brother's child."

"Yes. Yes. Of course."

And then he rushed off, leading Henry by the arm toward the gangplank that brought him down to the waiting crowd of hundreds, leaving her and the girls in an empty room with no one to greet them or say hello. Janet ran after him and spun him around.

"I need money for a hotel room and railroad fare back to Scotland. I need clothes and coats." She spoke to him directly without shame. She felt he owed it to her. Gordon Bennett and Mr. Stanley stood to make thousands, perhaps millions, of dollars off the name and fate of her brother, and without her, the trip would not have happened.

At first, Gordon just looked at her, and Mr. Stanley wanted her to go away like that day in Gordon's office, in December, when she told them she was going to Africa, too.

"Mr. Bennett, the trip was a success."

She made sure he heard her say "success." He took a checkbook from his coat pocket and a pen and just before he began to write, she added, "For me and the girls."

Although he hesitated when she mentioned the girls, he continued to write, tore out the check, and gave it to her.

"That should be enough, Miss Livingstone, to take care of your needs." With a stone face, he turned around and left.

"Come girls. We must go down the gangplank. We have to get a carriage to find a room." She made sure their coats were fastened tightly around their necks, for it was cold. Already, Chichi and a few others were sniffling.

"Baradi, Mamma. It's cold," Chichi said. Janet worried she might catch the flu not being accustomed to chilly weather, so she pulled the girls together and took off her scarf and wrapped it around Chichi's neck.

In a flash, she remembered how she pulled the girls together when they faced the lioness. Now, they had to come together again to stay warm and not get sick. Soon, she would have to find more sweaters and coats. What they had on was not enough, just different-colored animal skins, hides made from goats and cows stitched together with cotton cloth and canvas made hastily for them by the African children at the Jesuit mission. Janet was wearing three blouses and undergarments underneath a woolen sweater and her riding breeches to cover her legs.

"Who was that man?" Baraka asked as they began to walk. The gangplank descended in front of them.

"Gordon Bennett. He paid for this trip. Without his money, I would not have found you."

"Hapana rafiki. He's no friend. I don't like him," said Baraka.

"There will be many people you won't like." She thought of Goma once again, how he must have felt when he first came to England, his optimism dashed by hostility and indifference. "But, you know, there are many people who are not like him or Mr. Stanley, and that will make all the difference."

Janet was determined to show the girls that there were some decent English and Scottish people. She was determined not to allow the same thing to happen to these girls that had happened to Goma.

By now, the crowd of reporters had grown substantially, gathered before a stage, dozens of them, as well as government officials and curious onlookers. The newspaper reporters were most in evidence, jostling and joggling with each other to get closer to the stage where they knew Stanley would soon come down to speak. Correspondents were dressed in woolen or tweed coats with bowler hats or caps pulled down, smoking cigars or cigarettes and carrying small pads to take notes.

They came from the mass dailies such as *New York Daily Tribune* and *The Manchester Guardian*, *The Daily Telegraph*, *The Standard*, and, of course, the king of them all, *The Times of London*, Gordon Bennett's nemesis from the beginning. This event was international news, so reporters also came from France and Germany and from countries all over Europe and around the world.

Soon, they saw Henry coming down the gangplank, arm in arm with Gordon, who was carrying Livingstone's journal for all to see. Gordon wanted to show them that it was his newspaper and the reporter under his employ who had gotten the scoop. They had barely walked down to the middle of the plank when the reporters began to shout, all at once, drowning each other out. But Henry and Gordon kept walking down, as if they were royalty in front of their subjects, their faces bearing impudent smiles, smug and satisfied.

This was the moment Henry had been waiting for. Everything he had done and sacrificed for, including his close brush with death. It was for this that he had pushed and brutalized his caravan members, forcing them always to move faster and faster, thrusting guns in their faces if they talked back, and turning a blind eye to slavery and injustice, all for the sake of appearing before the world as the man who had found Dr. Livingstone.

Henry had reached center stage, dressed in a Mackintosh raincoat and, underneath, an ill-fitting suit, which he had borrowed from the *Carina* ship's captain. The reporters fought even harder to get closer, pushing forward to get a better view, scribbling their notes in their pads.

"Mr. Stanley. They say you're more famous now than Dr. Livingstone."

"I must say I'm a little shocked by all this attention."

"How does it feel?"

"Wonderful."

Meanwhile, Janet, together with her brood, walked down, holding Baraka's and Chichi's hands. Shali walked out in front, her bald head buried under a tight-fitting cap, her plaid skirt from the Catholic school covered by a goat-skin coat. As Janet and the girls inched down, they could see the large crowd assembled before Henry. They could see the outline of ships in other docks moored next to piles of timber. Dockworkers were unloading those ships. The sky was gray. They could see the cold white breaths of the reporters puffing in front of them. The wind lashed their faces.

To them, it was just another bleak, cold day. The crowd of reporters didn't see Janet and the girls coming, so they walked down without fanfare, without any kind of recognition. No one looked up. No one noticed them.

"But let's not forget those who made this trip possible." Henry turned to Gordon, who tipped his hat. "And there were many others."

For a moment, Henry glimpsed Janet walking down the gangplank with the girls around her, and she looked down at him. As their eyes locked, Janet remembered the eyes of the lioness just before she let them go, eyes that could see deep inside her. Henry's eyes bounced away, back to the crowd whose attention remained totally rooted to him.

He continued. "Let's not forget the African guards and porters who accompanied us through great trials and tribulations.

"Mr. Stanley, what do you mean by trials and tribulations?"

"Any caravan into Africa faces challenges."

They began to talk all at once.

"Were you ever in any danger? Did you get attacked by lions? What about hostile natives? Mr. Stanley! Mr. Stanley!"

Janet had reached the dock with eight African girls clinging to each other to buffer the wind. They turned and walked away from the crowd.

"And let us not forget Dr. Livingstone, the reason I went. I found him and was with him when he died."

Even when Henry mentioned her brother's name, Janet didn't flinch. She kept on walking away from him with the girls. She was worried now as she heard their teeth chattering. How long would it take to find a cab? They were in the middle of one of London's largest docks. How long would they have to walk? And where would they go? She had Gordon Bennett's check, but she needed to find a bank. She needed to get immediate cash, and she had to find a hotel. *Who will take us? A white woman with eight African girls, dressed in a motley array of shabby coats.* Their dresses were worn and stained from traveling. They looked like a circus troupe or a band of beggars.

Then, from out of nowhere, a ghost from the past came floating toward her, a woman holding her arms out. At first Janet thought she was dreaming again, or perhaps still touched by African fever. It was her sister, Agnes.

"Praise the Lord." She flew into Agnes's arms. They embraced and cried, long sobs of welcome and relief.

"Janet, Janet." Agnes rocked her from side to side.

"It's a miracle to see you." She really hadn't expected to see her sister again. "You couldn't have come at a better time."

"No miracle. I had to come. I just had to."

Agnes pulled back to look at her.

"I knew you'd come back, despite what I said before you left." Agnes turned and noticed the African girls. "Whose girls?" She smiled warmly but underneath she was shocked to see them. For the moment, her devotion to her brother and sister and to her Christian faith overrode the discomfort that she had.

"Our girls, Agnes. *Our* family."

London's docks. Henry and the African trip were now in her past. She had to keep moving forward. Henry's caravan trip had ended, and now she was on a new caravan, her own caravan, traveling across the British Isles back to Scotland. She would have to face new challenges ahead. And like the dawns of Tanganyika, when she rose from her tent to face the wilderness, a new day had come into her life, a new vision, a new consciousness.

She was a mother now, a mother with a very large family, and as she walked, her legs grew firmer. She had been tested, and she had won. She felt like the lioness. The power of life and death lay in her hands. She was no longer a victim, no longer a woman to be left behind or ignored. She would get the girls back to Blantyre. She would raise them as if they were her own. In the name of the two girls who had already fallen, in the name of Goma and her brother David, in the name of the people of Africa, and in the name of God, she would teach the girls how to read and write. She would help them to respect themselves and their African traditions, to stand up to the bigotry and hatred of whites. She would encourage them to achieve the happiness they deserved, and they would go on and on and on.

THE END

Kerry McDonald Collection
(Action and Adventure)

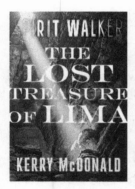

ISBN: 978-1-933769-98-1

When a wealthy playboy is paralyzed and near-ly consumed by depression, he discovers his ability to astral project to his estranged twin brother. Logan and Landon Flint embark on a high-stakes adventure to restore their relation-ship and find the Lost Treasure of Lima.

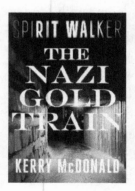

ISBN: 978-1-64630-000-6

When a neo-Nazi group discovers that the leg-endary lost Nazi Gold Train also contained a biological warfare agent specifically targeting Jews, Landon and Logan Flint must find the train first to avoid a new worldwide holocaust.

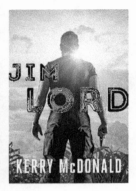

ISBN: 978-1-933769-96-7

After botching his response to a school shooting, a disgraced former cop, hiding out in Jamaica, is challenged by a local gang and decides to take down their powerful boss, seeking the redemption he so desperately wants.

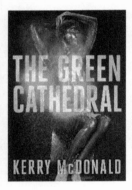

ISBN: 978-1-933769-92-9

When a corrupt DEA agent discovers an otherworldly alien girl lost in the South American jungle, he learns the true nature of beauty as he sacrifices everything to save her life.

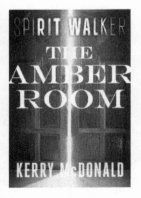

ISBN: 978-1-64630-040-2

When Landon and Logan Flint uncover evidence that the Amber Room contains holographic images from an alien civilization, they must locate the room before unknown alien technology falls into the hands of terrorists.

CPSIA information can be obtained
at www.ICGtesting.com
Printed in the USA
LVHW040600310323
743052LV00003B/340